Claddagh Pool

HEDI

Bringing it to life
is what it's all about

Denis

Claddagh Pool: a novel/Denis Hearn

ISBN-13:978-0615631301

ISBN-10:0615631304

Cover design by Nick Arnold

To Suzette, who helped bring me and Claddagh Pool to life.

Claddagh Pool

Prologue

Maelvadoog, the great grey hooded crow, stood erect and proud on the beech tree limb, his strong back absorbing the heat from the day-warmed bark. A rabbit stirred on the ground below hopping along the bank next to a pollen-covered pool. The grunts of the bullfrogs sounded deeper here in the woods. Dark eyes watched from above as the crow's black tail twitched from side to side.

The time to strike was now, immediate, inevitable. The rabbit emerged outside the cover of a branch and saw briefly the shadow; then darkness as black claws sank deep into its flesh. Diving death brought food and fable to the mighty bird.

High above, Showook spiraled in the rising thermals watching her mate tear pieces from the furry shape, still squirming in his deadly grip. She called, screaming with delight, as the yellow clouds of pollen spores blew inexorably through the magic wood below.

Maelvadoog flew higher into their nesting tree and waited there for her to join him in relishing the rabbit's flesh. Together they tore away the skin and dug deeply into the fresh meat below. Finishing up the meal, they cleaned their claws and picked the last morsels from their black beaks.

Maelvadoog spread his wings and soared skyward into the clear air above the forest rolling effortlessly along the winding river which lead to Brandon Abbey. He glided down the tree lined avenue and perched on the wrought-iron trim surrounding the library window ledge; tapping the window with his beak he nudged it open.

Hopping with well placed steps, he perched on the back of an ancient chair next to the leather covered desk and slowly his greyness and dappled feathers began to morph into the well worn habit of a monk.

His beak became the shadowed hood and his sharp, black claws moved slowly under the desk and slid, as feet into a pair of handmade leather sandals. The monk took a pen out of the silver holder and moved the sharpened point towards the whitened page of his scripted labor.

Outside the window he could hear the calls of his mate, Showook, as she circled high above the hallowed walls of learning.

She flew in through the window and perched next to him on the desk, her black eyes glinting in the hard, white light. They began to change color from black to blue as she turned her head to watch Maelvadoog's hand move toward the waiting page.

A rustling sound emanated from her feathered shape and slowly Showook became Peig, the seanachie.

"Well now Peig!" said the monk.

"What story do you have for me today, a gra?"

Chapter 1

A slight breeze stirred the water in Claddagh Pool next to the city of Galway as Lori Hanratty, an early morning runner splashed into a puddle next to the edge of the harbor wall. U2 music filled her head as she worked her way along the dock beside the water. Suddenly her foot slipped sideways and she staggered to her right landing on her knees and right shoulder as her body continued to slide periliously close to the edge of the dock, then stopped just in time before going over the side. She winced in pain as blood began to run down her arm. Raising herself up to view the damage, she looked at her skinned elbow and bent her arm to make sure there was no damage. She turned and sat up surveying her flayed and bloodied knees.

"Damn! Shit!" she blurted reaching down to

check her ankle. Then she saw it in the water, a black shape floating beside the wall. Leaning over to get a better look she realized it was a body dressed in black. *"Oh my God it is!"* As the black shape rose and fell in the undulating swells, she painfully stood up and took a few steps along the pier to get a better look. It was a man with gray hair, wearing a black suit and a purple vest. Screaming for help and still in pain from her fall she shouted, "Help, there's someone in the water. Somebody help me! Call an ambulance!" She scanned the dock area, but there was no one there to hear her cries for help.

Collecting her wits about her, she limped down the dock and up Market Street making the final blocks to Nealon's Bar, a well known watering hole for Galway locals and tourists alike. Pushing the door open she staggered into the building and up to the bar.

"What happened?" said Tom the barman, recognizing Lori with her blood stained shirt.

"I fell on the dock next to Claddagh Pool and twisted my ankle, but there's more. I saw a body floating in the water next to the pier."

"Are you OK? Let me get some towels to clean up the blood. Are you sure you saw a body?"

"Yes, get me a phone; I need to call the police!"

Tom pulled out his mobile and handed it to Lori.

"Officer, I was jogging . . . there's a body in Claddagh Pool . . . floating alongside the northside of the harbor wall . . . Oh my God. . .!"

"Are you sure it was a body?"

"I'm positive."

"What's your name?"

"Lori Hanratty."

"Where are you right now?"

"In Nealon's Bar on Market Street."

"Stay where you are. We're on the way!"

Tom took back the phone and began to talk to the two locals seated at the bar as Lori continued her conversation with the police.

"Hey Liam, you picked an interesting day to drop by."

"Yeah, Brian and I just drove from Caher to pick up some supplies for the business," Liam replied, then turned towards the runner.

"I'm Liam and this is Brian. I hope you didn't do too much damage with your fall. Let me get you a brandy."

"Thanks Liam, I'm Lori Hanratty."

"Hi Lori, that wasn't a good way to start your day," said Brian.

"Yeah, I run by Claddagh Pool every morning and happened to slip on the wet stones today and fall on to the pier, that's when I saw it," Lori replied.

"Are you OK now?" said Tom handing her a bar towel.

"Do you need a medic? Anything broken? "Would you like something else?"

"No thanks, I'll be fine, just need some time to catch my breath." She stood up, grabbing the towels and headed to the bathroom to get cleaned up. Tom turned to Liam.

"I've been a barman a long time and seen a lot of weirdness, but this beats all. Lori is in here sometimes on her way home and now she's a witness to finding a body. I wonder what happened to the bishop?"

"We'll find out in due course, I'm sure," said Brian.

"I wonder what he was doing down here at the docks, that seems very strange," said Liam.

"Speaking of docks, will you have access to the water at your new house?" Tom asked.

"There's an old stone pier about a mile away and I'm sure I could keep a boat there," Liam replied.

"By the way, how's the new house coming along?" Tom asked.

"It's nearly done. I'll be moving in soon and be able move out of my mother's house over the pub, that'll be a good thing."

Liam lived with his mother while his house was being completed and couldn't wait get a place of his own.

Lori returned from the bathroom and sat next to Liam.

"Hey Brian, how's baby Sean doing?" Tom asked.

"He's doing great Tom, thanks. Evie's such a great mother and we just love watching him grow like a weed every day."

"Yeah, kids are the best. How are things going with the job?"

"I'm really busy these days finishing up a research project, so that's taking me away from Sean more than I like."

Brian Conneally, Liam's best friend lived in Carraroe a small fishing village around the corner of the headland from Caher harbor. Brian, a marine scientist, worked at the Marine Research Center in Galway and was married to Evie. They were still getting used to their new son Sean with Evie snatching the odd spare moment to work on her art.

As Tom walked back down the bar to serve another customer the door in front of him swung open and a policeman with another man walked into the room and headed straight towards him.

"We're looking for Lori Hanratty, can you point her out to us?" the policeman asked.

"Yeah, she's right there sitting at the other end of the bar," said Tom pointing in Lori's direction.

Both men walked swiftly to the end of the room approaching Lori from her left side as she sat on the barstool talking to Liam who had moved over to sit beside her.

"Ms. Hanratty, I'm inspector Seamus O'Dowd and this is Officer Pat O'Brien. I'd like to take your statement about the body you saw in the pool, if that's all right."

"Sure, be glad to."

"Let's go to the booth over there where we'll have some privacy," said Seamus politely escorting Lori away from the bar.

"So what did you see?"

"It looked like a man in a black suit wearing a purple vest," Lori replied. "Who else wears a purple vest, other than a bishop? Oh my God! It was the bishop?"

"We don't know yet," Seamus replied.

Lori finished giving her statement to the inspector, returned to the bar and seated herself next to Liam and Brian who were still sitting where she had left them.

"You won't believe what I just figured out. The person floating in Claddagh Pool could be the bishop of Galway."

"Wow! That's too weird. Did he fall in or was it something else. What was he doing at Claddagh Pool?" said Brian.

Lori sat motionless on her stool trying to unwrap the scene developing around her. "I gotta go home; I can't deal with this anymore!"

"Do you need a ride?" asked Liam.

"No thanks, I called my Mum and she's coming to get me."

"The press and RTE will be all over this story soon, I bet," said Liam.

"What do you know about the bishop?" Brian asked Liam.

"He's been here in Galway for a while, and the only thing I remember about him was his controversial decision to transfer a priest to another parish a few years ago," Liam responded.

"That's right, I'd forgotten about that whole deal. Do you think that had anything to do with this?"

"You never know!"

"Let's go check it out," said Brian.

CLADDAGH POOL

They got off their bar stools and walked out into the street in the direction of Claddagh and back to the van. Arriving at the warehouse, they looked across Claddagh Pool and saw a number of police cars parked next to the pier. Their blinking lights created a riot of color reflecting in the puddles on the stone surface. The area had been cordoned off and no one was allowed on the dock so they walked back into the warehouse.

"What's happening now?" Brian asked one of the pallet truck drivers.

"The Guards identified the body floating in the water and they're saying it was the bishop," said the driver.

"Yeah, we were in Nealon's when we heard about it," said Brian walking towards the loaded van. They climbed into the cab and proceeded to turn west towards Caher before the light sank into the western sky.

Chapter 2

The diocese of Galway was in an uproar. The death of the bishop brought a huge press contingent to the city. Reporters were everywhere as the investigation continued.

Anne O'Gorman, a reporter for the Irish Times, was taking the lead for the readers on this unfolding story. She had driven to Galway from Dublin and set up base in a hotel in Salthill to begin a full-scale investigation of the event for the paper. Having settled in to the hotel, she visited the bishop's house in Galway, but was rudely turned away by Teresa O'Connor, the bishop's secretary, who told her that a press conference would be scheduled later in the day and a statement would be made at that time. Her gut feeling told her that Teresa O'Connor was stonewalling and was putting up a protection barrier for the bishop and the church hierarchy.

In the meantime she was interviewing other members of the clergy including the parish priests of the diocese in order to ascertain personal information about the bishop. She contacted Fr. Tom Leonard, a parish priest from Carna who had come to Galway to find out what he could about the death of his Bishop. Anne spoke to him about the bishop and learned that His Eminence was an educated and sociable person who had worked hard in the diocese to correct the negative behaviour of some of his priests. Using her investigative skills, she learned that Teresa O'Connor lived in a bungalow in the village of Spiddal on the coast of Galway Bay.

Anne, arriving in Spiddal to re-interview Teresa, parked her car beside Eilish Art, an arts and crafts store next to the shingle beach. She glanced in through the windows at some of the art before she crossed the road and proceeded to the O'Connor house where she rang the bell and waited for a response. The possibility of meeting Teresa would be slight as the secretary did not want to sully the bishop's name.

Anne knocked again. The door opened to reveal Teresa O'Connor in the hallway.

"Hello there, Miss O'Connor, do you remember me; Anne O'Gorman? We spoke earlier today. May I talk with you some more about the bishop's death?"

"Please do come in. I'm sorry I couldn't speak to you earlier. I had too much going on when you called at the church." Teresa ushered Anne into the living room.

"I understand."

They sat down and Anne began to use her well honed reporter's techniques to get inside the mind of the woman seated next to her.

"I'm sorry for your loss. I'm sure the bishop was like family to you since you worked with him for a number of years."

Teresa's face crumpled and Anne saw that she was struggling to gain control of her emotions.

"I got the call from the police early this morning and I'm still in shock. He was like an older brother to me. We liked the same music and had similar tastes in literature. He was godfather to one of my neices," Teresa began to sob. Anne handed her a tissue.

"Do you know of anyone who'd want to harm the bishop?"

"I don't know of anyone who'd want to do that. He was a good man," she said trying to recover.

"I'm sorry. I can't do this right now. It hurts too much," she began to cry.

"OK, I understand, maybe we can do this another time?"

"Of course, I'll feel better in a couple days," Teresa replied, walking Anne to the door.

On the drive back to Galway, Anne began to think about some of the things that Teresa had said.

Teresa is protecting him from something? What is she not telling me?

She sped up a bit, realizing there was much more to learn about the bishop and Teresa O'Connor.

Chapter 3

Brian and Liam continued westward along the coast road towards Carraroe. The sun had already begun to set, and its waning light cast a golden glow on the Twelve Bens Mountains.

"That's the damnest thing I've ever heard in Nealons," said Liam.

"It's going to be a big deal for the church, not to mention the city of Galway," Brian replied.

Liam hit the radio button and listened to an RTE reporter interviewing the female witness who had found the body of the bishop floating beside the pier in Claddagh Pool.

The woman continued, "I was jogging down the pier at Claddagh Pool when I slipped and almost fell over the side of the dock. Then I saw the body floating alongside the wall. I called the police and later they confirmed it was the bishop's body."

The reporter continued with his summation of the event explaining that according to his information the bishop had made a dinner appointment the previous day to meet a guest at the Star Hotel. He had been driven to the hotel by his driver but was seen leaving the hotel with his guest. It was assumed that they left in the man's car because the bishop had excused his own driver, and that was the last anyone saw of him until his body was found the next morning at the dock.

"I think there's more going on here than just a drowning," said Brian.

"Wonder why he left with that man at the hotel and didn't use his own car," said Liam. "NBCI will be all over this case, I'm sure."

At last the two friends arrived in the village of Carraroe and drove directly to Brian's house. "Thanks for the help today," said Liam. "We sure picked the right day to go to Galway."

"We sure did. Maybe next time a fishing trip would be a good idea?" Brian replied.

"Excellent idea, let's make it happen for sure! Give Sean a hug from me."

Liam turned his rusty beast out of Brian's driveway and headed back to Caher.

CLADDAGH POOL

*   *   *

There were still a number of cars parked outside the pub when he arrived. He went inside and asked one of the locals to help him unload the supplies. Grabbing a hand truck from the storage room, the two men unloaded the van, and Liam provided a pint as reward to his helper.

He went into the kitchen and looked to see if there was anything to eat. A piece of cold chicken stared at him out of the fridge, so he grabbed a skillet and proceeded to make an omelet.

"An omelet fixes everything," he thought, cracking fresh eggs into the pan. Sprinkling onions, tomatoes and cheese into the mix he flipped it once and sat down to finish it off with a tall glass of milk. Why would someone want to kill the bishop? Was it a robbery? Or blackmail? Liam didn't have much time for the church but killing the bishop was going too far.

Chapter 4

Conor Horgan, a young detective from Dublin, arrived in Galway to take charge of the investigation into the murder of the bishop. His superiors had selected him because of his experience in scientific analysis and psychological profilings of criminal cases. A science graduate from University College Dublin, his speciality was forensics. He lived in a condo in Dublin overlooking the city's refurbished docklands. Conor, in his early thirties with dark eyes and short cropped hair was in great physical shape. His body was constantly being put through a fitness regime of running and strength training. Sports, tennis, sailing and the outdoors in general was his life.

Conor booked himself into an old Victorian hotel in Salthill, a resort area located on Galway Bay and set up a base of operations in the room that would become his home for the duration of the case. Pulling the laptop out of its bag, he called up his custom crime software which allowed him to enter data, track leads, and build connections that otherwise would have to be completed on a white wall board with colored markers. He created a new file and inputed the information on the case. The following day he would monitor the autopsy of the bishop and all those details would be added to the file.

Googling Bishop Cronin, he discovered that Cronin had been a bishop for over ten years and had been involved with ecumenical activity with the Protestant churches and other denominations. He learned that Bishop Cronin had graduated as a priest from Maynooth College and was appointed bishop when he was in his late forties. Drilling a little deeper into the data, he uncovered the bishop's controversial transfer of a suspected pedophile priest from a parish in Galway to another part of the country. Conor was unable to find any personal information about the bishop's family and decided that he would be able to fill in that section after he had interviewed some of the locals and the bishop's secretary.

Chapter 5

Liam woke up to another bright, sunny day with blue sky and high clouds. He dressed and after a quick breakfast, drove to Clifden and west onto the Sky Road to see the progress on his new house.

Stopping in Clifden at the bakery, he bought some donuts for the workers at the construction site located high above the craggy rocks of the rolling sea. The drive along Sky Road reminded him of why he had selected this location for his new home; a spectacular site, overlooking the ocean, hanging on the western side of Ireland where nature created a new sunset masterpiece everyday.

Liam got out of the car and walked into his house. Carpenters were working on the first level installing the sub floor in all the rooms, while the electricians were running wiring to all the marked outlets and lighting fixtures in the upstairs floor.

"Morning, guys," he shouted, "Time for a break? I brought donuts and coffee, come and get 'em!"

Pat, the project manager, was the first person at the donut source. He handed out the grub to all his crew and then sat down on a box to talk to Liam.

"Did you hear about the bishop?" said Pat. "It was on the news last night."

"Yeah, I did. Brian and I were in Galway when the body was discovered," said Liam.

"No shit! You were there when it happened?"

"Not when it happened, but we were at Nealon's when the runner came in and told the police what had happened."

"And it was really the bishop?" said Pat.

"The woman who discovered him seemed sure because she noticed his purple vest."

"You know, Finbar, my lead carpenter, built all the cabinetry for the bishop's library," Pat replied, "and got to know him quite well during the job."

"That's right, I remember now," changing topic Liam went on, "You guys are making great progress on the house. It looks like the downstairs is nearly finished and the rough electrical upstairs is ready for sheetrock. I'm going to Galway tomorrow, so if you need me, call me on my cell-phone."

"No problem, I'll call you later and let you know how we're doing," Pat replied.

Liam walked upstairs and checked the bathroom and master suite. It was ready for fixtures. The view outside was still impressive to him as he checked downstairs and found Finbar working on some trim in the great room.

Finbar was a young man of small stature with short, black, spikey hair, blue eyes, with the sensitive look of an artist. His wide shoulders, tightly covered with a local hurling team T-shirt, led down to his wide belt that held up a well worn pair of jeans. He had strong hands with short fingers and battered nails permanently stained with wood dye. Finbar was whistling a traditional tune "She Moved Thru the Fair," when Liam walked in.

"Hi, Finbar, my da used to whistle that tune!"

"Is that right?"

"You're doing quite a job on the trim and have created a beautiful design feature around the windows and the bookcases," Liam continued.

"Thanks," said Finbar. "I really enjoy working on it."

"How do you plan to handle the glass doors on the display cabinets in the great room? Are they going to have clear glass or mullion doors? Either way, I think they should have glass shelves so I can light them from above," Liam requested.

"I think the mullions would look the best. They'd add variety to the door and frame the items inside in a unique way."

"I'm hoping to get the job as the shop teacher at Carraroe Tech, and if I do, I'd like you to teach a joinery class so my students could experience your expertise in constructing three-way, hand mitered corners," said Liam.

"No problem, I'd love to do it. Hope you get the job!"

"Me too," Liam walked out the door and down the stairs.

Chapter 6

Conor began his day of investigation into the death by eating breakfast in Nealon's. He steeled himself for the examination of the body later in the morning; cutting into a human body was a mutilation in spite of what it might reveal and he never looked forward to it.

As he continued to type notes into his Mac, he noticed a tall, blond woman approaching his table.

"Are you Detective Horgan?" she asked.

"That's me," replied Conor somewhat surprised.

"I'm Anne O'Gorman, a reporter for the Irish Times. I'm working on the story about the death of Bishop Cronin. The police department gave me your name and told me that I would probably find you here. May I ask you some questions?"

"Sure, have a seat, but you know I can't divulge details of the case. How about some breakfast?"

"Thanks, but I already ate. I'd love some coffee though."

Conor waved down the waitress.

"Do you have any idea about the cause of death?" asked Anne.

"Not yet, but we'll be examining the body later today. Are you working exclusively for the Irish Times?"

"I am."

"I suppose you'd like an exclusive source for your story?"

"You bet, maybe we can work together on this case. You scratch me; I'll scratch you!"

Conor began to study Anne as she sat on the other side of the table. She was very pretty with long blond hair and blue eyes that seemed to draw him into her world. Her long sweater covered a beautiful body with well-formed soft curves. It was fastened at her waist by a soft leather belt. He had not seen the rest of her below the table but assumed that the perfect picture would be completed when she stood up.

Anne continued to talk about her work on other cases and stories that had promoted her as a crime reporter.

"Have you worked many murder cases before?" she asked.

"Yes I have; that's why I wanted to get into this side of scientific investigation. I'm able to use all my skills and intuition to solve crimes."

Anne watched Conor speak about his life in Dublin as a detective. She was enthralled by his soft lilt and the descriptions of some of his previous cases; definitely an interesting person who could prove to be an endless source of info for her story.

"Let's get together for supper tonight at McDonagh's on Quay Street," said Conor. "We can compare notes. 7:30 OK?"

"See you then," said Anne, wondering how this back scratching thing was going to work out. She wasn't interested if he was going to do all the itching, and she all the scratching.

"Good luck with your investigation later this morning."

"Thanks." She stood up, shook Conor's hand.

Yeah! This itch is getting itchier all the time, thought Conor as he watched her walk out the door.

*   *   *

Brian Connelly walked into the Marine Research Center in Galway and headed for the office of Dr. Breda Woods, Chief of Aquaculture Research and one of his professors while he was a marine science student at UCG.

"Hi, Brian, how's the family?"

"We're doing great. Sean is growing like a weed and Evie is starting to get back to her art. Hey, what do you make of the drowning in Galway? I was there with Liam when someone found the bishop's body in Claddagh Pool."

"Yes, I saw that, too. I don't know much about him other than what I read about his connection with a child abuse case that was in the news a few years ago. I wonder how he ended up in Claddagh Pool?"

"I'm sure we'll find out in due course. It's just a matter of time."

"Speaking of time, how's your food source research going for the fishery?" she asked inquisitively.

"It's going great, that's why I came by to see you today. I'll be sending the research results to the lab in Derry shortly, and I've set up a meeting there with Susan Somers to combine our research results and prepare the data to the EU for approval."

"Well, show me what you have."

Chapter 7

Conor picked up a protective suit, put on the hat and mask, and snapped on a pair of latex gloves in preparation for the examination of Bishop Cronin.

The body of the bishop lay on a stainless steel gurney in the next room with focused lights illuminating the still covered corpse.

Conor would witness the examination of the body by the coroner's staff as they delved into the cause of death. Walking into the examination room he introduced himself, "Good morning, I'm Conor Horgan, chief detective on this case," he announced shaking the lead examiner's hand, "I'm here to observe."

"Good morning, Detective Horgan, I'm Mary Murray and this is my assistant Sheila Dempsey."

"Pleased to meet you both."

"Shall we get started?"

Sheila slowly opened the zipper revealing the white body of the bishop. The expanding light revealed the lifeless, gray form, as she undid the zipper ending at his feet. Death defined the departed as just another corpse. It did not acknowledge that the person might have been a king, a lowly working man, or a bishop. Death was the great equalizer.

Dr. Murray began to speak into the microphone attached to her collar, "We'll examine the entire body externally first for any trauma, old scars, or obvious indications of mortal wounds. I don't see any evidence of strangulation or blunt force trauma to the body. We'll learn more on the internal examination when we open the chest and examine the organs. Only then will we be able to tell approximate time and cause of death."

She took a scalpel in her hand and began the "Y" incision used in all autopsies. Conor watched as the examiner carved her way into the body, revealing the chest cavity and the vital organs.

"This person looks healthy," said the coroner. "We'll examine all the organs to ascertain the cause of death."

"I have more research to do on the case," said Conor excusing himself. "I'll be in the office next door, if you find anything important."

He left the room, tossing the protective gear into a large blue container on his way out. Walking into the shared office nearby he continued to add more information onto his laptop.

"This doesn't get any easier," he thought visualizing what was occurring next door. His pool of evidence was growing as he drilled deeper into the web to research more details about the bishop and his stint in Galway. Finding an old newspaper article about the transfer of a priest to another parish, he learned that the priest had been accused of child abuse and had only been reprimanded. Conor's thoughts were interrupted when Dr. Murray walked into the office having shed her protective attire.

"I've got a preliminary description of what I've found, so you'll have some immediate results for your file. A complete written report will be provided later," the doctor explained. "According to our examination, this person was deceased before he was put in the water. He did not drown. We found no strangulation evidence or blunt force markings on the body but did find a small puncture wound on the right side of his neck. His heart was healthy and there was no evidence of any terminal disease. The liver and kidneys were removed and we'll run tests on them to provide us with a clue to any substance that may have caused his death. Most likely the body was in the water for approximately eight hours, and as reported by the police, it was not attached to anything or anchored in any way. Therefore, until we get the scientific results of a substance in the organs, we are unable to indicate the cause of death. The body will be preserved for the undertaker and we should have biological and scientific results in twenty-four hours. I'll call you when the tests are back."

"Thank you, doctor."

It was late afternoon when Conor returned to his hotel. He showered, dressed and walked out the door into the waning sun as it slowly sank into the golden waters of Galway Bay. Walking down the promenade at Salthill, he tried to get the picture of the dead bishop out of his mind. He always needed a shower after an autopsy in order to wash away the visual and mental reminder of a body being defiled.

He could never get used to the smell of formaldehyde and the sight of the white-blue skin, glazed eyes now sightless but knowing everything. It was extremely bizarre seeing the mortal body of a man of God. One always thinks of them as being greater than other men, but in the end, their chests are hairy, their stomachs are paunchy, their testicles hang limply, an oddly corporeal sight for such a man as the bishop who purportly stood above his flock.

*   *   *

Anne stepped out of the shower, toweled off, and dried her long blond hair. She stood back from the mirror and checked the style and fall of it as it fell around her shoulders. Her twenty- six year old body was in great shape thanks to her morning running regimen and her work at the gym twice a week. She would need to maintain this schedule even under the stress of the current assignment in Galway.

She put on a custom pair of jeans, a shirt with oversized lapels and a fitted jean jacket. She pulled on her Luchese boots enjoying the oiled leather smell and feel as each heel thunked snugly into place. Standing up, she viewed the result. *That'll work, chic and practical.*

Looking at her watch, she saw it was 6:00. *I have some time, so let's find some background on Conor Horgan.* Opening her laptop she googled his name, then, for more information she checked Linkedin and delved into that source also.

After discovering he was a graduate of University College Dublin with a B.S. in Criminology Science, Google revealed interests in tennis, sailing and refurbishing a lighthouse on the Wexford coast. She continued her research of Conor into the world of sports and found out that he had competed in the Fitzwilliam Amateur Tennis Tournament in Dublin earlier in the year and also had raced in the Around the South Coast Sailing competition the previous year. Anne's journalism degree had prepared her well for this kind of fact finding work.

He's somebody I'd like to get to know. Wonder if he's in a relationship. No wedding band, but in Ireland, that doesn't mean anything.

Chapter 8

Fr. Tom Leonard walked into his living room in the parish house outside Carna, sat down and poured himself a drink. He gazed melancholy into the flames of his newly built turf fire and began to think about the horrific event that had just occurred in Galway.

Fr. Tom, as he was known, had been the parish priest in Carna since his installation by Bishop Cronin five years earlier. He had become a good friend of the bishop and could not believe that he was dead. When would the crime investigators be showing up at his door to ask questions and find out what he knew about the bishop and his friends?

Fr. Tom had been a student at Maynooth College in Kildare when he had met Eamon Cronin who was about five years older and about to complete studies before ordination and appointment to a parish as a curate.

CLADDAGH POOL

When Tom and Eamon were students in Maynooth, they would sometimes drive into Dublin to meet with other seminarians. They'd practice writing sermons and learning the process of public speaking. Staying at a friend's flat on Rathmines Road, they'd avail themselves of life in Dublin, frequenting the clubs on the south side of the city.

Fr. Tom enjoyed fulfilling the obligations of priesthood and guiding his parishioners toward spiritual fulfillment as well as the occasional hurling match or other social events often with the movers and shakers of the village.

The Church was going through the difficult time with the child abuse scandal and Fr. Tom was very aware of the issues that were occurring with priests and also with Bishop Cronin. He had seen the church ignore the pleas of the abused and watched the hierarchy make deals with the parents of the abused while the perpetrators of the crimes just walked away or were transferred. This was not the church to which he had dedicated his life.

Fr.Tom sat in his comfortable chair and tried to understand why someone would want to kill the bishop. None of the scenarios that entered his head made any sense, but there was a reason all of this had happened and he wondered if any of it had anything to do with the abuse. He gazed out the living room window and watched the black crows circling around a small copse of trees behind his house. They stood like sentries in the trees, waiting for the arrival of the leader and his court. *I wish I had their wisdom.*

Chapter 9

Anne walked out of her hotel to her car and drove to McDonagh's on Quay Street to meet Conor. It was a short drive and she found a parking space for her Mini right across the street. She walked into the restaurant and was ushered to a table where Conor was sitting.

"Glad you could make it."

"I remember being here before, while on another assignment in Galway," said Anne.

"They have the best seafood here," replied Conor.

The waiter approached and stood waiting for their order.

"What would you like to drink?"

"I'll have a glass of chardonnay."

"Jameson for me," said Conor.

"What's new on the case?" asked Anne.

"The autopsy is done and the results will be forthcoming when additional tests are completed."

"So, there's no cause of death at this point?"

"No, not until we get the complete results."

The waiter returned with their drinks and they chinked glasses.

"So, what do you like to do when you're not working?" asked Anne.

"Sailing takes up a good bit of time when I'm not fishing or playing tennis. Last summer, when I could catch a few hours of good wind, I taught sailing at the club in Dun Laoghaire."

"Where did you go to school?" Anne asked.

"Wesley College, where I got involved with rugby, it was the school sport and lasted for most of the academic year until the athletics program kicked in."

"What do you like to do when you're not working?" Conor asked, moving the conversation in her direction.

"I also play tennis but I'm not very good. I've been looking for someone to hit with and crank up my serve and backhand. Riding horses is a passion of mine. When I was six I had a pony and learned to ride. While *Sparks* is long gone, I still ride sometimes when I visit my cousins in county Wexford."

Conor chimed in, "In Wexford, really! I'm working on restoring an old Martello tower on the south coast of the county; my uncle, who had a small farm near the coast, left it to me. Remodeling this tower is a huge project; although I have it all weatherproofed at this point and need to start on the interior."

"That sounds exciting."

31

"I've been collecting antique furnit
wall hangings based on my research of tl
You know, a building with curved walls presents its
own special set of interior design challenges. *Tern,*
my sailboat, is moored at Dunmore, just across the
bay from Baginbun and the tower," Conor added.

"Do you know the Boland family in Wexford?"
Anne asked.

"I know Kevin Boland; he was at UCD with
me."

"Does he have a sister, Claire?"

"He does."

"Wow! Small world, they live next door to my
cousins outside Bunclody and Claire's one of my best
friends!"

"Really?"said Conor.

"Did Claire go to school with you?"

"Yes, we went to Alexandra College in Dublin
and got into a fair amount of trouble together."

"Great school, I enjoyed Wesley, especially the
debating society," Conor replied.

"Yeah, Wesley is known for its loud mouths!"
Anne grinned.

"How long have you worked for the Irish
Times?" Conor asked.

"This is my fourth year," said Anne, "This
case has a lot of twists and turns, kind of like sailing a
boat through choppy seas.

Sometimes the wind is strong and steady and
other times you're dead in the water. Pardon my
pun! Following a crime story is always exciting.

I love to connect the dots and see how my conjectures measure up to the final result. I constantly check myself. A good reporter can't let subjectivity skew her interpretation of fact. I need to intuit when I meet a source whether or not they are valid and then measure them against a source which has something to lose or gain."

"Now you have another source of information," said Conor, laughing.

"True."

The waiter returned and Anne ordered grilled salmon while Conor ordered sea trout.

"Any brothers or sisters?" Anne asked.

"I've a brother, Joe. He's a vet and lives in Naas; works with the horse racing business. How about you?"

"A sister, Miriam, who's a sophomore at UCD," said Anne adding some dill sauce to her salmon. "This fish is perfectly cooked and I like the capers on top. Now I remember why I came here before."

Finishing their meal, they lingered a little longer to finish their drinks before walking outside into the warm evening. The evening sun painted itself across the swells in the bay as herring gulls swooped slowly through the rolling waves.

"Thanks for supper."

"You're welcome. Maybe we can do this again."

Conor walked closer to her and realized that she was moving towards him. He gave her a soft hug and released.

"Good night," said Anne.

"See you tomorrow, maybe?" said Conor as he walked back to his car thinking about her jeans; her boots; that hair! She was a total opposite of the last woman he had tangled with, so real. No long red fingernails and artful makeup. Anne rocked the natural look. Conor could feel himself getting closer to her and wanting to, by the minute.

Chapter 10

L iam drove from Caher to Galway stopping outside the Board of Education building where he had an appointment with Frank Williams, the principle of Carraroe Comprehensive School and Bill McMahon, a department head. Hoping to be selected for the position of woodworking teacher, he walked into the office of the administrator for his scheduled appointment.

"Good morning. May I help you?" asked the receptionist.

"I have an appointment with Frank Williams,"said Liam.

"Please go right in, they're expecting you in the conference room just across the hall."

"Thank you," said Liam walking into the conference room. Frank and Bill stood up when Liam entered the room and both men walked over to greet him.

"Thanks for coming this morning," said Frank. "This is Bill McMahon, our technical program administrator."

"Glad to see you Liam," said Bill. Everybody went back to the table and sat down.

"Can I get you coffee, water?" Frank asked.
"Water , thank you."
"Bill and I have discussed your application. Your technical background in construction and education is a good fit for the position at CCS. Based on our previous interviews, we have decided to offer you the position of woodworking director. Your hands on experience and knowledge of all woodworking requirements, together with your fluency in the Irish language here in the Gaeltacht, make you the perfect candidate for this position. This is a new direction for us so you will need to supply us with your vision."

His fluency in Irish was a requirement for the job because the school was located in Gaeltacht, the Irish speaking part of Ireland.

"Thank you," Liam replied a little surprised because not only had the job turned out to be much more than just teaching, but they also had made the decision so quickly.

"I'm really excited about the opportunity and can't wait to begin my new program using interactive teaching in the classroom. I think all learning benefits from visual expression and hands on practice with tools. For example, Finbar, who is working on my house, is a graduate at Carraroe and I'd like to have him teach one of my classes."

"Good idea," said Frank. "We'd like you to attend an orientation session next Monday at the school and begin teaching the following week, if that will fit in your schedule. I know its short notice, but we have to get this program underway as soon as possible in order to make use of a technology grant from the EU."

"I'm looking forward to being part of the team," Liam responded with confidence.

"Looks like we're done with the formal meeting," said Frank. "I'm happy you made the decision to join us and look forward to you having you at the College."

"You'll need to go to the Human Resources department and fill out all the paperwork, before you leave today," said Bill. The three men stood up, and shook hands.

"Welcome aboard," said Bill.

"Go raibh maith agat," said Liam and walked out the door.

He spent about an hour at HR and realized that teaching required more paperwork than he thought. He couldn't wait to get started.

Chapter 11

Next morning Conor was awakened by the chirp of his cell phone. He looked at the number on the screen realizing it was a call from Dr. Murray at the coroner's office.

"Sorry for calling you so early,"

"No problem," Conor replied. "Did you work all night?"

"Yes," she continued, "We have forensic results from the body organs. They indicate some form of substance in the liver, but we haven't identified it yet so are initiating more tests.

The external, physical evidence on the bishop's neck indicates a puncture wound, possibly inflicted by a large needle, may be a veterinary needle because of the diameter of the puncture.

There were no other breaks in the skin or entry points anywhere else on the body; therefore we believe that the puncture wound was the entry point for a substance that may have killed the bishop. We're also going to request the resources of the Marine Research Center in Galway, to assist us in identifying the substance. We discovered traces of it in the liver and we know that MRC is the best source to identify it."

"That's great progress," Conor responded.

"Looks like you've discovered the how and the means and now need the substance that caused the death of this person," the coroner added.

"I'll check with MRC since my friend Brian Connelly, works there. He should be able to give me a more personal entre into the facility and avoid some of the red tape involved in getting forensic results from a crime scene. I worked with him, while I was studying at UCD. We were partners on a joint marine science project. I'll give him a call and let you know," said Conor.

He finished the call and stepped into the shower, then dressed and walked downstairs to the lobby, picking up a copy of the Irish Times. On the front page he read an article by Anne about the continuing investigation into the death of Bishop Cronin in Galway. She had quoted a police source for information on the story and indicated that there was still no precise cause of death. Conor was pleased that she was presenting the story in a factual manner not adding any speculation or opinions to the event.

He drove into downtown Galway and parked in Eyre Square. Walking past the sculpture of Padraig O'Conaire, the Galway born writer, Conor touched it as a sign of traditional good luck and respect and continued down Market Street to Nealon's where he sat in a booth and ordered breakfast then texted Anne. *At Nealons. Join me for breakfast?*

A few minutes later he got the texted reply from her. *Be there 30.*

He then called MRC and asked to speak to Brian Connelly. His call returned to the operator, who asked if he wanted to leave a voicemail. Conor dialed Brian's personal cell instead.

"Hi Brian, How's Evie? I'm sure Sean is growing like a weed!"

"Hi Conor, yes he sure is. Evie's doing great and picking up her watercolors again. What's up with you these days? It's been a while!"

"I'm working on the investigation into the bishop's death, and I need to get access to a lab to identify a substance that was found in his body. I know you have access to MRC and was wondering if you could give me a contact there to expedite some tests."

"Sure do. Try Dr. Breda Woods. Mention my name and I'm sure Breda will be able to help you out."

"Thanks for the help, Brian. What are you up to these days?"

"I'm finalizing food supply research for the proposed cod fishery off the northwest coast," Brian replied. "It's been a long process since it involves working with the government in the United Kingdom and the government in Dublin. Lot's of politics."

"That sounds interesting. I heard about the cod fishery, and it looks like a great idea. Let's get together soon for a meal and catch up with our lives. It's been too long. Now that I'm here in Galway on this case, we have no excuses."

"True, I'll give you a call and set it up at the house in Carraroe."

"Great talking to you again, and thanks for the contact," said Conor.

"No problem."

Conor put down his phone and ordered some more coffee just in time to see Anne walk in the door and over to his table.

"Glad you could join me."

"How are you doing with the case?"

"Nothing new at this point," Conor responded. "I'm still waiting for the forensics and may work this weekend."

"I'm going to Inishmore Island on Saturday morning and leaving from Rosaveal. I've always wanted to see the big island and now have a reason to make the trip. I discovered Peig, an old seanachie, who has agreed to tell about her childhood on the island. Hopefully I'll be able to produce this for print and radio," Anne confirmed.

"Good for you," Conor replied. "I've been there a number of times; I love the place."

"Why don't you come with me?" said Anne.

"There's an interesting offer. Let me see if I can still get a room."

"I'm sure they'll have other rooms in the B&B," said Anne.

"I'll bring my laptop," said Conor, "I can work on the case and take a little downtime as well."

*　　*　　*

Fr. Tom sat in the confessional listening to the murmur of the people lined up outside the door waiting to enter the secure, stuffy box.

He opened the slide on his side and a puff of stale air blew through the wooden screen into his private space.

"Bless me, Father for I have sinned," said a man kneeling down on the well worn step.

"How long is it since your last confession?" said the priest.

"Actually I'm not here to confess my sins."

"Why are you here, then?"

"Do you know Fr. Michael Godfree?"

"Why do you want to know about him?"

"I'm his cousin from Australia and in Connemara for a few days. I was driving by the church and thought I'd be able to find out where he is these days."

Fr.Tom listened to the words. *Why didn't this person come to the rectory and ask me?* He shifted his weight closer to the screen in order to get a better look at the person on the other side of his world and saw that the visitor was a large man with a shaved head wearing a black turtleneck sweater under a dark jacket. He had an ominous feeling about the person on the other side of the screen as the dim light reflected on the man's shaved head.

"Do you know where I can find him?" repeated the man.

"I believe he was moved to a parish somewhere in county Wexford, but I don't know where."

The man continued, "I'm sure you heard what happened to the bishop and his friend! Now it's time to deal with Michael Godfree!"

Oh God, I was right, Fr. Tom thought trying to take back his words.

"Did you have anything to do with the death of the bishop?" Fr Tom asked. There was no reply.

The bald man stood up, opened the door and exited the box as Fr. Tom closed the slide on his side pausing for a few moments to get his wits about him before opening the door and watching the bald headed figure leave the church. He re entered the confessional, opened the slide and listened to another penitent.

"Bless me father for I have sinned," said the stranger.

Fr. Tom pondered the words. *How true they are for me. What do I do with this information? I can't tell anyone about it.*

Chapter 12

Saturday began early for Conor and Anne as they made their way to Rosaveal and the waiting ferry to take them to Kilronan on Inishmore, the largest of the Aran Islands located far out in Galway Bay. They drove the forty-minute drive to the harbor in separate cars and arrived within fifteen minutes of each other.

"Morning," said Conor when he saw Anne walking from her car towards the embarkation point.

"Good morning to you."

She was wearing a blue jacket, blue jeans and hiking boots. A loaded backpack was slung over her shoulder.

Conor thought about her in a different way, seeing her in her outdoor attire. Now she was showing him her natural exterior, no longer dressed in the garb of a professional journalist but a flesh and blood woman ready to take on the weekend with gusto.

They paid the fare at the window and got on board the ferry. Engines rumbled to life beneath them and lines were cast off releasing the ferry from the safety of the harbor. The ferry navigated down the bay and out into the open Atlantic stretching westward before them.

"I'm glad we got a good day to make this trip. You never know what'll happen with the weather on this side of the country," said Conor.

"Yes, I was here in November once working on a fishing story and the weather was terrible," Anne replied. "I was supposed to be here for a weekend and had to stay a whole week because of a storm!"

"Hope that doesn't happen to us! That would really put a kink in my investigation!" said Conor.

The wind was getting stronger now as the ferry eased out into the rising swells and began to slowly roll with the motion of the waves.

"Are you OK with the rolling?" asked Conor.

"I'm fine, so far," she replied.

"It's not a long trip, so it shouldn't be too bad."

Conor scanned the horizon and noticed a build up of clouds towards the west over the open sea. The immediate weather was sunny and reasonably warm for the end of August.

"It's a little chilly," said Anne.

"Let's move to the lee side out of the wind," said Conor steering them around the deckhouse.

"That's better," she said, sitting down next to him.

She felt his body warmth through his jacket as they rolled their way towards Kilronan.

"What did you bring in your backpack?"

"Just the basics for the weekend, snacks, water, change of clothes, first aid kit. You never know when you might need an aspirin or a Band-Aid," she continued moving closer to Conor. He could smell her subtle perfume wafting in his direction.

"I'm sure we'll be able to buy more supplies, at the dock," she continued, "before we begin to explore the island and set up a time to interview Peig. They have mini buses on the island if we need a ride, but I think we should walk unless we need to go to the other end of the island of course."

The ferry continued its rolling journey to the approaching harbor and slowly entered the safety of the craggy cliffs. With an experienced hand the skipper eased the bow of the boat towards the pier and spun the wheel to port to line up the hull positioning it parallel to the dock. While the crew threw the mooring lines to the waiting shoreman, the skipper put the vessel in reverse forcing the lines to tighten the hull snug up against its barnacle covered mooring.

They disembarked down the ramp onto the hard surface of Inishmore and began walking in the direction of a small store built with its rear wall embedded into the ancient rock.

Conor and Anne trudged up the hill from the pier at Kilronan and entered Joyce's Grocery Store and Public House. Anne spoke to the man behind the counter.

"Dia is Mhuire Dhuith," she said.

"Dia is Mhuire dhuith'gus Padraig,"

"Bhuil Bearla agath?" Anne asked.

"Yeah, I speak English. I'm Peadar Joyce and this is my wife Moira. Who do we have here?" he asked Conor.

"Conor Horgan and this is my friend, Anne O'Gorman."

"Welcome to Inishmore."

"I'm wondering how far it is to Peig Moran's house," Anne asked.

"Oh, it's a couple of miles up the road on the left hand side. Peig lives there with her younger brother who, by the way is over seventy years old. He's a widower and recently moved in with his sister to take care of her," Peadar continued. "I'd be happy to give you a ride to her house, if you need one."

"That'd be great if it's not a problem," said Anne.

"No bother," said Peadar.

"Let me call Peig and see if she's free after lunch."

Anne dialed Peig's number and a soft voice answered.

"Is mise Peig Ni Morain."

"Is mise Aine O'Gorman."

"Go maith," replied Peig.

"May we speak in English?" Anne asked.

"Of course."

"I'd like to come and talk to you after lunch. Would that be okay?" Anne asked.

"Sure, that'll be fine; I'll put the kettle on."

Anne and Conor walked outside, sat down at a table, and began to eat a light lunch of fruit and sandwiches with two bottles of Harp.

"I'll stay here and hang out at the bar with my laptop and continue working on the case," said Conor.

"When I come back, I'll find the B&B and check in," said Anne. "I only booked one room since I was originally going to be by myself," she continued.

"I'm sure I can get another room," Conor replied. "I'll give them a call."

"Good, then let's finish lunch and I'll go meet Peig. I think this'll be a great story told by a true seanachie. She's a wealth of information, I'm sure. I just have to weasel it out of her and let her do the rest,"

"How did you find Peig?" asked Conor.

"I discovered her the last time I was here reporting on a fishing story but didn't have time to talk to her. She may be the last true storyteller on the islands to carry on the oral tradition. I also heard she's a shapeshifter."

Conor walked back inside the pub and sat at the bar as Anne and Peadar left the driveway and drove up the hill to Peig's house in Peadar's beat up truck. He settled onto a stool at the bar and ordered a pint of Swithwicks.

"Moira, did you hear about the bishop's body being found at Claddagh pier?" Conor asked.

"Yeah, we sure did. It was a sad day indeed," Moira replied. "There're all kinds of rumors about his death, rumbling around the island. You know his mother was born on Inishere, the smallest of the Aran Islands, so the islanders have suffered a personal loss with his death."

"Is that right?" said Conor,"What are the rumor mongers saying about him?"

"It may be just pub talk but you hear everything in here. Some people say he was too easy on the priests when it came to the issue of child abuse. Then the other camp talked about the bishop like he was a saint. You're always going to find that when it comes to the church or anyone connected with it."

"Did you hear anything specific?"

"No, just general gossip!"

*   *   *

Anne arrived at Peig's house and got out of Peadar's car. She walked down a narrow path lined with a flowering fuschia hedge. Bees buzzed in the blooms plying their trade in aerial pollination. In a small open space in front of the house she noticed a pile of turf stacked neatly like old dried up boots resting in the sun.

Two noisy brown hens pecked incessantly at some grain scattered outside a weatherbeaten red door that led into a hen house with nest boxes built against the back wall. Wooden flaps on the outside of the boxes facilitated the outside collection of the eggs without disturbing the hens.

She walked around to the front door of the house that overlooked the wide expanse of Atlantic. Lifting the old brass knocker, she banged the green patinaed stop three times and waited for Peig to appear. The door was layered with bright red paint built up to a high luster. It opened quietly revealing an old woman wearing a fine knitted stole and a pair of ancient pamputies on her feet.

"Failte, a Lana! So glad you were able to come today."

Anne was led down a whitewashed hallway into a living room with a big open fireplace on the back wall. Two wing back chairs were angled toward each other in front of the fireplace. Between the chairs was an old wooden slab table with piles of books and papers stacked on one end.

"Excuse the mess, Miss O'Gorman. I'm working on transcribing some poetry and haven't had time to put it away."

"Please call me Anne. It's a real pleasure to be here today."

Peig was very spry for her age as she moved about clearing some space on the table.

Her lined face, framed by gray-white hair was tied in a bun and two cowrie shell earrings hung pendulously from their silver settings in her ears. Her kind blue eyes looked out from beneath a pair of tortoise-shell half glasses.

Anne sat down in one of the wing backed chairs and pulled out her note pad and tape machine. Peig sat in the other chair and waited for her guest to get settled.

"Would you like a cup of tea before we get started; the kettle's on?"

"Maybe after a while when we both get thirsty from all the talking that we are about to do. I'm going to just sit here and disappear into your voice."

Peig had an aura of mystery about her. Anne felt that she had always known this old lady who seemed to connect with her. Her azure blue eyes created an instant link to a woman who was more than a storyteller; she was magical. Anne clicked on the tape machine and asked Peig to tell her about her childhood growing up on Inishmore over the past seventy years of her life.

Peig began to speak, first in Irish, her native tongue. She described her primitive life on the island and how difficult it was to live with next to nothing around her. She recounted having to drag water from a well in one of the fields to a big black kettle that hung from a wrought-iron crane over a roaring turf fire.

"My ma baked bread and we always had a good supply of potatoes stored in a clamp outside in the yard."

She continued with her memories.

"A small black range sat beside the open fire that was used to bake the brown bread and fry rashers and eggs on cold drafty mornings before my brother and I had to walk to school with all the other children on the island; some of them had no shoes. They all carried a lunchbox with a double ended tin can nested inside, containing sugar and cocoa. The school children also had to drag water from a well and bring it back to the schoolhouse to prepare the lunchtime snack. I learned to write and found my calling as a storyteller. It was then that I discovered another skill; I could change myself into a herring gull and soar in the thermals along the ancient cliffs of Dun Aengus four hundred feet above the crashing waves below. This was my secret, I told nobody about it, not even my mother. Sometimes I would fly back to the mainland and land on the old spire of Brandon Abbey in the middle of Connemara, watching the monks parade their liturgy in the cloisters below. Shapeshifting was part of my being. It freed me from the anchored life of a human and I loved the noise of the wind whistling under my wings."

"When did you realize that you had the gift?"

"I was lying in bed one morning wondering what it would be like to be able to fly. I just let myself go and realized that I was flying, high over the island. I could see the harbor, the pathways between the stone walls and the waves crashing below me at the base of the fort. I flew down lower and through the spray from a wave. It splashed water on my wings. Then I knew it wasn't a dream."

Anne related, "I was raised on stories of shapeshifting in the Irish culture but never met anyone who claimed to actually do it. I suppose it wouldn't do to ask you to shift while I'm here? Most cannot show on demand how it's done," said Anne.

"How did you learn about shapeshifting?" Peig asked.

"My mother told me about the gift when I was a little girl. She believed that her mother was a shapeshifter because of some of the stories she had told her when she was growing up," Anne replied.

Peig continued on with her story about her family.

"I would have liked to have you meet my brother, Mike today but he left on the ferry a couple of days ago to go to a funeral in Clifden. I'm sure he'll be a while in getting back here. My brother was a fisherman and worked with our father on a small lobster boat here in Kilronan. There were no roads back then, just rutted lanes that wound their way around the high stacked stone walls of the island." Peig showed Anne a picture.

"That's where I went to school," she said handing Anne the old faded, brown photograph. "Nobody knew English out here back then, so I had to learn it in school."

Anne listened spellbound as Peig described the custom of Wren Day when people in costume would parade a wren on a stick from one end of the island to the other as little boys covered in straw tried to attack the King of the Birds.

"Do you know the story 'bout the Wren?" Peig asked.

"I've heard about it, but we never experienced it in Dublin."

"After Christmas, people called Mummers would dress up in straw outfits and walk through the village, playing whistles and parading a wren on a decorated pole. They'd collect money for the wren in order to keep it alive and then the money would be given to charity."

"Would they kill the wren if no one gave money to the crowd?" Anne asked.

"I never heard of a wren being killed for money but in the old days the wrens were sacrificed because they had betrayed the Irish warriors when the Vikings invaded the country."

"That's a strange tradition," said Anne, "but we Irish have a lot of Druid customs, maybe that's where it came from."

"You're right, now it's just another reason for a parade, drinking and dancing. . . a good craic!" said Peig.

Anne listened intently as Peig continued, "As you probably know, the people of the Aran Islands have a long history of survival. Catholic families were expelled from their lands on the east coast during the English conquest to the barren lands of the province of Connaught in the west of the country. Ultimately the Irish were driven onto the Aran Islands where there was little or no soil, so they had to make it out of kelp. It took generations of islanders to continue the task and the present day islands bear visual witness to their work and endurance to make a home and survive the harsh world of wind, waves and persecution."

CLADDAGH POOL

*　*　*

Back at the pub Conor was studying an older man standing at the end of the bar wearing a black donkey jacket, black pants and an old cap that covered his graying head. The figure swayed back and forth as he sipped his creamy Guinness. His face was lined and leather like, sculpted by the weather, the salt spray and years of boat handling as a fisherman. His hands were brown, gnarled and weathered like the wooden bar that held him in place. Conor got up and moved closer to the older man.

"Dia's Mhuire dhuith," said Conor.

"Dia's Mhuire dhuith's Padraig," he replied. "Cad as dhuith?"

"I'm Conor Horgan from Dublin."

"Padraig O'Hare from Kilronan," said the chiseled figure in black shaking Conor's hand.

"Sure, 'tis a great day for a visit to Inishmore," said Padraig.

"That it is, though it looks like we may be getting a storm," Conor observed. "How long have you lived on the island?"

"Oh, I was born here, many years ago. . . Went to school on the island then became a fisherman like my father before me. I've fished around these islands and the coast of Galway for many years. My family left for the mainland after my wife died from TB, so I continue to keep busy here and make a few trips to the mainland once in a while. My son Donal owns two trawlers and is based out of Killybegs in county Donegal."

"So, I'm sure you know everybody on the island."

"That, I do."

"Did you hear about the death of the bishop?"

"I sure did and it's a sad day for all of us. Ta bron orainn."

"Does he still have family here on the islands?" Conor asked remembering his online research.

"No, all his family moved to the mainland. Eamon Cronin studied theology in Maynooth College and became a priest and then Bishop of Galway. Some of his relatives still live in Galway and I think his brother lives in Dublin."

"I'm here with a friend of mine, Anne O'Gorman, a reporter for the Irish Times, writing a story about the history of the islands. She's interviewing Peig Moran about her life here on the island. I'm sure she'd like to talk to you about your life here as well," Conor continued.

"Oh yeah, I know Peig; she's the best storyteller I've ever heard," said Padraig. "Some people say she has the magic!"

"Would you also be interested in talking to Anne?"

"Sure, I would. I've a lot of stories as well."

"She'll be back shortly; how 'bout another pint?"

"Sure."

"Moira, two more pints please, when you have a minute."

Moira pulled two more pints and placed them in front of the two men.

"Slainte," said Padraig as he slowly worked his way through the creamy head on the pint and tasted the black brew underneath.

"Slainte mhaith."

A few minutes later Conor's phone rang. It was Anne.

"I'm just about finished here; should be another hour or so."

"Peadar'll be there to pick you up when you're done just give him a call."

"See you soon," Anne replied. "Peig's a total free spirit with wind beneath her wings!"

"Oh by the way, I met another interesting character here. He'd like to tell you his story about growing up on the island."

"Tell him that I'd love to meet him."

Chapter 13

Brian woke early, turned over onto his side and ran his hands down Evie's back to the rise of her derrier. *I never tire of her smell and touch.* On his way down to make coffee, he stopped outside Sean's room and peeked in watching the little guy sleeping soundly in his crib. Brian knew that this calm time would end soon and Sean would need his diaper changed and breakfast with Evie.

He walked into the kitchen and began to make the coffee. Sitting down at the table, he looked out the window. Saturdays were good days for his family. The early morning sky was blue with a bank of clouds sitting on the western horizon.

Checking his email, he discovered a message from Conor indicating that he was taking the weekend off and would be back on Monday to begin work on the investigation. Conor wanted to set up a lunch meeting with him on Monday to discuss his request for research help on the case at MRC lab.

His thoughts were interrupted when Sean woke up and began making noises for attention. Going back upstairs, Brian walked into Sean's room, picked him up, gave him a big hug and carried him to the changing table. Sean grinned up at his dad as his diaper was changed and Brian put him in a new outfit making him ready for the day ahead. Then he carried Sean into the bedroom and put him next to Evie, who was already awake and ready to give him his breakfast.

"It's a beautiful day, my love," said Brian.

"I love you guys," said Evie. "Thanks for bringing our little guy for his breakfast."

"Sure. Let's go for a drive to Clifden today and visit Liam's new house. You know he expects to move in at the end of next month."

"Sounds like a great idea," Evie replied.

"I'll get the stuff packed up and maybe we could stop in Clifden for lunch."

*   *   *

Brian, Evie and Sean set off from Carraroe to Clifden. In the sunny western morning, they sped along the road which twisted and curled around the rocks and stonewalled fields.

"What a great day for a drive!" said Evie.

"Yeah, weather looks good but it can change so quickly."

"How far along is the construction on Liam's house?"

"He told me a few days ago that he could move in by the end of September. He also said that he was offered a director's job in Carraroe and begins work on Monday."

"That's good news!"

"Now he needs to find a wife!"

Evie smiled, "Right!"

They proceeded on R366 to Maam Cross, turning west past Lake Shindilla and on to Clifden. The barren landscape was dotted with lakes and clumps of trees bent over with their backs to the wind. Peat bogs lay between the rocks with uncut turf waiting to be harvested and made into fires. An occasional donkey with turf creels on it's back stood placidly on the bog as its owner threw sods of turf into the baskets. The ancient scent of Connemara mixed with the smell of heather blooming on the wind. They arrived in Clifden, capital of Connemara and drove down the main street stopping at a new deli restaurant where they ordered sandwiches and drinks. Evie took Sean out on the patio and fed him his lunch. Brian joined her and when Sean was satisfied placed him in his stroller.

"Remember I need to make a trip to Derry and meet with Susan Somers to go over the research for the cod fishery at UMR," said Brian.

"When do you have to go?"

"In about two weeks, I have to complete one more experiment for the project and then I'll be ready. Conor called yesterday. He was looking for a forensic science contact at MRC to expedite some tests on a substance that the coroner found in the organs of the bishop, so I gave him Breda Wood's name. Let's get together with Conor, before I leave for Derry," said Brian.

"Good idea," Evie replied. "We'll have a meal and grill out."

They finished their sandwiches and rolled Sean out to the car, where they installed him in his car seat. The Sky Road to Liam's house wound around the rocks and climbed higher above the cliffs below. The view westward was breathtaking with rolling sea, soaring seabirds and two trawlers returning to port after a night of fishing.

Brian stopped the Jeep at a recently paved driveway that led towards a house built of faced stone and plastered walls. They walked up the driveway toward Liam's house. There were two trucks in the driveway and hammering noises coming out of the front door. They walked through the door and into a very impressive hallway made of natural wood and stone trim decoration that continued into the family room.

The focus of the family room was the view westward with large windows overlooking the ocean and capturing all the western sunsets. The opposite side of the room was balanced by a large fireplace incorporating a cut stone mantelpiece. Brian and Evie continued into the kitchen where they found a carpenter installing the remainder of the wall cabinetry.

"Hi there; I'm Brian Connelly and this is my wife, Evie and our son, Sean. We're friends of Liam's. He told us to come by and look at the house. It's spectacular."

"That it is. I'm Finbar Joyce," He stood up and shook their hands.

"Did you design it?" Evie asked.

"Yes, as well as installing all the trim work here, in the kitchen and other rooms. I live down the road in Roundstone so that makes it easy for me to work out here on the house. I went to school at Carraroe College, that's how I got to know Liam."

"You do beautiful work," Brian observed looking around the room,"What other projects have you done?"

"I had a big job at the archdiocese in Galway," Finbar replied.

"That's right, Liam, told me that you'd done some cabinetry work at the bishop's house," said Brian.

"Yeah I designed the area at the rectory and then completed all the trim work.

I was working on the design for my own house at the time and the bishop introduced me to an architect, who helped me with my plans," Finbar continued, flicking sawdust out of his eye.

"Why would anybody want to harm Bishop Cronin I wonder?" Brian asked. "You have any ideas? Or do you think it was just a senseless murder?"

"I've no idea although you never know what goes on behind closed doors," Finbar replied changing the subject. "Why don't you walk upstairs and take a look around; it's about finished except for a final coat of paint and carpet installation," said Finbar.

"We sure will."

Brian and Evie walked up the stairs to an open mezzanine and entered the master suite. This room also overlooked the ocean and the view was even better from this height. The bathroom suite was complete with walk-in shower and tiled bench, two vanity sinks and a sitting area with heated seating as well as under floor heating in the rest of the space to take care of the cold winter months.

"Wow!" said Evie. "This is spectacular. Liam has really put some thought into the design of the entire space. I can't wait to see it finished."

They completed their tour and headed back down the stairs to the main floor with Sean bouncing along happily on Brian's back.

"Good luck with finishing the rest of it, Finbar," said Evie as they stepped out the front door towards the Jeep, "Keep up the great work."

"Thanks for stopping by, see you all again, I'm sure."

* * *

Brian, Evie and Sean drove back to Carraroe via the coast road. As the sun began to work its way farther westward and downward into the gathering clouds, they made their way through Roundstone, a quaint fishing village around the corner from Dog's Bay and Errisbeg Mountain.

"I bet Finbar's house is impressive," Evie commented.

"I'd like to see it sometime and get to know Finbar better. There's something interesting about him," Brian observed.

"I noticed that too. He had a strange reaction to my comment about the bishop though, as if there is more to that story."

They continued their drive around the headland in the direction of Dog's Bay.

"Isn't this a beautiful place," Evie remarked looking at the expanding scene before her.

Brian stopped the Jeep on the road below Errisbeg Mountain to look at the sunset over the bay. He remembered camping there many years ago with his family in their house trailer. He leaned over in the seat and gave Evie a gentle kiss, running his hand languidly behind her waist.

"I love my life with you and Sean. We sure live in a special place on this ancient island".

"That's what I love about you Brian," said Evie, "You never forget where you are and your connection to the land and family."

"Let's go home," she said smiling at Sean sleeping in his cozy seat.

Brian started the Jeep as the evening began its slow journey into night to continue the drive back to Carraroe.

Chapter 14

Conor sat at the bar using the program on his laptop to add more details about the murder. When Moira finished serving the locals she walked back to where Conor was sitting.

"You've a really nice place here, Moira, looks like you've remodeled it but kept the stonework and its original atmosphere," said Conor.

"Yes, we did. Tourists love it so we're careful about the tradition of the place including the open fireplace we light when the weather gets cool. What do you do back on the mainland?" Moira asked.

"I'm a detective from Dublin now working in Galway to investigate the death of the bishop Cronin."

"Is that what brings you to Inishmore?"

"Partly," said Conor, "I'm also taking some time to unwind."

"This is a good place to do it," said Moira. "Do you have any suspects?"

"No, but it's early yet."

"You know the bishop's mother used to live here," Moira continued.

"No, I didn't know that; what else can you tell me about his family or friends?"

"His brother, Declan, comes here in the summer once in a while with his family."

"How long have you lived here?" Conor asked.

"I moved here when Peadar and I got married," said Moira.

*   *   *

Daylight was growing shorter as the clouds continued to build from the west and a steady wind began to blow. A car appeared from over the hill and Conor saw that it was Peadar and Anne returning from her interview. Peadar pulled the car into the driveway and Anne got out.

"Thanks for the ride, Peadar. I'll see you later."

"Ceart go leor."

"It must have been a good interview," said Conor. "You were gone a while."

"Yes," Anne replied, "It'll be a great series for the Living Section of the Times. Peig has a terrific memory and I'll recount her life as an islander here on Inishmore together with her memories of her parents. She also told me about Peadar and Moira who own this pub. She said they've a son called Finbar who lives in Roundstone. That's the same Finbar who's working on Liam's house, isn't it? She also talked a little bit about the bishop and mentioned that his mother's family used to live on Inishere, the small island. Peig knows everyone here and tells a great story. Did you know she has a pet crow on her outside porch and it's true, she's a shapeshifter! What have you been up to?"

"I've been talking to Moira and also to Padraig O'Hare, one of the locals here, who has another story for you. Maybe you can set up some time to meet with him, before we go back tomorrow," Conor asked. "I bet you're ready for a drink now, after all that talk."

"That's for sure."

"Let's go inside and take care of that and meet Padraig."

They turned to walk into the pub, just as a gust of wind blew the blond hair away from Anne's face and Conor again realized how pretty she was.

"What would you like?" Conor asked.

"A glass of chardonnay and some kind of munchie."

Moira brought Anne the drink and crackers as Conor continued to lower his disappearing pint.

"Do you want to meet Padraig now and set up a time for tomorrow?" he asked.

"Good idea, but let's sit here and unwind for a minute before I do that," Anne replied.

They sat and talked about the pub and all the antiques that inhabited the old place. The rear end of the pub had been built into the cliff leaving the exposed rock as a unique feature. Ancient dust-covered beams held up the ceiling but also provided hanging space for old copper jugs and the occasional oil lamp.

"I'm getting ideas for the tower," said Conor.

"I bet you are!" replied Anne.

Anne finished her drink as Conor got up out of his seat and walked over to Padraig still in his usual position, propped up at the end of the bar.

"Padraig, I'd like to introduce you to my friend, Anne."

"Conas a ta tu?" said Padraig.

"Taim go maith!"

The two men walked back to where Anne was sitting. She noticed Padraig was dressed in black wearing a cap which seemed to be permanently anchored on his head. His ancient weatherbeaten face was etched with the history of many storms, hard times and immense character.

"Padraig, this is Anne."

"Hello Anne, a gra, you work for the Irish Times?"

His low voice echoed into his past as he spoke with a Connacht Irish lilth which seemed to sing his phrases rather than speak them.

"Yes, I do. I'm here to write a story about the islands and its people. This is a great opportunity for me, meeting you and hearing your stories."

Padraig and Conor sat down with Anne to discuss a good time to meet Sunday morning.

"Let's meet here at 10:30," said Anne looking at Padraig. "Will that work for you? I know its Sunday and I can do it later in the morning, if you wish."

"No problem, I gave up going to church years ago, ever since my wife died," said Padraig. "There's no future in that."

"I'd like to ask you about your life growing up here, changes you have seen and where you think the future of the Gaeltacht and the island economy is headed. I'll be recording this interview for radio if it's all right with you and hope to have it broadcast on Radio Na Gaeltachta. Maybe you could mix both English and Irish when you're telling the story, whichever feels right at the time."

"Either one works for me. I've been telling these stories for many years and now I've found someone who'd like to hear some of them," said Padraig with a grin.

"Thanks," said Anne. I'll see you here tomorrow morning."

"Ceart go leoir," said Padraig as he stood up and walked back to his mooring spot at the bar.

Anne and Conor sat together outside and finished their drinks. The sun was slowly sliding towards the rippling water on the horizon into the building clouds of a possible storm.

It's beams displayed a cacophony of color as the moving clouds painted a magical blend of red and orange. Conor slowly moved his hand over Anne's, "Thanks for asking me to come with you; it was a great idea."

"Yes it was," she replied.

* * *

Conor and Anne left the pub and walked about a mile up the road to a steakhouse called "The Edge". Entering the restaurant, they sat by the window where they could see the waves breaking below them.

"I drove past this place when I visited Peig earlier and thought it was worth a shot," said Anne.

"What a great location and I'm sure the food is good judging by the number of cars here," Conor remarked.

"Yes, Peadar told me they have the best steaks and the seafood is tremendous."

"Let's start with a drink."

Conor called over the waitress and she began to get her pencil ready for the orders.

"I'm Una, and I'll be helping you make your food choices this evening."

"Let's order a bottle of Rombauer," Conor requested.

"Be right back," said Una.

"This was a great opportunity to come to the Aran Islands and interview Peig about her life here on Inishmore, and now I can add Padraig to the mix. I'm so glad you came with me," said Anne.

"Me too, I'm doing more internet research on the child abuse issue with the church. I've a hunch there may be a connection to the death of the bishop somewhere in there."

Una returned with the wine and two glasses letting Conor and Anne taste the special reserve. They chinked glasses and sampled the bouquet. Anne watched the film of alcohol slide down the curved glass.

"Now that's a beautiful wine," said Anne letting the smooth liquid loiter in her mouth.

"I was in Napa two years ago and went to the vineyard where this wine is grown, so I got hooked," Conor added.

The waitress returned to check on their food selection.

"Sorry, we're still deciding and need a few more minutes," said Conor.

"Just for your information, we have fresh lobster and scallops tonight as well as our prime steaks. I'll come back when you're ready."

Conor watched Anne sipping her wine and his eyes held hers for a few seconds. There was something in the look that was more than a casual glance.

"You seem to be a very outdoors sort of person, quite at home with the elements and the gear that goes with it," Conor remarked.

"Yeah, I really like what I do in my job but for me it's all about getting outside and having fun; sailing, playing tennis, hiking. I can't imagine been chained to a desk for eight hours. When I was in school I had a teacher who turned on my ability to write and as a result, I've been able to make a great career of it investigating stories and events as a journalist."

Conor flagged down Una.

"Ready to order?"

"Yes, we are."

Anne spoke first, "I'll have lobster tails with saffron rice and a Caesar salad."

"Ribeye steak, medium, with onions, mushrooms and dirty potatoes," said Conor.

"That's an interesting combination," said Anne.

"It's time for a steak; I hardly ever eat red meat, but I've got to keep my strength up."

The day slowly crept toward darkness as a brisk wind began to stir up the dust and whirl it around outside. The sea was becoming more irritable as the wind continued to build up the swells and hurl them onto the jagged rocks. Farther out, a pointed beam of light from the lighthouse flashed full into the window leaving a trail of illuminated raindrops in its wake.

"Looks like we might be in for a storm," Conor observed.

"Let's hope it blows itself out tonight," said Anne. "We need to get back to Galway for work on Monday morning."

"Let's not worry about that now."

"So what's the deal with Peig and her pet crow?" asked Conor changing the subject.

"I don't know, but I think it might be her mate."

"So you really believe in shapeshifting."

"Yeah, now I really do, having spoken to Peig. I was skeptical before but she's convinced me. I'm a journalist and my analytical, rational brain keeps nudging me to question however my romantic Irish psyche wants to believe. Maybe it's the magic of the island . . . or being here with you . . . or maybe it's the Druid in me."

The food arrived and they began to savor the taste of succulent lobster and a perfectly grilled steak.

"Peadar was right about the food here, this steak is really good. How's your lobster?"

"Like it just came out of the water and into the pot; the sauce is perfect and all this melted butter!."

They finished their meal as the sun sank sullenly into the bank of clouds on the horizon creating a spectacular sunset. It cast a red glow on the water through a hole in the clouds, creating a window of red light before disappearing behind the gathering night.

"I'm ready to burn off this food with a walk to the place up the road. I understand they have traditional Irish music, and we could get some apple pie and ice cream at the same time," said Conor.

"That sounds like fun. Let's go!"

Conor paid the waitress and they walked outside into the windy evening.

"Looks like we're going to get it," Conor said looking at the impending clouds.

"OK let's get going."

They walked up the narrow road and came to a pub called Doolin's perched at the top of the hill. Before they reached the building they could hear the drone of uilleann pipes and the busy strains of fiddles playing happily in the wind.

"Sounds like a fun place," said Anne.

Music got louder as they arrived at the door and walked in, setting down their backpacks. The place was really jumping and full of people stomping their feet and enjoying the bodhran beat.

"Let's sit here at the back and we can order some of this great pie that everybody seems to be eating."

As they took up residence on a bench; a server came by to take their order.

"Now we have the true music to go with the rocks and the sea," Anne commented. "I just love those pipes."

Uilleann pipes were a masterful concoction of turned wooden tubes, reeds and valves, powered by air through a bellows attached at the player's elbow. A flute like piece called a chanter created the notes and the instrument was played in a seated position, not like its relative the Scottish war bagpipe that was blown thru the mouth and played standing up.

They ordered two pieces of pie and proceeded to demolish both with ease as the classical drone of the chanters filled their ears with the native pulse of the islands.

"This seems to be the place to be on a windy Saturday night," Conor remarked.

The pub was full of tourists and natives and a couple of dogs nestled under the table at the back of the room.

Conor sat monitoring the players, following the words and notes as the songs and melodies played their way to completion. He also watched Anne, deep in concentration as she connected with the people and the players. Her blond hair fell around her face as she laughed at the impromptu players manifesting their art and talents as musicians. He wondered what else was stirring inside that pretty head with its laughing eyes and smiling lips.

She turned to him focusing her eyes on his and said, "We're going to have to go soon in order to check into Mrs. O"Shea's before 10:30."

"I'll call her right now and make sure she has another room," said Conor. He began to worry about the sleeping arrangements but was sure they would have other rooms. It was important to maintain a working relationship with Anne but it was becoming more difficult and he didn't want to sleep with her at this point. Not only was there the conflict of interest issue but also he needed more time to feel her out as it were, before moving to the next step.

"Okay," Anne responded. "It might be a little late for that, but we'll see what happens,"

Conor dialed Mrs O'Shea's.

"O'Sheas Bed & Breakfast, may I help you?"

Conor explained the situation regarding the last minute decision.

"All my rooms are full, but there's a pullout bed in the room that Ms O'Gorman has booked, if that would work?"

"Thanks," said Conor. "Hold on a minute please, while I ask her."

He turned to Anne and explained the situation.

"I hope it's comfortable!" replied Anne.

Conor replied to Mrs O'Shea, "That'll be fine."

This is going to be an interesting night.

"How far is the B&B from here?" Anne asked.

"Mrs O'Shea said it is about four miles down the road. I'll see about the mini bus. There was one parked outside when we walked into the pub," Conor replied.

"Sounds good."

Conor extricated himself from the bench and walked out the door, returning a few minutes later sitting down on the bench. She moved closer to him and asked, "How's the weather?"

"It's getting windier and the rain can't be too far away. I spoke to Pat, the driver, and he said it would only take a few minutes to get to O'Sheas and we were to let him know as soon as we're ready."

"Good, let's stay here a while longer. These guys are great. They're going to play a few of my favorite tunes."

The music began again and the lilted pipes wrapped vancient chords around the appreciative audience.

Chapter 15

Finbar Joyce finished his Saturday evening meal and walked out of the house and into his wood shop where he was in the process of constructing built in cabinets for the ground floor bathroom in Liam's house. The wind had become stronger and the murder of crows that normally roosted in the trees behind his house had departed for more shelter. He finished sanding a door and began to prepare the frame of the cabinet for assembly, inserting the glue into the joints, spreading it with a flat knife making sure all the surfaces were in contact with the adhesive; then setting the piece on the bench to dry. The process of handling wood, sanding it smooth and feeling the texture of the grain, gave Finbar a feeling of peace and satisfaction. It made him feel whole and provided him with healing renewal and personal pride in his work.

He had just finished gluing the last cabinet when his phone rang.

"Hello, this is Finbar."

"Finbar, Eistigi liom, I have some more information for you and need to know if you want to proceed with the job as discussed. Tuigeann tu?"

"Tuigim, I'll call you next week and give you my decision then," Finbar replied.

"The first part of the job is done and I'm sure that the rest will be completed as planned," said the caller. "Talk to you next week? Oiche Mhaith."

Finbar hung up the phone, went back into the shop and started his router to create some dado joints in the frames for the door panels. He noticed that the wind had now increased in velocity and the rain had begun to play staccato music on the large windows next door in the living room. The dark and on-coming storm was going to give him time to think about the decision he would have to make the following week.

Chapter 16

Conor and Anne stood up while still applauding for the final tune on the pipes and walked toward the door. Pat standing at the back of the room came toward them.

"Are you ready to go?" he asked.

"Yes we are."

"It's started to pour down rain so we'll have to make a run for it," said Pat.

"No problem."

Pat opened the door and the wind whipped it out of his hand, "Wow, there's a small gale blowing out here!"

Grabbing their backpacks they ran after Pat who opened the side door into the bus so they could jump in.

"I think this'll be a quick storm," said Pat wiping the rain off his glasses. "When they come in fast like this from the west, they leave just as quickly. It'll be gone by morning."

They drove down the island road, through blasts of rain and strong gusts of wind to arrive at the B&B. Through the rain streaming down the windshield, they could see the welcoming light in one of the windows steering them toward the front door as the rain streamed down the windshield of the van.

The driveway gravel crunched loudly as Pat applied the brakes and the wheels came to a halt.

"We're here," said Anne, "It sure looks cozy inside."

Conor jammed some money into Pat's hand and said, "I'll call you in the morning. We have to get back to Kilronin to interview Padraig at 10:30, but we'll see what the weather is like at that point. Thanks for the lift."

"No bother!"

The two friends scampered out of the vehicle and ran to the already opened front door of the B&B. Mrs O'Shea was standing in the hallway. The old stone floor swallowed up the dripping water from the two travelers as they shook off the outside world onto the flag stones and lowered their hoods. A peat fire burned in the parlor and the house smelled like fresh baked brown bread.

"Come in. Come in. Get in out of the rain. I'm so glad you made it on such a bad night. If you need anything dried, just let me know. I've a dryer in the back."

"Thanks very much," said Anne. "Your home is beautiful."

"Thank you. We had it built for comfort and of course the views which you can't see right now, but maybe in the morning. Here's your room with the bath ensuite."

The wet travellers scurried into the large room and immediately felt the warmth of a fire burning in the limestone fireplace. Antique furniture was everywhere. A true ecletic mix of carved chairs with brasses adorning a dark tallboy in one corner and a sea chest in the other

"I lit the fire for you about twenty minutes ago. I thought you'd like it on a wet, windy night even though it's August!"

"Great idea," Anne replied.

"There's the sitting area with the pull out bed and a microwave in the kitchenette. There are extra blankets in the chest of drawers."

Anne smiled, "Thank you."

"If you need anything else, let me know."

Conor walked into the sitting area and put his backpack on the pull out bed. "This'll work fine for me."

"I hope it's comfortable," said Anne. "If you don't mind I'm going to take a shower and get to bed."

"I'll start unpacking and do the same when you're done," said Conor.

Anne walked into the bathroom and Conor heard her turn on the shower. A few minutes later he heard the shower door close, and the theme of the water changed.

He imagined the water washing over her smooth body as she washed her long legs. Tension mounted as he waited for her to finish. He continued to unpack and prepare the roll out bed, getting a blanket out of the closet.

The sound of water ceased and a few minutes later Anne walked back in the room dressed in a long tee shirt leaving little to the imagination. He walked over to her and wrapped his arms around her feeling her breasts and hard belly push against his anticipating frame. He kissed her softly and began moving his hand under the back of her tee shirt. Her skin felt like silk as his hand moved up her back. He pulled back unsure of his journey into another relationship. Anne sensing his hesitation gazed into his dark brown eyes, "It's OK, you know."

"I know," said Conor nibbling on her bottom lip. "I haven't felt like this for a long time and it would be so easy to ..."

Anne interrupted, "I know, but it could complicate things, right?"

"Sure would," Conor went on. "We're both involved in our own ways with the bishop's story and some people might see a conflict of interest here."

"You're right but it would be a perfect ending to a perfect weekend." The rain lashed furiously at the window and Conor kissed her again, smelling the soft scent in her hair.

"Let's take it slowly," he groaned. "Good thing one of us has some self control!"

Anne walked over to the bed, slid under the covers and plugged in her IPhone, "I'm listening to a great book right now," she said, "it's written by Lorcan David about sailing solo around the world." She continued snuggling under the covers.

"Interesting," said Conor, "now there's a challenge; twenty-four thousand miles alone!"

Conor walked in to the bathroom and turned on the shower. He felt the warm water washing over his tense body and wondered when he would be able to satisfy his feelings for Anne. Besides the work conflict, he had just ended a recent relationship and realized that he might not be ready for another. He finished his shower and walked back into the darkened room. Anne had already turned out her light. He pulled out the rollout bed and lay on his back thinking about what had just happened between them.

"Good night Conor. Thanks for coming with me. I had a great time tonight," she said pulling up the covers.

"Me too, it's not over yet, we have another day tomorrow."

They lay separated from each other as the storm increased outside and the pelting rain began to rattle the windows. Conor found it hard to go to sleep, thinking about Anne's warm body and her soft skin a few feet away. The fire flickered and he watched the dancing images move the shadows around the room.

*   *   *

CLADDAGH POOL

Early morning sun crept slowly around the walls of Conor and Anne's bedroom, its bright rays illuminating the roll out bed and shining into Conor's eyes. He awoke but didn't move, remembering where he was. He listened to Anne's breathing in the other part of the room and heard her beginning to stir.

"Are you awake?"

"Yes, I am," she replied. "What time is it?"

Conor found his watch. 8:00 AM

"Time for breakfast," said Anne walking into the bathroom. Conor got up and walked over to the window. There was the view that Mrs. O'Shea had talked about. An angry sea crashing out its last waves of fury after the storm had blown itself out, a new day and a new beginning.

Anne came out of the bathroom already dressed in her hiking clothes and caught Conor pulling on his pants. She smiled and walked over to her bed picking up the rest of her stuff. Conor took her place in the bathroom, shaved, dressed and emerged back into the room. He walked over to her, gave her a long soft kiss, and said, "Good morning, let's go get some breakfast, we have miles to go."

They walked down the hallway and into the dining room where there were three more couples working their way through food and early morning conversation. They took a place by the window putting their bags under the table. Mrs. O'Shea had prepared a spectacular breakfast with home baked brown bread, fruit, cereals, rashers and poached eggs.

"What a great feast!" said Anne. "The eggs taste better out here."

"I have my own hens. That's the reason I bet," said Mrs O'Shea. "Did the storm keep you awake last night?"

"I heard it in my dreams," replied Conor, glancing towards Anne.

"I woke up once when the rain was really hammering on the window," said Anne, "but it was so warm and cozy inside, I had no trouble going back to sleep."

The storm had blown itself eastward and now the morning sun rising over the mainland had illuminated the islands, creating a stunningly clear image of the slabs of limestone as the waves crashed on the jagged rocks.

They finished breakfast with enough time to look out the picture windows at the wonderful view laid out before them. Pat was waiting outside with the mini-bus and ushered them inside.

"That was quite a storm last night!" he said. "And now look at the weather, its perfect, that's the way it works out here, a pattern of extremes. You never know what to expect."

They arrived at the pub and knocked on the door since it was Sunday. Moira opened the side door and bade them inside, "Good morning to you both."

"Good morning, Moira, and thanks for being here early so I can spend some time with Padraig," Anne replied.

"You're welcome. He's in there in the living room; that's where he likes to hang out on Sunday. I'm sure he'll be ready to go with his stories."

"I'll go in?" Anne asked walking into the living room. Padraig rose from his chair to greet her.

"Dia duith Padraig, grand day after the storm. Thanks for your time to tell me your stories."

"Sure, you're welcome."

Anne listened with total attention to Padraig's tales of walking to school in the winters, swimming livestock to the steamer to transport them to the mainland, building the soil from seaweed, creating food from edible seaweed, enduring the constant fight against nature and the elements; going fishing for basking sharks in tar covered canvas currachs. His memory of the events was clear and he succinctly described the events in his life with detail and emotion. He continued at his own pace, and Anne asked a question only when she needed some more details or elaboration of an event or his family.

Conor remained outside and walked down the pier to look at a wide array of boats and the gear that linked the island to the rest of Ireland; much of it a tribute to the island's history as a bastion of survival. Kilronin had been a natural harbor since fishermen had ventured out from the mainland many generations ago escaping from nine hundred years of trials and political turmoil on mainland Ireland as the country struggled under the oppressive rule of the English.

He began to think about the upcoming week and the investigative tasks into the death of the bishop. He would get in contact with Brian and schedule some time with Breda Woods at MRC to generate an expedited result of the substance that may have caused the death of the bishop. He'd also complete more internet research about the legal issues concerning some of the clergy in the Catholic Church. Conor was more convinced than ever that this was the direction the investigation needed to go after his interview with Moira made it clear that there were no long standing family feuds or grudges.

Anne finished with Padraig and walked down the pier to join Conor who was sitting on a bench talking on his cell phone. When she got closer to him he stood up and closed his phone. She joined him on the bench. Raucous calls of the seagulls were all around them. Giant birds swooped down to dive bomb a solitary black crow that had taken up its position on the mast of one of the trawlers. Proudly, the crow ignored their screams as it watched the acrobatics around it. Odor of diesel fuel mixed with seaweed created its own sensuous familiarity with the place as the tide crept up over the swirling kelp among the rocks and pools below the dock.

"How did it go?" asked Conor.

"He was fascinating, and thanks for a great lead, by the way. I got plenty of information from Padraig about life on the islands and the history of the people who've lived here.

His story will play well for radio and print. I just loved his character and his idiomatic Irish and English will have everyone hooked up with his amazing voice and adventures on the islands," Anne replied. "What have you been up to?"

"I just spoke to my friend Brian. He told me that he would be setting up a meeting with Dr. Breda tomorrow, so now I'll have access to all the lab resources at the MRC facility," replied Conor. "I just checked with the ferry office, and the boat leaves at 3:00, so we'll have time for lunch before we go."

"Sounds good, we can go back to the bar and get caught up with Moira and Peadar," Anne put her hand on Conor's arm as she continued, "We made a very mature decision last night and my mind has cleared just like the day."

"True!" Conor replied continuing her train of thought, "but sometimes being an adult is not as much fun as it's cracked up to be!"

Holding hands, they walked back up the pier to the pub, sat down at the bar and looked at the food menu.

"Let's have something different. How about fish and chips?" said Conor. "That's what I'm having."

"Good choice," Anne observed, "back to the healthy routine tomorrow."

"Moira! Two orders of fish and chips, please?"
"Coming up!"

*   *   *

Conor and Anne finished lunch and walked outside. Angry clouds had moved out leaving calmer weather behind but waves were still churning from the storm and big swells rolled past the mouth of the harbor.

They walked into the ferry office and bought their tickets to Rosaveal boarding the waiting ferry with the other passengers.

"Let's get a seat on the sunny side," said Anne.

"Good idea. It may be a little rough after we get out of the harbor."

Walking up the ramp they found a seat on the starboard side of the boat. The seagulls were wheeling overhead emitting their sad cries as they dived and chased each other. One of the gulls landed on the ferry's mast where it reared up and with a wide-open beak released a piercing scream.

"I think it's trying to make us leave," Anne observed.

"We don't have any food to give it, so it's frustrated."

They felt a deep rumble as the engines started, and the crew became animated, going about their tasks of casting off the mooring lines and clearing the ramp from the port rail. The skipper blew the horn and began to back slowly into the rising swells out of the harbor and steer eastbound towards the mainland.

Conor remarked, "There's quite a swell out here in the open water. Are you doing okay?" he looked at Anne.

"Yeah, I'm fine. I get used to the motion and don't think about it anymore."

Anne sat closer to keep warm and Conor put his arm around her. As the ferry moved farther from land Anne remarked, "What a great weekend. We had a storm, I got two potential award winning stories and now we go back to Galway and start a new week."

"Yes, it was a lot of fun especially the music and the storm. I'm glad the weather moved out," Conor remarked with a sense of relief.

"I feel the same," said Anne. "It's quite a transformation from the stormy night to a nice warm sun with a gentle breeze."

Chapter 17

F r. Michael Godfree finished Sunday mass and walked outside to meet his parishioners. He had been the parish priest for ten years in Bridgeville in County Wexford. The day was warm and a soft breeze blew through the old beech trees behind the church. Two crows cawed loudly to each other on a branch as they watched the pastoral scene below their shiney feet. The priest shook hands with many of his flock, discussing the weather and other local issues that had happened over the past week.

"Did you hear about the death of the bishop in Galway?" someone asked.

"A sad day for all of us; Bishop Cronin was a great man and a good friend."

"Will you be going to his funeral, Father?"

"I may go. I don't know yet because I have to be here for the Retreat. If I do decide to make the trip, Fr. Doyle will be here to take my place."

CLADDAGH POOL

As he turned and walked back into the church he was distracted by the two black sentry crows watching him from their perch high up in the yew tree. He opened the heavy oak door and glided down the aisle to the sacristy where he shed his vestments and stood in front of the altar removing the alb, the last piece of the wardrobe. A sudden shiver went down his spine causing him to remember the reason the bishop had transferred him to Bridgeville.

Having completed the sacristy, he walked into the office and sat down with his head in his hands, fear overtaking him. He thought about the death of the bishop and the ramifications of the event as it pertained to his "problem."

I can't go to the bishop's funeral. It'll stir up all those memories and I really don't want to see any of those people again. Gazing at all the junk piled up on his desk, he saw an old picture of himself and Bishop Cronin standing outside Galway Cathedral; its dusty glass covering the last ten years of veiled secrecy.

*   *   *

DENIS HEARN

I've been exiled here for ten years and never heard anything from Bishop Cronin. Now he's dead and all the turmoil of that time has come crashing back on me. The bishop protected me as one of his flock and forgave me. I've worked hard to become virtuous. I've prayed for forgiveness and led a mostly chaste life. Even Christ wasn't perfect. Didn't he fall to the vice of anger? God doesn't judge us by our faults, he is merciful. Each one of the deadly sins is mortal and a major offence against the church. Is Christ's anger toward the moneylenders in the temple worse than Fr Francis's gluttony at the table, or the pride and self indulgence that Fr Gabriel has with his new Mercedes, or my lust after young boys? Does God quantify our sins? I have defeated that devil through prayer and good works.

Chapter18

Somewhere inside Brian's sleeping world was the sound of a baby crying. He opened his eyes and knew that Sean was waking up and getting ready for the day.

"I got him," said Evie rolling over to give Brian a kiss.

"I'll start breakfast after I get out of the shower," said Brian.

"Great."

Brian finished in the bathroom and began a breakfast of coffee, toast and poached eggs. Evie joined him in the kitchen putting Sean in his swing.

"What's on the menu for you today?" she asked.

"I'm going to meet with Dr. Breda and Conor at MRC. He needs to use the facility to complete a substance analysis and I need to wrap up the seafood research for UMR in order to have it delivered to Derry by the end of the week."

"You've been on that project for quite a while now."

"Yeah, it's taken up the last two years of my life and now it's done. The team collected sea-water and food organisms off the coasts of Killybegs and Derry, and lured Dr. Woods away from her own research on the "Red Tide" algeal blooms. Now we're ready to present the findings to the government in Dublin and Belfast."

"What did you find out?"

"We found an abundant supply of krill in the area that would support the new fishery as long as catch controls are enforced by both governments. That's going to be the hardest part; all the politics."

"Sounds like you're going to have a busy day. When are you going to Derry?" Evie asked.

"Next week."

"Good, because my Mum is coming for a few days and that'll work great. How long are you going to stay?"

"Oh, just one night, I think I can get everything done in that time. We have to integrate all our research and prepare our presentation for both governments."

"Just one night. Good," Evie replied.

"Well, I've got to get ready to go to Galway. I'm sure Conor will be calling me about the meeting later this morning."

They finished breakfast and Brian got ready to hit the road.

Packing up his laptop, he grabbed some cookies off the countertop, "I'm leaving!"

He stood up, walked over to Sean giving him a big gooseberry kiss on both cheeks, then turned around and took Evie in his arms.

"I love you both," he said giving her a big hug.

"See you for supper," Evie replied. "Be careful out there."

Brian kissed her, walked out the door, and got into the Jeep with Evie's perfume lingering on his shoulder. The stone walls rushed by and the miles galloped away beneath him as he headed for Galway. His phone rang interrupting the road induced monotony. It was Dr. Breda, "Good morning Brian, let's get together this afternoon."

"Sure, how about two-o-clock. I'll call Conor and let him know."

"Good, I'm more than happy to help him with the analysis."

"Thanks a bunch," Brian replied.

"You're welcome, see you soon."

Brian hung up and called Conor.

"Hi, Brian."

"How was your weekend?" Brian asked.

"A lot of fun, we had a good time."

"We?" Brian exclaimed, "Who'd you go with?"

"Anne O'Gorman, she's a reporter with the Irish Times and is covering the story about the bishop's death. She had an interview set up with a storyteller on the islands and asked if I'd like to go with her. I did and we had a great time. I'll tell you more about it later," Conor answered.

"Can't wait to hear it. I just set up our meeting with Dr Woods; her office at 2 PM. Will that work for you?"

"That's fine! See you there."

* * *

Conor finished the call from Brian and checked the time as he continued the drive to his morning meeting with Dr. Mary Murray, the coroner. It was going to be a busy day. Pulling up at the building, he walked into the place which had the old hospital smell of strange chemicals and used up air.

"Morning, Detective Horgan," said the receptionist.

"Morning!"

"Dr. Murray is waiting for you in her office."

"Thanks," Conor continued down the hallway and into the doctor's comfortable office which was decorated with pictures of her family and a small toy collection on the window sill. The room was newly carpeted and the space created a small personal oasis in the desert of clinical sterility.

"Morning doctor!" said Conor.

"Morning Detective, looks like it's going to be a good one."

He sat down and waited for her to pull up some details on her desktop.

"We ran final tests on the organs and results indicate only one unknown biologic which we sent for analysis. The deceased's medical records indicted no diseases although he was allergic to shellfish and had been prescribed an Epipen." she replied.

"Interesting, I'm meeting with Dr. Woods over at MRC this afternoon and hope to get a quick analysis of the unknown substance. Thanks for the update and for sending the biological samples to MRC. I'll let you know the results of the tests as soon as possible; hopefully then we'll have the cause of death," Conor replied.

"The undertaker has the body now, and will prepare it for the lying-in-state service at the cathedral," replied the coroner.

"Thanks for the help," said Conor as he walked outside. His phone rang. It was Anne.

"Hi there!"

"Morning! Which one of your stories are you working on today?" Conor asked. "Let me guess!"

"I've compiled my story about Peig and hope to get it written for print by Wednesday. Then I'm going to Radio Na Gaeltactha to produce the show from the audio files that I recorded on the island. What are you up to?"

"I'm meeting with Brian and Dr. Woods this afternoon at 2:00 to hopefully get an answer about this so far unidentified substance."

"Great, I'm also preparing for the bishop's funeral coverage and will cover that story as well. Looks like we'll both have our hands full this week," said Anne.

"Maybe we'll have time to get together for another meal at some point," said Conor.

"Just let me know, and good luck at the lab."

Conor left the coroner and drove to the MRC lab, stopping for a sandwich to go at Nealon's. While waiting for the sandwich he picked up a copy of the Irish Times. Thumbing through the lead stories he read; *Bishop Cronin's funeral will be attended by a large number of dignitaries including the Auxiliary Bishop and Jack Moran, the local TD.*

Conor dialed the local NBCI branch and requested a meeting with Tomas Ashe, their lead investigator, hoping he would provide some local assistance with the case. Conor wanted to have some undercover personnel at the funeral to observe members of the public at the event.

He had met Tomas at a regional meeting earlier in the year and knew that he was a seasoned detective. While driving to MRC, Conor finished his sandwich and arrived just as Brian was turning into the parking lot.

"Hi Brian, good to see you again. It's been a while since we worked on that old college project together."

"It sure has and a lot has happened since then," Brian replied. "You need to come and see Sean while you're here in Galway. Evie would love to see you."

"Looking forward to it as soon as we get some time to make it happen. Thanks again for getting me into the lab."

"No problem. Let's go meet Dr. Woods, I know you'll like her," Brian responded.

Walking into the building, they stopped to check in with the receptionist before heading toward the lab.

"Please go on in, Mr. Connelly, you know the way," she directed. Dr. Woods met them at the door of the research department.

"Dr. Woods, this is Detective Conor Horgan, the lead investigator on this case."

"Pleased to meet you, Detective Horgan," she responded.

"My pleasure," he replied shaking her hand. Dr. Woods was in her mid-thirties with long black hair and dark eyes. She was dressed in a well fitting skirt topped with a white coat. Conor noticed that she spent a little too much time observing him and wondered if that was part of her intrinsic research mode or if she was attracted to him.

"I understand you need us to complete some forensics on the sample that we received from the coroner's office."

"That's right."

"I've already begun the testing and will have identified the substance by lunchtime tomorrow. Hopefully we'll be able to see if it is a substance that has a DNA signature so we would be able to find out where it came from."

"You've saved me some leg work by identifying this substance, otherwise I would have had to bring the samples back to Dublin and that would waste a lot of time. I really appreciate your help," Conor replied.

"No problem, I'll call you as soon as we have an answer."

"Thank you, doctor."

"Always glad to help out a colleague, and please call me Breda. I hope you find out who did this soon." She shook his hand holding it just a fraction too long, smiling coquettishly at him.

The friends walked out of the lab.

"I need to stay here at the lab but I'll call you later to set up a time to get together for a catch up meal," said Brian. "Say, did I detect some electricity back there between you two!"

"What do you mean?" Conor replied.

"Dr. Wood's a great catch, Conor. She's smart, interesting, and definitely not hard on the eyes!"

"Well when it rains, it pours!"

"You mean, Anne?"

"Yeah, that's the direction I'm heading in at this point."

"Well Conor, as long as I've known you, there's never been a drought in that area!"

Conor laughed, "My life is interesting, especially when it comes to women. They always seem to be part of the action. You know how it goes! Thanks for introducing me to Breda Woods and helping me with the case. It's all scientific with her from here on out!"

*   *   *

Brian left Conor at the lab and walked back down the hallway into the fisheries food research department.

"Have you finished the results on the new batch of samples?" he asked Jackie, the technician.

"Yes, I'll have all of them completed by tomorrow and arrange to have them shipped directly to the Ulster Marine Research facility on Friday morning," she replied.

"Great!" Brian applauded. "I'll be there next week to meet with the staff. Hopefully by combining data we'll be able to continue our environmental research on this food product and move on with the process."

He had been working on the cod fishery food supply-program for over a year now in hopes that the establishment of a new cod fishery off the northern coast would breathe new life into one of Ireland's oldest industries. It would also establish a partnership between the fisheries department in Northern Ireland and Britain. Cod fishing had been the mainstay of the fishing industry in Newfoundland across the Atlantic but had been depleted due to overfishing.

The governments of Ireland and the United Kingdom wanted to establish a new cod fishery, creating a controlled catch area off the coast, but not make the same mistakes that had been made in Newfoundland.

Brian's research with MRC could provide the necessary food documentation for this new venture involving both governments and verify the Donegal coast as a viable growth area for the species.

"I've prepared all the required paperwork for the shipment using the contacts from Dr Woods so this shipment should go through without a problem," Jackie confirmed.

"Excellent," said Brian, "I'll be in touch, thanks for taking care of the shipping."

"No problem."

He walked out of the lab and got into his Jeep to make the trip home to Carraroe. The sun was slowly working its way behind the Aran Islands, sitting out there in the open sea like giant whales waiting to submerge and bring another western day to an end.

*   *   *

Brian drove the last few miles to Carraroe listening to music by U2. Their distinctive sound and the dynamic pulse of their music helped him put the miles behind him. When he stepped out of the car onto the pebbled driveway the evening air was salty with a scent of gorse. He was home.

"Hi, love," said Brian as he walked into the living room where Evie was playing with Sean. He kissed both of them.

"How did your man do today?" he asked.

"Great! We went for a walk, and I found a new weaver just outside the village. He has done some beautiful work and I bought a throw rug for Sean's bed. How was your day?"

"I finished the samples and they'll ship them this week in time for my trip," he replied. "I also met Conor at the lab. He needed to get some evidence expedited through Dr. Woods," Brian replied. "He also told me that he had spent the weekend on Inishmore, with a new friend, Anne O'Gorman, a reporter with the Irish Times!"

"Sounds like Conor has recovered nicely from his previous relationship with that evil bitch!" said Evie. "That's cool! Can't wait to meet her and get all the details."

"Let me help you with supper," said Brian. "I'll make the salad."

Evie carried Sean into his room put him in his crib. He was tired after a busy day of exploring and his feeble, grumpy cries soon gave way to sleep.

Chapter 19

Teresa O'Connor returned to her office in the bishop's rectory to finalize the arrangements for the funeral.

Bishop Cronin's body would be brought to the cathedral on Tuesday morning and lie in state until Wednesday morning. The burial would take place on Wednesday afternoon at the cathedral cemetery with all the ceremonial protocols. She had heard from the office of the Cardinal in Armagh that an auxillary bishop would be appointed to the diocese as soon as possible. Teresa wondered if she would be asked to stay during the transition and was completing the final VIP list when her phone rang.

"This is Teresa O'Connor."

"Teresa, this is Declan Cronin, Eamon was my brother. I think we met many years ago."

"Yes, Declan, so good to hear your voice again. It's been a while."

"It sure has, thank you. Can I meet with you tomorrow to go over the final funeral arrangements and the invitation list?"

"Of course, I'll be here all day."

"I'm in Dublin right now but will be leaving for Galway this afternoon and stay until my brother is buried."

"Declan, please call me when you get settled and we'll set up a time to get together tomorrow," Teresa replied.

"Sounds good," Declan responded. "Bye for now."

Teresa wondered why she had infrequently seen Declan in Galway since his brother's installation as bishop. She had been the bishop's secretary for many years, and had met Declan at the inauguration of his brother. She remembered that he was an attorney, and had helped the bishop during that unfortunate business with the child abuse cases in the diocese. *I wonder could the abuse issue have had anything to do with his murder?*

The police had already picked up the funeral schedule, and were making plans for crowd control at the cathedral. Teresa continued to look at the list and began checking off the confirmations. Because the death was so sudden, she was surprised at the number of people who had confirmed.

Chapter 20

The next morning Liam drove to Carraroe Technical College and parked in the faculty lot. It was a good day to begin a new job. The storm was over and the fine weather seemed to be welcoming him to the campus as he walked into the classroom and checked out the shop equipment making sure that the facility had all the tools required for his framing class. The session bell rang and the students began to file into the room.

When the clock showed five minutes after the hour, Liam asked the students to come together in teams of four. The program was set up to teach blueprint reading, framing techniques, tool selection and a hands-on section using power nailers and saws.

"How many of you have done any framing before today's class?" he asked.

About six hands went up in the air.

"Not too many, but that's OK. When we're done with the class today everyone will know the basics of framing. We'll continue with roof layouts and learn how to use a framing square during the rest of the week."

Carpentry was Liam's first love. He was a master carpenter and preferred to design and build custom cabinetry with a fine hand rubbed finish. His father had taught him the secrets of joinery using age old tricks to make the process seamless.

He gazed out over the sea of faces. *Now I'm getting somewhere. I'm teaching something I love and soon will be out of the house in Caher and into my own new house. Life is good. I can't wait to show some of these students first hand how this whole process goes together.*

*   *   *

Conor called Tomas Ashe to schedule a meeting. He had received the final report from the local police with all the documented interviews and eyewitness reports and began to formulate a timeline for the last day of the murder victim's life.

According to his timeline, the bishop had been driven to the Star Hotel by his driver for a dinner appointment with an unknown guest. After the meal both men left the dining room and walked outside to the parking lot.

The bishop had dismissed his driver and both men were picked up by a third party outside the hotel. There was no CCTV camera in the parking lot and therefore no video record of the departure. *Need to pick up that driver for questioning.*

The dining room staff at the hotel gave a good description of the bishop and his guest, a well built, middle-aged man with salt and pepper hair, a manicured beard, wearing a sport coat with gray pants. The bishop paid for the dinner with a credit card so there was no record of any financial transactions by the guest. The bishop's phone records had been included in the report and numbers were still being checked but so far all the calls seemed to have no connection to the dinner meeting.

The coroner's report was also included. It indicated the cause of death as a possible homicide, because of a puncture wound on the neck of the victim and traces of an unknown substance in the liver. Tests were still being made to determine the identity of it. The bishop had not been drowned because there was no water in his lungs. He was apparently dead before he was put in the water.

So far, Conor had an identified body recovered in Claddagh Pool, a puncture wound on the neck of the victim, an unknown substance in the liver and a vague description of a dinner guest. He had no motive, no weapon, no suspects and no eyewitnesses to the crime, and as yet, no phone records or email records connecting the meeting with the bishop and a dinner guest. Not a lot to go on.

He arrived at the police station a little sooner than he expected as he was eager to get this crime solved.

"Hi Tomas, good to see you," said Conor. "Let's see where we are with this. I don't have all the pieces yet but I'm getting more and more information and with your help and your team, I'm sure we'll get to the bottom of this," said Conor. He began to read Tomas's report and made some comments.

"Whoever this guest was, the bishop sure kept it quiet. He also was not afraid to appear in public with this person so it looks to me that the person was a friend and not a threat to him. Both men apparently left in the same car and whatever happened after is still a mystery. Have an officer pick up the bishop's driver and bring him here for questioning. Have you discovered any other information since you finished this report?" Conor asked.

"We've received a few calls, from members of the public who want their fifteen minutes of fame, but nothing relevant.!" Tomas said indignantly. "I've checked with the department and they have a record of a missing car on the night the bishop disappeared."

"Who reported the stolen car?" Conor asked.

"A woman living in Galway reported it missing on the day that the bishop's body was found. She'd been in Dublin on a business trip and got home to find her car was missing from her driveway. She described it as a green BMW 5 with a Galway license plate. We're still looking for it."

"Do you think this is a coincidence?" Conor asked.

"Maybe, but we need to find the car. We'll have the toxicology results tomorrow from MRC and should be able to have a definitive cause of death," said Tomas.

"Let's stay in touch and let me know about the car," said Conor.

"I'm going to talk to the staff at the hotel one more time. Maybe someone saw the two men leaving and could describe the vehicle," Tomas responded.

"I'll call you tomorrow as soon as we receive the results from MRC," said Conor.

Conor drove back to his hotel and flopped onto his bed. He lay there thinking about the car and the driver. Then he called Anne. She didn't answer, so he sent a text message, then sat down and turned on the TV just in time for the RTE evening news. His phone chirped and he checked the text message.

Dinner2night? He typed a response.

No plans. Nealons 7?

Anne responded. *K! 8-)*

Conor turned up the audio on the TV to watch a segment on the bishop's funeral arrangements and a short bio on his life and career including a brief mention of his past involvement with some legal issues in Galway.

* * *

An hour later Conor and Anne settled into a booth at Nealon's.

"I met Tomas, the local detective working the case this afternoon and compared notes about the investigation so far. There's nothing new. We're still dealing with the same facts. I hope to get the toxicology report tomorrow from MRC. At that time we'll know what type of substance was used," said Conor.

"I'm not going to report anything until I get your go ahead on the facts," Anne explained. "But I'll make notes on a daily basis and file the story as soon as you OK it. Meanwhile, Peig's story is going together really well and I'm planning to get it in draft form before Wednesday, besides covering the bishop's funeral."

"I appreciate your discretion on this. We would not be having this discussion, if I didn't trust your journalistic integrity. You've had plenty of opportunity to break the details of this story but you've shown a lot of professional restraint. There'll be plenty of opportunities to talk to members of the public at the funeral and get more feedback on the bishop's history in Galway and Connemara. We don't know a lot about him as a person, but maybe the locals can give more insight into some of the friends he had in the city. Let's order some food. How about a salmon salad?" said Conor, "I'm starving, must be the sea air!"

"Sounds good."

While Conor was giving his order to the waiter, his phone rang.

"Excuse me a minute."

Anne continued with the order.

"This is Detective Horgan!"

"Detective Horgan, this is Sergeant Keenan with the Galway police. We found the missing green car in the Corrib River and there was a body in it."

"Where's the car now?"

"We have it at the forensics lab and the body has been sent to the coroner. She'll have to do the examination tomorrow morning; she's on her way back from Dublin this evening."

"Do you have a description of the body"? Conor asked.

"Yeah, let me find it here. It's a middle-aged man with salt and pepper hair, a beard, wearing a sport coat and gray trousers."

Sounds like the same person who had dinner with the bishop Conor thought, remembering the description from a witness at the hotel.

"How do you want us to proceed?"

"I'll be right there," Conor replied.

"Did you hear all that?" Conor looked at Anne.

"More or less," she replied, reading between the lines.

"I have to go. This may be the break we need. It can't wait till tomorrow. You stay and eat. I'll call you later," Conor picked up his backpack and walked out the door.

Anne pulled out her Mac and began to type: Green BMW found in the Corrib River with a body inside. *Looks like this crime is expanding its reach to other members of the bishop's circle.* Note to self: Get more details about this person. She continued to type while picking at her salmon salad. Wouldn't be the first time she had had a working lunch.

Chapter 21

T uesday morning dawned with a bright sun illuminating the dome of Galway cathedral. The casket of Bishop Cronin was carried down the short side aisle to lie in state on the bier already in place in the sanctuary. Two tall candles were positioned, one at the head and the other at the foot of the casket. Ropes were strung around the area and a walkway had been established to allow mourners to pass by and express their condolences to the man they had called their pastoral leader for the past ten years. A book of condolences lay opened at the exit door. The public would be allowed into the cathedral at noon and the place of worship would be transformed into a place of departure for the bishop, awaiting his funeral mass and burial the following day in the bishop's Plot.

Tuesday was also a busy day for Conor and his team as yet another autopsy would be performed. He arrived at Dr. Murray's office and walked directly into the examination room where a team of technicians had assembled along with coroner.

"Good morning, Detective Horgan," said Dr. Murray. "I apologize for not being here last night when the body was brought in but I was on my way back from Dublin at that point."

"Morning, doctor!" said Conor. "I understand."

Sergeant Keenan and Tomas Ashe stood on one side of the body.

"What do we have so far?" said Conor addressing the coroner.

She looked at the body of the man lying on the stainless steel table.

"We have a middle aged man who appears to have a broken neck, found in the green BMW that was submerged in the Corrib River. My assistant did a preliminary examination of the body last night and discovered that the occupant sitting in the car was not wearing a seatbelt and was found on the floor under the dash of the vehicle. We will perform the autopsy after this meeting to discover the actual cause of death."

"How long do you need?" Conor inquired, "bodies are starting to pile up around here!"

"We should be done by 2:00," Dr. Murray replied.

"Let's get the bishop's driver here and see if he recognizes this man," said Conor.

Conor wondered why the bishop's body was found first, and then the green BMW with the other body. *If this is the man that left with the bishop, why was he found days later?* He turned to Tomas, "Let's go next door and look at what we've got so far. Excuse us," said Conor.

Once in the closed door office, Conor began, "We have another body, found in the front seat of a stolen car underwater in the Claddagh location where the bishop's body was discovered. Do we know if both of these deaths occured at the same time? If so, why wasn't the car discovered when the area was searched after the bishop's body had been found? Or was the second man killed later in the week? Why was a stolen car involved? Who is this other person?"

Tomas didn't respond.

Conor speculated, "Let's assume that one of the victims, or both, knew the driver of the BMW who picked them up after their dinner. Furthermore, let's assume that the bishop was killed sometime that night and dumped in Claddagh pool. The other man must have been killed later. That's the only logical explanation. Tomas, we don't know the connection between the bishop and his guest other than they had set up a dinner appointment. I need the identification on this other victim and also his connection to the bishop. I need you to canvas witnesses who may have seen the two men get into the green car after the dinner. We have to find the driver of that car. The bishop's body is now lying in state in the cathedral. Let's monitor the crowd and take some pictures. We might get a lead at the funeral."

*　　*　　*

That afternoon, Anne crossed the public parking lot and glided into the cathedral entering through the main entrance. She walked down the center aisle. The closed casket lay on its bier like a cold, carved statue. Shafts of afternoon light illuminated the dark wood and ornate brass-work of the casket creating a solemn picture for the forthcoming funeral event when throngs of people would walk past their bishop and express their condolences.

Anne stopped at the end of the aisle, absorbing the entire mood of the scene and began to work on the layout of the piece she was about to write for the paper. She noticed a man walking down the aisle towards the casket. He stopped, genuflected, and knelt at the altar rail to pray. When he had finished, he shuffled to the casket and leaned over to kiss it then continued down the transept toward the red-flickering votives eerily illuminating the statue of St. Jude, the patron saint of lost causes. The solitary figure paused to light a candle before opening the door allowing a shaft of bright light to enter the chamber. The silhouette of his body created a dark shadow down the aisle that was swallowed up as he closed the door. *Who is that guy?*

Anne's thoughts were interrupted when the rear doors of the cathedral opened and the parishioners began to file into the hallowed space to express their sorrow. They were led by a host of acolytes with flickering candles, then a group of priests followed by the mayor, political party members and finally the Auxiliary Bishop. Encircling the casket they bowed their heads in prayer and followed the cortege down the left transept and out into the noon day sun. Anne followed the group and exited through the same door.

"Afternoon!" Anne turned as Conor walked up behind her.

"Hi, what have you been up to?"

"Sorry I had to leave you last night at Nealon's."

"I totally understand. I'm finishing my report about Cronin for tomorrow's edition," said Anne.

"I went to the autopsy for the second victim this morning and needed to come over here to check out the protocol for Bishop Cronin's funeral tomorrow."

"What did you find out about the second victim?" Anne asked.

"I should have the autopsy report later this afternoon. I also had the bishop's driver come to the morgue to identify the second victim. He couldn't identify the body."

They walked into the parking lot and began to look at all the people in and around the parked cars. Suddenly Anne said, "There's Teresa O'Connor sitting in her car with someone."

They made their way to the parked car and saw Teresa O'Connor in the driver's seat with the man Anne had seen in the cathedral, sitting next to her.

Teresa lowered the window.

"Good afternoon."

"Good afternoon, Teresa. This is going to be a difficult day for you. I hope you're doing all right in spite of everything."

"I'll get through it," she replied. "Oh, by the way, I'd like you to meet Declan Cronin, the bishop's brother."

"Declan, this is Conor Horgan, the lead detective investigating the death of your brother and Anne O'Gorman, a reporter with the Irish Times."

"Pleased to meet you both," said Declan. "Do you have any more news about the cause of my brother's death?"

"Yes, I do and there'll be a news conference this evening to discuss all the information we have so far. We'll be asking for additional public assistance in solving this crime," Conor responded. "Did you know of anyone owning a green BMW, who may have known the bishop?"

"No, I don't," Teresa replied.

"Detective, I hope you find out who killed my brother," said Declan.

"It's my job to get to the bottom of this and find the perpetrator. I'm so sorry for your loss, Mr. Cronin. Do you have a few minutes, now, to talk to me about your brother?"

"Of course."

Anne, sensing Conor's need for privacy made her excuses and left to post her story.

Declan got out of Teresa's car, and walked with Conor to his car. They sat inside and Declan began, "My brother attended Maynooth College and was ordained to the priesthood. He was appointed a curate in Kildare for a few years and then transferred to a parish in Galway where he became the parish priest of Cashelore. He served the parish of Cashelore for ten years and was then called by Rome to become the bishop of Galway over ten years ago."

"I understand from the records that while he was Bishop of Galway, there were cases of child abuse by priests in his diocese," said Conor.

"That's correct," Declan confirmed.

"I also understand that one of these priests was removed from the diocese and given a position as a parish priest in County Wexford," Conor continued.

"That's true."

"Why were charges not brought against this priest?"

"The church didn't want a scandal and also didn't want to release the name of the minor child so no charges were filed,"

"Did this boy or his parents receive any payment to maintain their silence?"

"Yes, they did."

"Where did that money come from?"

"A fund had been set up by the bishop to take care of these issues."

"So there were additional cases of abuse?"

"There were other deals made with the parents of other victims."

"Did you play any part in the resolution of this case or any others?"

"I'm an attorney in Dublin and I gave my brother some advise in this case. I was familiar with similar cases that had occured in Dublin and was aware that the Archbishop of Dublin had created a fund to take care of any issues pertaining to child abuse by the clergy. So I suggested to my brother that he set up a fund in Galway to tap into it if the necessity arose."

"So you knew about this abuse and didn't report it to the authorities?"

"I was aware but assumed incorrectly that the church would take care of the abuse charges and deal with the priests while monitoring their behaviour in the future."

"What about the abused children? Did they not have any rights to confront their abusers?"

"They did but were advised of the scandal it would create for their family and were persuaded to take the money and keep it quiet."

"So you were essentially breaking the law having knowledge of a crime and not reporting it?" Conor exclaimed dumbfounded.

"As I said, I thought the church would take care of the problem and I'm sure you've heard of client confidentiality."

"Do you know the identity of any of these abused children?"

"I don't. I deliberately didn't want to know for legal reasons. It was a matter of attorney-client priveledge - like a priest breaking the seal of the confessional. I would loose my license as a barrister."

"Do you know the name of the priest who was transferred?"

"I do, his name is Fr. Michael Godfree."

"Do you know where he was transferred?"

"I believe it was somewhere in south Wexford County. You could call the Diocese of Clody. I'm sure they'll be able to help you. Do you think this abuse issue had anything to do with my brother's death?"

"I don't know, it may have," Conor replied, "To your knowledge was there anyone else other than yourself who may have known about this abuse situation?"

"My brother had a good friend in Dublin with whom he kept in touch. He was an architect and lived in Donnybrook outside Dublin. I played golf with him at Monkstown a few times."

"What's his name?"

"Brendan Duffy."

"Why do you think he may have been connected or known about the abuse?"

"Brendan is a good friend of mine and also my brother's; I'm sure my brother confided in him about the abuse issue because Brendan was on the Ryan commission."

Declan continued, "My brother Eamon was a compassionate man who found himself in the unfortunate position of having to mediate between the abused and their abusers.

" On the one hand, you have these boys whose lives were ruined. What would be best for them? A trial which would expose not just the guilty priest but also their personal lives to the world? Or a cash settlement which could provide them with counseling and a chance at a new life? On the other hand there was the church position. If all this was made public, one of these bad apples could rot the entire structure. Would not remediation, repentance and remorse be better than vengeance? My brother was a broken man emotionally. He became a confessor to these men and as such took on their sins. He had to live with that on a daily basis and it weighed him down."

"Mr. Cronin, thank you for your insight about your brother. I hope to see you again while you're here. Please feel free to come to the press conference this evening. Again, I am so sorry for your loss."

"Thank you. I want you to do everything in your power to find his killer. Please call me if I can help in any way."

Declan Cronin dragged his long body out of Conor's car and walked back across the parking lot to the cathedral. The crowd grew larger in hopes of seeing his brother's casket lying in state in the stark, limestone edifice.

*   *   *

Conor left the cathedral and drove to Dr. Wood's lab at the Marine Research Center.

"Good afternoon, Doctor!"

"Good afternoon Detective. I received the file from the lab and was just about to call you."

"What did you find out?" he asked expectantly.

"We found a substance in the liver called Saxitoxin," said Dr. Woods.

"What? You mean the WMD Saxitoxin? My God, this adds a whole new dimension to the investigation. That's an extremely dangerous and potent poison!" Conor interrupted, "That's why it's classified as a WMD. Why would someone use that type of poison and where would they get it?"

"There are only two places in Ireland that have secure facilities to keep Saxitoxin. One is here in MRC and the other is in Derry at UMR. They're the only two licensed facilites in this country," Dr. Woods continued, "Saxitoxin is a neurotoxin and was developed during the cold war. In the fifties the CIA provided it in pill form to the U2 pilots who flew reconnaissance missions over the Soviet Union in case they were captured. It is a thousand times more potent than ricin or serin. Whoever used it in this instance must have had knowledge of its lethal power and been able to create it or steal it. All Saxitoxin has a DNA biomarker so we should be able to find out where it came from. It must have been injected into the bishop and immediately entered the bloodstream where it caused anaphylactic shock and paralysis, exacerbated by the fact that the bishop was apparently allergic to shellfish."

"Can you refresh my memory on how it is produced?" Conor asked.

Dr. Woods continued, "The toxin is generated in shellfish that have ingested contaminated algeal blooms. The blooms are filtered by the shellfish and the resulting by-product is the neurotoxin. There have been algeal blooms off the north and northwest coast, and I believe that may be the source for the raw material. Our supply of Saxitoxin in this facility came from a secure lab in the U.S. I'm not sure where the UMR supply was produced. They may have created it for research purposes during one of the "Red Tide" episodes off the coast of Ireland. I'll check with my counterpart, Dr.Somers in Derry, and let her know what I've discovered here in Galway."

"By the way, she went on, "it also has beneficial uses. It can be used for medical research on nervous disorders and diseases related to spinal column paralysis."

*   *   *

Conor finished the meeting and proceeded to the coroner's office to get the autopsy report and any other physical evidence on the victim who had been found in the BMW. Dr. Murray was sitting at her desk when he walked in.

"Hello there, Doctor."

"Hi Detective, I have the autopsy report for the new victim."

"What do you find out?"

"We have a middle-aged man with grayish hair and a beard. No I.D. on the body, yet. The external exam revealed a broken neck and severe upper body bruising consistent with an auto accident. The body was clothed when recovered and was dressed in a sports jacket and gray slacks. There was also a puncture wound on the neck of the victim, consistent with the similar mark on the bishop's body. The internal exam revealed a similar substance to that taken from the bishop and we now know that this substance was Saxitoxin from the results faxed to us earlier from Dr Woods at MRC. Therefore I'm indicating Saxitoxin poisoning in the report as cause of death, not a broken neck. That injury occurred later after he was already dead. The victim would have died instantly from this poison. We did find traces of skin under the fingernails and that tissue will be tested for DNA if it is still intact. I believe he was a professional of some sort based on his tailored jacket and fitted shirt. The police also took fingerprints for identification."

"Saxitoxin again! These murders are being committed by someone with sophisticated technology and intimate knowledge of a WMD, but why? There are easier methods available to kill a person. I'll notify Interpol in case we have something more than just two murders," Conor replied.

"We also did an XRay of the body and discovered that the victim had a steel rod and pins in his left leg, indicating an old accident, thought you would want to see that."

"That should help speed up the I.D. Thank you doctor, we'll be in touch."

Conor left the building and drove to the NBCI office to meet with Tomas Ashe and prepare a statement for the press conference. On the way he began to suspect that the person in the BMW might have been Brendan Duffy, the bishop's friend as described by Declan Cronin. He dialed NBCI at Phoenix Park in Dublin to check missing persons. After pulling over on the side of the road, he googled *Brendan Duffy* and discovered that he was indeed, an architect. *It had to be him.* He called Sergeant Dolan at the Park.

"Sergeant Dolan, this is Detective Horgan. I'm working on the bishop Cronin case in Galway. Can you research a Brendan Duffy? I believe this person lives in Foxrock and may be an architect. I also need his home address and phone number."

"Call you back as soon as I get it," the sergeant replied.

Then Conor called Tomas and told him about the X-Ray.

"I'll check hospital records in Dublin right away and see if we can get a match," Tomas replied.

Chapter 22

Brian finished with the food samples at MRC and walked down the hall to Dr. Wood's office. He knocked on the glass wall and walked in.

"Hello Brian."

"Hi Doctor, the food samples are ready to ship to Derry and I just spoke to my counterpart at UMR and set up an appointment to meet with her next Tuesday to discuss the research to date. I know both government entities; BIM, that's the fishery board, and the Northern fisheries are waiting for the results."

"Excellent! By the way, I met with your friend Conor; we were working on identifying the substance that may have killed the bishop. It was Saxitoxin."

"Saxitoxin! Wow! That's deadly stuff."

"We have some of that here at the lab to use for research purposes and I know they also have some at UMR in Derry. We're able to account for all of ours here in Galway so either they are missing some in Derry or it's been manufactured locally," said Dr. Woods.

"Or brought in from the outside!" Brian interjected.

Dr. Woods continued, "Your friend Conor is using the latest technology on this case. I hope he finds the killer before this toxin gets into the wrong hands, like a terrorist organization. Let's hope it isn't that. I very much doubt a terrorist would want to kill a bishop, maybe the killer got it from a terrorist cell. Who knows? I'm calling UMR to let them know that they might have a security breach and ask them to check their stock of Saxitoxin. In fact I'll call Susan Somers right now."

Dr Woods keyed in her number and received voicemail. She left an urgent message. A few minutes later she received a reply from Susan Somers, "Sorry, Breda, I was on another call, what's going on?"

"This conversation between us is confidential. We've had a poisoning incident here in Galway and the police believe Saxitoxin was used to kill two people,"

"Oh my God."

"I need you to check your facility to see if any of your secured Saxitoxin is missing and call me back immediately, thanks Susan," said Dr. Woods hanging up.

Brian looked at Dr. Woods and continued, "I need to get home. Call me if you get any info from Susan Somers."

"I sure will. Brian you know all of this information is confidential. We don't need to give any assistance to whoever has this WMD."

Brian walked briskly to his car and drove westward into the setting sun as it worked its way back into the ocean. He'd driven a few miles when his phone rang. It was Breda Woods.

"I just heard from Susan Somers. Her staff ran a security check and found that some of their Saxitoxin was unaccounted for."

"That's bad news."

"I'm calling Conor to let him know," said Dr. Woods.

"Thanks Doc, we'll talk more about this tomorrow."

The light continued to fade in the west as Brian drove towards the warmth of Evie and the giggles of Sean. *Shouldn't he tell her about the Saxitoxin? Sure, Conor would mention it at the news conference.* He reached Carraroe and drove the short distance to the welcoming light glowing inside the place he called home.

* * *

Dr. Woods called Conor, "Hi Conor, I've some very disconcerting news about the substance. Are you able to talk?"

"Sure, I'm just preparing for tonight's press conference."

"I just spoke with Susan Somers at UMR in Derry and she has discovered some missing material."

"That's not good. We don't need that news right now. Thanks for the information. I'll call the authorities in Derry immediately and let them know."

"I'll be sure and watch the news conference when I get home," Dr. Woods replied.

"Be careful, Conor," she warned.

"I will, don't worry."

"We'll talk later, have a good evening."

*   *   *

Conor sat in Tomas Ashe's office finalizing the talking points for the press conference due to begin in forty five minutes. The adjacent conference room had been set up to accommodate press and television news reporters as well as the social networking bloggers. His phone rang. It was Stephen Dolan returning his call from Phoenix Park.

"I have the information you requested for a Brendan Duffy. He was indeed an architect and I have his home number if you need to make the call. A missing persons report was also filed by his wife."

"Thanks, you need to find his dental records so we can make a positive ID. I need these records tomorrow morning, without fail."

"I'll get on it. Do you need anything else before the press conference?"

"No that's it, we'll talk tomorrow."

Conor looked over at Tomas, "Are you ready?"

"Yeah, I'm ready to go."

They walked out of the office and into the flashing lights of the digital world. A large crowd of reporters greeted them as they took their places at the podium.

Conor began, "Ladies and gentlemen, welcome to NBCI Galway. We're here today to update you on the murder of Bishop Cronin, and now apparently, another victim."

Conor glanced around the room to see who was there and to prepare for the follow-up questions. His eye caught Anne standing at the side of the crowd. She smiled at him.

"I'm Detective Conor Horgan. Here's where we are with this case. Bishop Cronin's body was found in Claddagh Pool, an autopsy was performed and we determined that the bishop didn't die from drowning, he was poisoned."

A gasp went out from the crowd as Conor continued, "We also discovered another male victim that we believe is connected to this case. This man was found in a submerged car in the Corrib River, at a location close to where the body of the bishop was found. We have performed an autopsy on this new victim but have no final results and still don't have any identification on this person. We hope to have more information later tomorrow."

He continued, "We need the help of the public to solve this case. Anyone who saw the bishop and another man getting into a green BMW the night before the bishop's body was found, should call NBCI. All information obtained will be kept confidential. We need to speak to witnesses who may have seen this green BMW in the dock area of Claddagh pool on the same night the bishop disappeared. We're still looking for the driver of a car stolen the day before the incident. A picture of this vehicle will be available after this press conference."

"I'd like to thank Detective Tomas Ashe and his support team here at Galway NBCI for their continuing assistance with this case. I wish to extend my condolences to the family of Bishop Cronin in this tragic crime. Now I'll now take some questions."

"This is Sean Murphy with RTE News. Do you have any people of interest at this point?"

"No, we don't."

"You said in your statement that the bishop was poisoned. So was he dead before his body was dumped in the water?"

"According to the autopsy, that is a correct assumption."

"Do you know what kind of poison was used in this instance?"

"Yes, but I cannot discuss that at this point."

"Why?"

"Rules of evidence."

"Karen Powers with Ulster TV. Was the second victim killed before he went into the water?"

"We will not have the information to confirm that hypothesis until we complete the autopsy."

"What was the connection between these two victims?"

"We don't know the connection at this point, or if there even was one."

"Why was the car not found when the bishop's body was discovered?"

"When we found the bishop, there was no car in the Corrib River. We used sonar to check for evidence on the night we found the bishop's body. We also scanned a stretch of water in the Corrib River at the same time and found nothing."

"Chris Hynes with the Irish Independent, "Do you have a description of the person who was driving the green BMW?"

"At this time, we don't. We're canvassing the area and getting statements from possible witnesses. We're still compiling that information."

The reporter continued, "Do you think any of these murders had anything to do with the bishop and the child abuse issue?"

"While there has been speculation in the media, I don't have any connection at this point."

Conor finished the press conference, "Thank you ladies and gentlemen. There'll be another press conference tomorrow evening and we'll update you at that time."

Conor walked away from the podium as the television lights clicked off and the room returned to normal punctuated by the murmur of conversations.

Chapter 23

Wednesday morning dawned with a warming breeze that wound its way through the still streets of Galway, the City of the Tribes. The limestone cathedral sat like a solid statement of power in the midst of the present day turmoil of the Catholic Church. It held the body of one of it's chosen who had guided the spiritual lives of the people of Galway. His cold corpse lay in state in the adorned casket under the dome in full view of all the assembled that had gathered to hear the final words of the liturgy preparing his soul for the transfer from physical to spiritual. The limestone interior with its praying arches and ornate ceiling personified the space as massive and motivating. Lights flickering from hundreds of votive candles painted the texture of the cold stone-walls with shadows of gold and orange. The public sat or kneeled in prayer waiting for the service to begin.

CLADDAGH POOL

Two altar boys walked towards the center aisle from each side of the sanctuary. Coming together they stopped, genuflected and walked in unison up the steps to the main altar. With tapers raised they added flames to the waiting wicks of ceremony, returned back down the steps, bowed and disappeared into the sacristy.

Organ cadences began to play solitary staves from Johann Bach as the minutes ticked by allowing the additional parishioners including the mayor of Galway, council members and the local members of parliament, to progress down the aisle. A group of priests in starched surplices led the Auxiliary Bishop wearing a gold mitre and carrying a crooked staff. Immediately behind this group a lone male figure walked in reverence, the bishop's brother. There were no other family members.

Conor stood outside the main doors of the cathedral and watched the mourners as they entered the building. He made notes in his IPhone and took the occasional picture. When the line of mourners ended, he walked into the building, down the east aisle taking a seat behind the pews that had been set up for the press. Anne was sitting on the end of the pew and turned toward him. Looking into his dark eyes, she smiled.

"Good morning!" she whispered.

"Good morning to you."

The Auxiliary Bishop and other members of the clergy walked around the casket, paused for a few minutes and went up to the altar. The bishop removed his mitre and began with a welcome to the dignitaries and mourners and finally, Declan Cronin the deceased bishop's brother. He asked for God's forgiveness for the killer or killers of the bishop and proceeded to begin the service with a blessing.

The Funeral Mass continued and incense ignited in the thurible to anoint the soul of the departed. The bishop walked around the casket blessing it with the smoking thurible. Smoke spiraled up into the circular dome imbuing the sanctuary with a strange blue veil of mysterious scent.

The bishop walked to the center of the altar and began the solemn portion of the Mass with the consecration of bread and wine. Transubstantiation was complete when he raised the bread and the wine and the altar boy rang the bells beside him. He then served communion to the dignitaries and to the bishop's brother. The service ended with the placing of the remaining pieces of the consecrated bread into the paten. The paten was wiped off into the chalice and the bishop consumed the last drops of the transubstantiated wine. Ending the ritual, he covered the chalice with the purificator, the paten and the pall and then covered the entire setting with the humeral veil and burse, then walked to one side of the altar to complete the readings.

Fr. Tom Leonard sat motionless with his fellow parish priests as the ceremony continued. He realized that he had been given valuable knowledge from a secret source looking for information concerning the bishop but was unable to divulge it to the authorities. The seal of confession couldn't be broken. *Deponatur sacerdos qui peccata penitentis publicare præsumit.* Let the priest who dares to make known the sins of his penitent be deposed.

He knew about the bishop and his dealings with the abhorrent behaviour of some of the clergy with minors. He knew about Michael Godfree and his removal after the bishop had made a deal with the abused boy's parents to keep the incident from becoming public. He knew the police turned a blind eye to this issue unless the abused had the will to come forward and expose the crime.

Information from an anonymous voice from behind the screen of the confessional was proof that something was happening again in the clandestine world of clerical abuse. Did this have anything to do with the death of the bishop and now apparently another victim? Could he approach Detective Horgan with this information? Absolutely not! He had received it under the seal of the confessional. He now realized that he had too much information and something inside his gut began to tighten and make him afraid.

Deep Coronach vibrations from the organ brought him back to reality as it droned out its final farewell. The bishop made his way down the altar steps and stood next to the waiting pallbearers. Bishop Cronin's coffin was lifted onto strong shoulders and in unison the cortege filed out of the cathedral into the bright afternoon sun followed by the bishop who entoned the last prayers. The body of Eamon Cronin was lowered into his place of rest next to the graves of prisoners interred decades earlier in the same site which ironically had once been old prison yard.

*   *   *

Conor and Anne walked out of the cathedral and stopped as Declan Cronin approached them.

"A beautiful service, Mr Cronin," Conor exclaimed.

"Thank you," he replied. "Have you any more information on the case since the press conference last evening?"

"Nothing new at this point, but information is still coming into the Bureau and I'll be having another press conference this evening."

"If I can help in anyway, please call me, I'm leaving after lunch tomorrow."

"Thanks, I will."

Declan walked away from the couple.

"Where are you off to now?" Anne asked.

"I have to go back to the coroner's and hopefully get a positive ID on the second victim. I'm expecting some more records from Dublin and expect to have a name before tonight's press conference."

"What's new with your stories?"

"I'm still writing the script for Peig's island story. RTE is going to broadcast it on Radio Na Gaeltachta."

"Congratulations."

"I have to finish my report on the funeral today and post it ASAP."

"Well, I'll see you at the press conference," Conor said.

He drove away, still smelling the heady scent of her perfume. He arrived at the coroner's and went straight into Dr. Murray's office.

"Hi Conor, how was the funeral?"

"Over with. I don't like funerals."

"I understand. I received dental records from Dublin and medical records for St. Vincent's Hospital and there's no doubt that the second victim is indeed Brendan Duffy," she continued.

"That was quick," Conor replied.

"Yes, but get this, he was also poisoned and died of cardiac arrest before he was put in the car and dumped in the river! He didn't drown; neither did he die of a broken neck."

"What's with this poison deal?" said Conor.

"The killer must have found a source for this type of poison and was familiar with its speed and toxicity. Duffy was injected with the substance through a puncture wound in his neck. The poison would have gone directly into his artery causing cardiac arrest."

"Thanks, doctor, for your help. When will the body be available for the undertaker?"

"Later this afternoon."

Conor left the coroner knowing that he had to call the Bureau in Dublin to get a phone number for Brendan Duffy's next of kin. While he was dreading the call, he knew it had to be made before the next press conference. He picked up the phone and dialed the Bureau.

"Sergeant Dolan, this is Detective Horgan again."

"Hi Detective, I understand the dental and medical records identified the other victim," the sergeant replied.

"They sure did, now I need the home number for next of kin."

"Let me check the file. Here it is. His wife's name is Betty Duffy."

"Thanks for your help. I'll be in touch."

Conor drove to the promenade at Salthill and walked to a bench overlooking the bay. His head whirling like the giant herring gulls that were screaming down out of the sky, before pulling up at the last minute to crash into the waves. He dialed Betty Duffy's number.

"Duffy residence," a voice responded.

"This is Detective Conor Horgan with NCBI, may I speak to Betty Duffy?"

"Oh my God, Brendan's dead isn't he?" screamed Betty.

"I'm afraid he is," Conor replied with a tremor in his voice. "I'm so sorry."

Conor heard gasps of sorrowful cries as his words sank in to the mind of the distraught woman recoiling from the tragic news. A few minutes passed as Conor listened to her sobbing.

"How did it happen?" Betty finally asked through her sobs.

"We believe Brendan was murdered."

"Brendan, No! Oh my God! No, Not that! Why?"

"We don't know why, we're still waiting for more information. Betty, do you have anyone there with you at the house?"

"My daughter Jean, is here."

"Do I need to call any other family members?"

"No, thank you. I'll need to do it. Thank you Detective Horgan, for letting me know, I hadn't heard anything from the police since I reported Brendan was missing, and now he's dead. Murdered!" she wailed.

"Thank you Mrs. Duffy. I'm so sorry for your loss."

Conor ended the call.

I hate this part of this job. There's no easy way to tell someone about the death of a loved one. I'll meet her in Dublin at the funeral and extend my condolences in person.

He looked at his watch, 5:30 PM, and called Tomas Ashe to tell him that he was just leaving Salthill on his way over to prepare for the next press conference. Tomas was sitting in front of his computer, busily typing a report, when Conor walked in.

"So Tomas, what do we have so far?" Conor asked. "We have no suspects. We have a connection between Brendan Duffy and Declan Cronin, the bishop's brother, who's an attorney and assisted the bishop during a child abuse case over ten years ago. We have a possible source for the poison, the lab at UMR in Derry. They have reported to us that some of their material is missing and they have notified the authorities. We have no motive as yet, there may be a connection to the child abuse cases but we have no direct linkage and no names.

Why was Brendan Duffy killed? Did he know the killers? Did he have information about the killers and come to Galway to warn the bishop? Who picked up the bishop and Duffy after the dinner and why was Duffy found in a stolen car? Why was Duffy killed after the bishop was found in Claddagh Pool? And where was he being held until then?"

Conor continued, "We need to revisit the email records from the bishop's personal computer and also the records from Duffy's phone and computer. I'm going to Dublin to his funeral and interview his wife, Betty, to find out what she knows and examine the computer files. We need to know more about the connection between the bishop and Duffy. We need to find the name of the person in Galway who Duffy was planning to see and find out the reason that Duffy had called the bishop in the first place. If the killer or killers wanted to kill them both, why didn't they do it at the same time? It looks to me like Duffy was interrogated after the bishop was killed, and then disposed of to maintain the secrecy of the murderers."

"We need to go back to those abuse cases, Tomas, and learn the names of the players in each of those instances while Eamon Cronin was bishop and a priest. There is so much secrecy attached to these abuse cases, I believe it's going to be difficult to get information unless we contact the minors who were abused at that time. All of them are now adults. Some may come forward now because there's a crime involved."

Tomas interrupted, "I think we should add a new page on the police website to enable the public to respond to this crime, using chat, phone or texts. We may get more leads that way since it is more impersonal."

Conor continued, "Do we have any witnesses that may have seen both men being picked up outside the hotel? Did anyone see the car on the same night or during the next day? What evidence was found on Duffy to indicate where he might have been, before he was killed?"

Tomas replied, "So far we have canvassed the streets and the dock area and haven't heard from any witnesses who may have seen the car. We'll be getting a scientific report from our own investigation of Duffy's body and may find more forensic evidence. We already know that skin was found under his finger nails. We have to wait until we get the DNA results in order to run that search data. We're still working on the car and completing the forensic evidence file on the vehicle. This may lead us in the direction of the killers, if any of it is useable."

"I'll prepare a statement for the press conference. Tomas, thanks for your help."

Conor completed the statement just as Anne walked into his office.

"Anything new on the case?"

"It'll all be in the statement," he replied hurredly as he walked toward the conference room door.

Anne thought, "He's getting stressed out. I wonder if I should keep my distance at this point?"

*   *   *

The press conference began exactly at 7:00 PM. As Conor waited for the rowdy press corps to quiet down, he scanned the room noticing RTE, BBC, The Irish Times and even CNNI.

He began, "We have the identification of the second victim. His name is Brendan Duffy, an architect from Dublin. His next of kin have been notified. Apparently he was a friend of the bishop's and was visiting him in Galway. He was poisoned with the same substance that killed the bishop, before he was placed in the car and dumped in the Corrib River. We're completing additional forensic tests on the body and also the vehicle and will have more results later in the week. To date we have circumstantial evidence but no witnesses to any of these events. I believe there are people out there who may have seen something and don't realize that what they know is important. Now that we have presented a scenario, maybe witnesses will be able to provide information to help us with this case." Conor concluded, "Now I'll take some questions."

Sean Murphy with RTE, "Do you know what type of poison was used?"

"Yes, it's a classified substance."

"Since it is classified, does that mean that there may be terrorists involved?"

"We have no indications that this crime is terroristic."

"Do you know why a stolen car was used in this instance?"

"We don't and as I said in the statement, we don't have all the material evidence from the car at this point."

Paul Warren with BBC, "Do you have a connection between the bishop and Duffy?"

"Other than being friends, no we don't."

"Do you believe these killings have anything to do with the abuse of children by the clergy?"

"We have no reason to believe that is the case at this point."

Pat Duggan with The Irish Catholic, "Are you investigating any other motives in these murders?"

"We're looking at all our options at this point but don't believe that these murders were just isolated incidents because of the method and the timeline involved. We believe they were planned not random."

Conor concluded, "Thank you. There'll be another press conference as soon as we have more information, and I'd like to reiterate to the public; we need your help in solving this crime. Please call the Bureau if you have any information.

The lights were turned off in the room and the rumble of conversation continued to spill outside as the press dispersed and began to transmit their reports to various media connections. Conor and Tomas went back into the office to plan the next day's agenda.

"Tomas, question Teresa O'Connor again and crank it up this time. I believe she has more information and we need to turn up the heat," Conor said forcefully.

"Will do."

Conor continued, "I'm going to Dublin to interview Betty Duffy and hope to get more information from her that may lead us to the driver of the car or the call that was made to Duffy asking him to go to Galway. I'll also meet with Declan Cronin to see if he has any more information about the child abuse cases that involved his brother. I think there's a connection there. Let's hope we get a lot more information about Brendan Duffy's friendship with the bishop. We need to research the court records concerning the child abuse cases to see if it's possible to get any names of any of the victims. We'll need a warrant to unlock that source."

Chapter 24

Finbar watched the press conference from his comfortable chair wondering how long it would take before the authorities would solve the murders. He had made his final decision and now had to live with it. He would never forget the years of closeted abuse while he was an altar boy. Life had moved on from that point, but then he had discovered that his friend, Colm, had also been abused while he was a student in the Christian Brothers School. Colm, a successful fisherman, worked out of Rosaveal on a Norwegian-built trawler. He had been Finbar's friend since school and now they were both members of a survivor group. Finbar had monitored the continuing abuse by the religious orders and the regular clergy through the years hearing from other friends that they also had been abused and demoralized as young children. When he discovered that he wasn't alone; that there was an entire underground of abused boys out there, he was spurred to action. It was oddly comforting to find others; to not feel so isolated. Together, they were stronger, a fraternity of sorts.

The government had established a Commission into child abuse asking the abused to testify in confidence to the committee members. Finbar and Colm had decided not to testify. They were too psychologically wounded and realized that nothing would come out of it anyway. The committee would never punish, prosecute or change the grip of secrecy that the Catholic Church held on Irish society.

Finbar turned off the television. He walked into his workshop and out the back door to the forge where he was completing a piece of ironwork. He felt the need to get back to reality by using his hands to mold metal into a shape that would make its mark on the people of Ireland.

Skillful hands, beveled, chiseled and reheated the piece of metal into the shape of an emblem. Four swirling heads intertwined in metal made the design come alive. When he completed the polishing process, he stood back to view the final piece, scanning the detail by cross lighting the embossed image with a hand-held LED light. It looked perfect. He turned out the light, walked into the house, took a shower and went to bed.

Chapter 25

Conor and Anne sat in the window of The Bay Restaurant in Galway.

"This has been an incredible day," Conor remarked.

"Yeah, I believe this was the busiest day I've had since I came to Galway. Things are starting to happen with this case and it's only going to get worse," Anne replied as they sipped their wine and perused the menu.

"I'm off to Dublin as soon as I find out the schedule for Brendan Duffy's funeral," Conor explained. "I'll be back here as soon as possible. Let's order some food, I'm starving." He tracked down the waiter.

"Right, I'll have sea trout, rice and a salad," said Anne.

"I'm having the curried chicken," said Conor.

The waiter took their order and topped off their wine glasses before returning to the kitchen.

"I'd like to set up another weekend getaway for us at some point when this case is over."

"Great idea!" Anne responded. "Maybe we could plan a fishing trip on one of the lakes?"

"Yeah, I used to fish on Lough Mask with my Dad and I'm sure we could stay in Ballinrobe and get a boat from there. I'll check it out."

Their food arrived and they continued to discuss the idea of a future get away weekend. Conor slid his hand across the table and covered Anne's soft hand. He remembered the feel of her warm body. Communicating through her eyes, she responded by smiling into his eyes. Her eyes held a promise of heated passion. Annoyingly Conor's phone rang interrupting the quiet moment.

"Hi Brian!"

"Evie and I would like to set up some time to get together for a meal. How about 6:30 this Saturday at the house here in Carraroe?"

"That'd be great!"

"Why don't you ask your friend, Anne to join us as well?'

"Let me ask her, she's sitting here with me at the restaurant."

He turned the phone away, "Brian and Evie have asked us for a meal on Saturday evening at their place."

"Sure, I'd love to meet them."

"Brian, thanks for the invite, we'll be there at six thirty."

"Great, looking forward to it. We can catch up and hang out with Sean before he goes to bed. See you then."

"That sounds like fun," Anne exclaimed.

They finished the meal and went outside to see a rising moon, glowing large over the Twelve Bens.

"Let's walk down the beach," said Conor.

They scrambled over the rocks and tufts of grass, and began their walk down the western crust of Ireland's shingled beach.

Warm hands and a comfortable silence between them greeted the incoming waves. A band of rock appeared out of the sand and they stopped and sat down. Conor placed his hands underneath her jacket and held her close to his body kissing her soft lips. She responded holding his body tightly to hers as their closeness warmed the rocks below.

*   *   *

Brian finished the call with Conor and walked into the living room where Evie was giving Sean his supper.

"It's going to be fun getting together with Conor and Anne on Saturday," said Brian.

"I'm glad he's found a new friend in spite of the circumstances."

"How about we have steaks and lobster. I'll pick it all up during the week and we'll grillout!" said Brian.

"Great idea!"

"Did you watch Conor's press conference?" Brian asked.

"Yeah, I did. Looks like these murders could be connected to child abuse with the clergy according to the press. It seems to be pointing in that direction."

"Well, we'll see this weekend when Conor is here to talk about it," Evie continued. "He also mentioned some kind of poison at the press conference. What was the name of it again?"

"It's called Saxitoxin and it's one of the most potent of all poisons."

"Where did the killers get something like that?"

"It probably came from a lab or a chemist who knew how to create it without a lot of suspicion. We have a sample of it at the lab in Galway to use for research but none of it was missing according to our records. Each sample of the neurotoxin has its own DNA so it should be easy to trace. I spoke to Susan Somers in Derry last week and she said some of their stock of Saxitoxin was unaccounted for."

"That's scary! Have you heard anything from Liam about his new job?" she asked, changing the subject.

"I haven't talked to him since he started. I'll call him right now and find out."

Brian sat down next to Evie and Sean and dialed his phone. Liam picked up on the first ring.

"Hi Brian, what's new with you?"

"Just checking in with you to see how the new job is going."

"Great, it's going to take a while for the students to get up to speed with the classes and the schedule. What's new with you guys?"

"Sean is growing like a weed and Evie has him on schedule with sleeping and eating. As a result, we both have a better schedule. I'm off to Derry on Monday and have a meeting at the lab to go over the new food samples I just finished. I'll be back Wednesday."

"Good deal, I'm getting closer to finishing my house and hope to move in at the end of next month. There's a lot of trim to finish, and Finbar's doing a great job. I understand that you and Evie went over to look at the house?" said Liam.

"Yes, we did and it's spectacular especially the views. You really nailed the design and made the best of the location. Finbar gave us the tour. Speaking of Finbar, what do you know about him; he seemes to be a very intense guy."

"He's a cabinetmaker and a bit of a character. I met him while I was a student at Carraroe. He's from Inishmore where his parents own the pub in Kilronin. Why do you ask?"

"While we were at your house the bishop's death came up during our conversation and Finbar had a kind of cryptic response. We thought that since he had worked with him that he would have had more to say."

"I don't know. I never discussed any of that with him. You know he too, has a great house in Roundstone."

"Yes, we drove by it on the way home the other day. I bet it's fantastic inside."

"It sure is. He designed a custom wood shop into the house, so he can just walk to work from his living room. I helped him with the layout," Liam said proudly, "Very cool!"

"Oh by the way, Conor's coming over for supper on Saturday night with his friend, Anne. Why don't you join us too?" Brian asked.

"Sounds good, we can all catch up then. What time?"

"How about 6:30?"

"Perfect, see you then.   Hi to Evie, I'll bring the wine."

Chapter 26

Fergus, the leader of *Dies Irae* sat in his home office and continued to write software security code for a customer in Dublin. *Dies Irae*, a group of four men: Fergus, James, Martin, and Colm, was dedicated to gaining justice in Ireland for victims of child abuse by priests. Two of its members, James and Martin, had been abused by the clergy.

Fergus's I.T. business had slowed down due to the recession so he decided to move the thrust of his talents into industrial security and expand his customer base in Ireland and the United Kingdom.

His upbringing as a boarder at Blackwater School in Dublin an all male enclave managed by a religious order, had introduced him to a classical education. His academic life in the school was punctuated by athletics, membership in a camera club, and a position as a successful debater on the school team. He and James met at Blackwater. James, who had come from a Christian Brothers' primary school, was going through an emotional crisis trying to forget the pain of being abused by one of the brothers. While having never experienced any abuse during their studies at Blackwater, they had heard horror stories by members of the clergy at reformatories and religious schools in other areas of the country.

James told no one of his abuse other than Fergus and tried to forget about that wound in his life, but in the back of his mind, it was always there, tearing away at his self esteem and leaving him with a feeling of violation and worthlessness.

When they graduated from Blackwater they went separate ways but continued their friendship. Fergus attended Dublin College of Technology to study IT and James became a chemist working with a Dublin pharmaceutical company on the Naas Road. Their friendship continued thoughout James's battle with the trauma of his early abuse.

Searching for a link to other abused boys on the internet James found a website called *Dies Irae; Day of Wrath*, a resource group for abused minors. He connected with the group using a fictitious username in the hope of finding some redress or counseling for the damage done him by the Christian Brothers.

Dies Irae offered counseling, legal assistance, and a confidential outlet for the abused. He signed onto the site where he found a few acquaintances he had known while a student at the Christian Brothers' School in Connemara and became one of the leaders of *Dies Irae*. They met in secret locations and always disguised their identities. It was not the first time Ireland had need of a secret group to free itself from tyranny.

Two more members joined and emerged as leaders in the group. Colm lived in Rosaveal and had been abused by a priest while an altar boy in his home parish. He now owned a thriving fishing operation with two trawlers and lived with his wife Sheila in the village by the sea.

Martin, an ex-military munitions expert, completed the tetrad; he owned a security business on the outskirts of Galway and lived alone in an old stone house that he had remodeled off the Galway-Dublin road. His successful security operation had a wide range of customers and connections, some with dubious backgrounds. Retired from the military, he had been involved in peacekeeping duties in Kosovo and had seen first hand the horrific effects of ethnic cleansing between the Serbs and Albanians. The experience had left him a wounded man with nightly terrors ringing in his head. He had tried treatment but couldn't deal with the mind numbing drugs that left him emasculated and useless.

CLADDAGH POOL

After a few years of retirement he gave up the drugs and decided to return to Kosovo as a security consultant for one of the Serbian leaders. This mission involved clandestine operations including the ethnic cleansing of Albanians who were trying to establish power in Kosovo. He had become what he went there to eliminate, a killer with skills and technical know how that enabled him to operate with impunity.

Now, his connection with *Dies Irae* gave him the opportunity to carry out his own cleansing operation. He hated the church for allowing the pedophiles to go free without any redress from society or the church hierarchy.

Fergus recruited Martin to the group having discovered his business online. Martin became an enthusiastic member providing overall security expertise to the group. While never having been abused, both he and Fergus were determined to help their friends find solace and retribution.

The Catholic Church had a history of responding to accusations of priestly abuse with cavernous silence by sheltering the names of both the perpetrators and victims. The Justice Department left the Church to handle their own problems internally, but the four founding members of *Dies Irae* believed that this approach amounted to a conspiracy of silence. The civil authorities looked the other way until the government, forced by public opinion, established a Commission to investigate the causes, nature, and extent of abuse and report its findings to a Board consisting of a Chairman and five members.

161

Recently another person, calling himself Neil, had asked the group for help. He had recently remembered the stigma of being abused by a priest when he was an altar boy in Connemara, and how his parents, believing it was for the best, accepted a financial settlement from Bishop Cronin. Neil had tried to move on with his life in spite of being a victim of this pedophile but the hurt continued so he contacted the group. The bishop had chastised the priest and moved him out of the parish while Neil had been persuaded to keep quiet about the incident, but had spent the last twenty years trying to delete the guilt and mental torture that had become part of his life. Now, with *Dies Irae*, he had the opportunity for some kind of retribution.

Dies Irae met with Neil and decided to help him track down his abuser and question the bishop about his decision to relocate the priest. They decided that Colm would take care of the interrogation details while Martin would handle the physical and security issues for the operation.

Chapter 27

Friday morning Conor and Tomas met to review the physical evidence from the car and the two victims. Faint fingerprints were found on the car and diluted traces of blood on the front seat. The forensic division had run a search on the prints but found nothing other than the prints of the victim. Some of the blood matched Brendan Duffy but the remainder was unknown. They also analyzed the DNA profile of the skin found under Duffy's finger nails: still no suspects.

Conor received a report from a witness who had seen the green BMW parked outside a warehouse in the dock area the day after the bishop's body had been found. The forensic team had investigated the empty warehouse and found traces of blood on a chair in the office.

One of the samples matched Brendan Duffy. They also found a small trace of Saxitoxin on the floor of the office and sent a biohazard team to remove it and file it for evidence.

Conor continued to key in the evidence on his laptop and began to connect the pieces. His experience told him that this case would be solved by connecting the evidence to an individual or individuals who had both scientific knowledge of the poison and the physical power to kidnap the victims and administer the lethal dosage. He deduced from the evidence in the warehouse and from the physical evidence found on the body, that the victim, Brendan Duffy, must have been questioned or tortured before he was killed. He reviewed the emails from the bishop's computer as supplied by Teresa O'Connor. There was one email between the bishop and Brendan Duffy concerning the dinner appointment. Duffy did indicate to the bishop that it was very important that they should meet because he had received a warning from someone in Galway who told him that the bishop's life might be in danger. The bishop had not asked for the details but seemed to take Duffy's word for it as a close friend. From this exchange Conor decided that the bishop had known why the meeting had been scheduled. All the other email communication between the two friends was just social discussion. His cell phone records indicated a number of calls between Duffy, Teresa O'Connor and two other recurring numbers.

Based on the timing of the calls, the cell numbers had been traced only to find that they were from disposable phones. Conor wondered if one of these numbers could have been the number of the person who had picked up the two friends after the dinner on the night the bishop was killed. There was also another call to a number in Carna. He called the number getting voicemail, discovered it was the home of a parish priest, Fr. Tom Leonard.

Conor scheduled a time to have Tomas re-interview Teresa O'Connor. He believed that she knew more about the person who may have picked up the two friends. He finished moving pieces of evidence around the program and turned to Tomas.

"We've collected a lot of forensic evidence and made certain conclusions about the victims and the evidence but it hasn't led us anywhere," he observed. "We have no motive other than the possibility of a connection between the bishop and child abuse cases. That assumption came from Declan Cronin but there's no physical link to connect this motive with a person or the evidence. While I'm in Dublin, you need to re-interview Teresa O'Connor and also Fr. Tom Leonard to see if they can shed any light on the case. They both had a connection with the bishop, so we may get lucky."

"Will do," Tomas confirmed.

Conor added, "I've received the personnel list from MRC, and none of the technicians or scientists who worked with the Saxitoxin material have any criminal records. They were all able to account for their whereabouts over the forty eight hour period prior to the murder. I got a message from the undertaker this morning telling me Brendan Duffy's body would be removed from the morgue tomorrow and taken to Dublin for burial on Monday."

Tomas replied, "There has to be some connection to all of these players concerning the motive for these killings. We're missing a key piece of information. More interviews, more information."

Conor agreed, "We'll continue the search and regroup as soon as we've collected more information from Teresa O'Connor, Declan Cronin, and Fr. Leonard. Let's touch base after the interviews and hopefully, at that point, we'll be able to establish a motive. I'll let you know my schedule for next week as soon as I confirm the meetings in Dublin," Conor concluded as he walked out of the office.

Tomas continued to type more information into the calendar on his laptop and then reached for his phone to set up the appointments with O'Connor and Fr. Tom. He dialed the number for Fr. Tom and a voice answered, "Good morning, this is Father Leonard."

"Good morning, Father, this is Detective Tomas Ashe with NBCI. Do you have a minute to talk about the death of the bishop?"

"I do", he replied, "and please, call me Father Tom."

"Thank you, Father Tom. I've a number of questions and wondered if I could meet with you tomorrow morning. Are you available at ten o clock? I know its Saturday, but this is important."

"Ten o clock'll be fine."

"Thank you, Father, see you then."

He dialed Teresa O'Connor but got her voicemail.

"Miss O'Connor, this is Detective Tomas Ashe with NBCI. I'd like to set up another appointment with you this afternoon about 3:00 to discuss the case. Please call me back if this time will work for you. Thank you."

Chapter 28

Martin sat at his desk writing a program for a customer in Galway who had requested security for a new product being developed to thwart terrorism. It was a three pronged attack: erecting barriers in buildings to prevent unauthorized entry, installing a palm-scan identification reader and developing anti-hacking software. Completing the last paragraph he filed the project under New Business.

He stood up, stretched, and walked through the kitchen down the hallway to a locked door. The blue light of the iris scanner read his retina and the door opened. The heavy security door shushed shut behind him. Now he could proceed with his personal passion; that of removing the next pariah from society. Bishop Cronin and Duffy had succumbed easily to the poison and been cleansed from society through the ritualistic baptism by water.

Both men had played their role in the coverup by the church and received their just punishment. Martin began to plan the scenario for the next target. This situation would be different as it involved the actual pedophile. He wanted this pervert to have time to think about what he had done to young boys including Neil, before his punishment would be carried out. Martin re-lived the killings of Bishop Cronin and Brendan Duffy. He remembered the satisfaction of plunging the needle into the necks of these enablers. He was haunted; not by guilt but rather by the fear of leaving an evidence trail at the crime scene. Had he left something behind at the warehouse or maybe on the bodies? No, he was too careful for that. Surely the cleansing water would have removed any evidence linking him or *Dies Irae* to the victims. He opened the door of a refrigerator and looked at a small phial of poison. *That should be enough to finish the job.* He closed the door of the mini fridge and opened a drawer under the desk which held a wooden box containing a large syringe, some cotton pads and latex gloves. Walking to a closet, he took out a set of disposable, black, coveralls which he checked for tears or damage. A small mask hung from a strap on the coveralls. This would not only protect his identity but also prevent him from inhaling any of the toxins. The next cabinet contained a black, twelve gauge Mossberg pistol grip shotgun loaded with six rounds. He opened a drawer below the shotgun and took out a Sig Sauer P 229, 40 caliber pistol with a fully loaded magazine. He re-checked the weapons and closed the cabinet. Turning off the light, he left his lair, the security door closing tightly behind him, and sat down at his desk to continue work on the new assignment.

James had provided him with a source for the poison which had been successfully smuggled into the Republic. As a chemist, James was able to safely handle the material and advise the other members of the group regarding the delivery protocol. The next mission would require two of them so he would have to be doubly careful. He knew from the conversation with the priest in confession that the next target would be in the Diocese of Clody. Using one of his many disguises, he would make a trip to the location to plan the logistics of the execution. Then he and Colm would set a date to complete the final phase of the operation. This was his expertise. He knew they could execute a clean get away as long as they were prepared and careful. One iota of physical evidence left behind during the reconnaissance missions could bring the whole thing down around them.

Chapter 29

Tomas drove along the ocean road to Spiddal and stopped for lunch at the Basking Shark Pub in Barna. Fish and chips seemed like the perfect meal, so he picked a table overlooking the ocean and bit into warm crispy codfish. The day was bright and the rolling sea moved effortlessly onto the beach, etching bands of spent foam on the grained tapestry of sand. Tomas was hypnotized by the banded progress of the waves inching farther and farther up the beach. It occurred to him that progress on this case also came in waves, each wave bringing his team closer and closer to the inexorable truth. Stuffing the last few fries into his mouth he got back in his car and continued down the road to Spiddal, arriving at the home of Teresa O'Connor at 3pm on the dot. He picked up his materials from the front seat of the car, including the voice recorder, and walked up the path to the front door. The doorbell sounded inside the house and Teresa appeared.

"Good afternoon, Ms. O'Connor, thanks for meeting me today."

"You're welcome, please come in."

Tomas walked into a well manicured home. Nothing was out of place, even the books were standing straight and orderly in the bookcase. He made his way over to a stiff-backed chair, not meant for lounging, and sat down.

"May I get you something to drink? Water, or tea perhaps!"

"Water would be great."

Teresa returned with two glasses of water and two napkins. Tomas wondered if she had just polished the glasses, they were so shiny.

"I'm hoping you'll be able to give me more information about the bishop's meeting with Brendan Duffy."

Teresa began, "The bishop and Brendan were friends, as you know, and it looks like Brendan had discovered some important information that he needed to pass on to the bishop. He didn't discuss the details of this information, other than it related to some of the bishop's decisions about child abuse cases."

Tomas looked at the log and the print out of the email about the proposed meeting. He realized that Brendan Duffy may have found something on the internet or through a phone call that could have put the bishop's life in danger, and as a result wanted to meet the bishop and discuss what he had learned. Duffy had indicated that they would have dinner and then meet with someone else after the meal.

"Do you have any idea who this may have been?" asked Tomas.

"I don't."

"Are you sure?"

"That's what I just said, Detective," Teresa huffed becoming irritated.

"Did the bishop have a lot of contact with Brendan Duffy over the years?"

"He did. They often met in Dublin when the bishop had to go there for ecclesiastical meetings and sometimes in Galway so they could play a round of golf at Lahinch. He always made time to visit the bishop. They were good friends."

"Did the bishop have any other close friends here in Galway?"

"He was friends with many people in Galway including TDs, the mayor, other priests and bishops but he didn't have many close friends as far as I know,"

"Did he have a lot of contact with his brother in Dublin?"

"He spoke with Declan by phone on a regular basis. There are some emails here that he sent during the time when the bishop was involved with the transfer of a priest to another parish," Teresa said handing the file to Tomas.

"Thanks, I'm impressed that you still have all these records."

"Oh, I keep everything. You never know when you might need it."

Tomas began to high-lite names, dates and opinions from the emails. He observed, "I see that the bishop mentioned an altar boy who had been abused here in Connemara. He indicated that he had given this boy and his family a financial settlement based on their promise not to prosecute the priest. It looks like the bishop's brother advised him to make that deal. Do you think his brother knew the identity of this family?"

"I don't know. All of those records are confidential to protect the abused and the abusers. I've worked for the bishop for twelve years and all this happened before my employment. I do know that Bishop Cronin and his brother had many phone conversations, and the bishop visited him when he went to Dublin. I never saw Declan Cronin here in Galway, until his brother's funeral."

"Are you sure you don't know the identity of this boy?" Tomas asked more sternly.

"Believe me, this all happened before I started work for the bishop," said Teresa, her neck stiffening.

Tomas continued to browse through the emails looking for any names that might have a connection to the murderers.

He began to study the persona of Teresa and observed, "Here is an unmarried woman in her early forties, living alone in a clinically clean house. She wears no makeup and no perfume. Her hair is tied up in a French bun and her sensible clothes do nothing to accent her femininity. She seems totally asexual and has an aura of a nun, like someone he remembered in kindergarten. Why did she choose this career, hiding herself away in the cloistered life as a bishop's secretary? He knew without a doubt that she'd protect the church at all costs.

"Would you like some tea?" Teresa's voice broke back into his world.

"No, thanks, I think I have all the information I need for now. I really appreciate your time and your observations about the bishop. I may have more questions later."

Teresa answered him with a wry smile, "Of course, glad to help."

Tomas stood up, collecting his paperwork and he putting it in his portfolio, he walked to the front door.

"Slan," he said stepping off the front step.

"Slan abhaile," said Teresa closing the door behind him.

She knows the name of that boy and a lot more.

Chapter 30

Anne continued to edit her interview with Peig and finalize the script for the radio show. The twenty minute presentation would use narration with excerpts from her audio interview.

She planned to produce the show in two parts. The first part would describe Peig's early childhood on Inishmore with her family and her experiences at a National School. National Schools were public, typically two room with boys on one side and girls on the other. They provided a comprehensive education through Irish for children in the surrounding community. The rest of Peig's early story would describe her later life on Inishmore with her husband and two children.

The second part of the program would add Padraig's life story to the mix and include the details of his life as a fisherman, a poet and an oral historian. The entire program would be a blend of Irish and English. Anne decided that the mixture of languages would provide a cultural interest to her stories and leave the listener with a truer expression of the islands' character.

She had also been able to provide The Irish Times with a constant stream of information about the murder case because Conor kept her in the loop, allowing her access to important details. The newspaper's webpage had received a large number of hits on her story. The large amount of public interest made her feel like her writing and communication style was striking a chord with her readers. She stopped writing and called Ronan, the producer of the radio show at (RNG) in Cashla.

"Ronan, I'll be ready for air early next week with the first part of the show."

"Go maith! I can't wait to hear it. Send me the file when you're ready."

"I need to add some music and sound effects to complete the story. I've an audio session booked for next Monday in Galway and will bring you the completed version after that."

"Are you going to put it on the Times webpage as well?" Ronan asked.

"Yes, I finished the promo for that and will be able to put it up early next week."

"Grand! We may have some airtime for another story next month. Do you have any ideas for another show?"

"I may have something by that time. I've been working on a western writer's show for the past year and may have it completed by that time. I'll let you know," Anne advised. "I've been really busy reporting on the bishop's murder, as you know."

"I understand. Your writer's story sounds interesting, how much of it's in Irish?" asked Ronan.

"All of it, the narration, the writers and their readings will all be in Connacht Irish. I'll bring you an outline next week."

"Always ready for the next great story. Hope you can take some time off this weekend to take a break."

"I hope so too."

"Slan."

"Slan go foil."

Chapter 31

Liam walked around the students in his classroom and watched their technical progress using shop tools. Some of the students were completing joint construction with saws, routers and hand tools. They were settling into the program while learning all the details of joinery, design and final finishing. He spoke individually to some students to offer personal guidance with their work as they struggled with some of the double mitered corners.

After gaining their attention, he spoke to the class, "When we're making a double miter joint, think of it in two steps and complete one before you think about the other. If you try and figure out the entire joint, you'll become totally confused."

One of his students asked, "If I'm making a frame, do I make all the dados first and stop the cuts before I get to the corners?"

"No," Liam answered. "If you're making a frame to inset a glass door, you need to make the complete frame first; then create the dado for the glass, using a router. You can clean up the corners with a straight chisel or a corner chisel. Everybody understand that process?" They replied in unison, "Tuigamid, Mr. Duggan."

"Grand, now it's time to clean up the shop, put away all the tools, and leave your work on your benches. We'll have our first critique on Monday. Have a great weekend everybody, you're making great progress."

Liam walked into his office and looked at his schedule for the following week. It included the construction timeline for his house which was about ninety percent complete. The last ten percent was always the hard part, with all the details. Furniture would be arriving in three weeks so one way or another it had to be done.

Liam would teach a wood turning class for some of his more experienced students while beginners would continue with their framing skills. He was going to design a student built gazebo that would create an outside conversation area where they could talk over completed framing projects and world issues at the same time. He was an advocate of the Socratic approach.

Saturday night he was meeting Brian, Conor, and Anne for dinner at Brian and Evie's. The wine was already chilling in the pub cooler, and he was ready to have a good evening with his friends.

I need to grade their work today, so I'll have some time for myself tomorrow.

He realized that he had run out of printer paper so went down the hallway to the supply closet to get more. On the way back he passed Niamh O'Malley's classroom and noticed she was working at her computer. Niamh, a dark haired Irish beauty with deep brown eyes, could be described as black Irish because of her family's mythical connection to the scattered remains of the Spanish Armada that was wrecked in 1588 and washed ashore at Carna where they eventually interbred with the local population.

Niamh's ancient pirate relative, Grainne O'Malley had ruled the seas around the coast and her domination of the English ships made her a legend in the area. Niamh grew up in Galway with her two brothers, Frank and Larry. Her father, a doctor managed his practice in Galway. She had had a previous job as a technical school teacher in Galway City and then moved to Carraroe.

"Hi Niamh," Liam said walking into her classroom.

"Liam, how's it going with the new job?"

"It's going great, my students like working with wood and can't wait to complete their projects. How's it going with your guys?"

"I'm teaching CAD and they're picking it up fast. This generation is fearless with all things technical."

"I use CAD too but need to get up to speed on the new software. I used it to design my house."

"Yeah, Finbar told me that you were building one."

Liam continued, "I began designing it when I was in school and over the past few years the dream has become a reality. It has also become a great teaching tool for my students; I can take them over there to see the construction process in real time. You know Finbar?"

"Yes, we've been friends for a few years. He's an interesting character and a really talented cabinetmaker," she replied. "Have you seen his house?"

"I have and used some of his ideas in mine, especially the built in cabinetry that he designed around the main windows overlooking the bay."

Niamh went on, "He keeps to himself and is difficult to get to know but a great friend once you get past his facade. His life has been tough and he only has a few good friends."

"Do you like hiking?" Liam asked changing the subject.

"Sure do," Niamh replied. "I like to hike through the Twelve Bens and do a little trout fishing at the same time."

"Me too, I've camped on the Aran Islands a few times and found out a lot about the history of the place. It's the only real way to get in touch with the people."

"Sounds like we ought to talk about this some more," Niamh exclaimed. "I need to finish up this grading and get out of here."

"How 'bout we go to Spiddal for the craic Sunday night?" Liam asked anticipating a positive reply.

"That'd be fun!"

"Owen, a friend of mine has a new band and they have their first gig tomorrow night at *The Sunset Bar* in Spiddal," said Liam.

"What kind of music do they play?"

"Traditional Irish with a twist is how he described it."

"Fun, what time?"

"They'll start around 8:00," Liam confirmed. "How about I pick you up at 7:00 and we can get something to eat before they get started! I need directions to your house."

"I live on the Carna road just outside Carraroe, in a small bungalow called Flower Hill. You can't miss it."

"Sounds great, see you Sunday."

Liam walked back to his classroom looking forward to learning more about Niamh and her life.

Chapter 32

Friday afternoon turned into evening as the western light crept across the parish house in Bridgeville. The old stone house stood behind the church and was centered in a grove of gnarled yew trees. A flagstone path with dandelion weeds sprouting through the stones led from the church to the front door of the house; its painted plaster a strange ochre with color chipped away at the corners. The long neglected windows lacked paint and a splash of color needed to be added at the front door to soften the harshness of the mildewed walls as they dove down into the ground. Inside, a pock-marked floored hallway led past the stairs into the kitchen where a solid fuel Aga cooker stood with a large black pot of stew simmering on the cast iron burner.

A scrubbed, wooden table sat between two windows overlooking an un-kempt vegetable garden. One end of the table against the wall was occupied by a pile of dog-eared books while on the other end a single place setting lay ready waiting for the occupant of the dingy place to partake of an evening meal.

The large main floor bedroom which occupied the area at the back of the house contained an antique bed with a carved oak headboard and a panelled footboard. Above the bed, a broken crucifix hung on the dusty wall, its dying image personifying the gloomy existence of a tortured soul. Another pile of books was stacked on a side table next to the bed and a small brass lamp shared the remaining space, its worn tasseled shade spilling feeble rays of measured light onto the bed. Through another door an old fashioned claw-footed bathtub squatted on the cracked tiled floor. A brownish-green scum line wrapped around its rusting enameled finish and a shriveled rubber plug lay rotting in the drain. The window in the bathroom overlooked the pathway back to the church.

An ancient shower curtain rail ran around the top of the tub and was anchored into the peeling plastered walls. Above the white pedestal sink opposite the bathtub was a grungy mirror and a dirty glass, which hung in a chrome ring loosely attached to the wall, contained old toothbrushes that had seen many years of use. On the other side of the sink, a wall mounted bracket held a shaving mug containing a balding shaving brush. An open razor was stuck into a round, rusting hole on the other side of the bracket.

The upstairs of the house contained two bedrooms and a small bathroom that had not been used in many years.

Back in the church, Fr. Michael Godfree opened the doors of the confessional box and walked back behind the altar into the sacristy. He had heard the final confession of the day and was ready to eat his evening meal, put an end to another day of ministry, and relax for a while.

He removed his purple stole, kissing the cross symbol on it's back and hung it on a wooden peg next to a row of other confessional stoles he had received as gifts from parishioners and family members. The sacristy had been set up for the following day but he took a cursory look to make sure everything was in place. He noticed a small white card embossed with four swirling heads entertwined around the Celtic letters D and I lying on the chalice table. Picking it up, he flipped it over and saw the Latin words *Dies Irae*. He knew what they meant; Day of Wrath. . The words on the card sent shivers through his body and his heart missed a beat.

Holy Mother, someone has discovered my past. I've lived in dread of this day for a long time. They know where I am.

He walked outside into the soft evening on his way back to the house and saw four black crows chasing a sparrow-hawk into the setting sun. Looking down he continued the few steps toward the faded front door.

Chapter 33

Tomas Ashe rolled out of bed and into the shower. Savoring the hot water soaking into his body, he relished the time before the day ahead. He finished his ablutions, shaved, and got dressed in a pair of slacks and a polo shirt. Before putting on his jacket, he made sure his Sig Sauer 9 mm. pistol was firmly installed in the shoulder holster under his left arm.

The timer on his coffee machine had done its job and he poured himself a large cup of dark steaming brew. It was Saturday, but he had a scheduled appointment with Fr. Tom in Carna. He finished his bowl of cereal and poured a second cup of coffee for the road. The hour's drive to the priest's house, would give him plenty of time to reflect on the questions and drill deeper into a possible motive for the killings.

Taking the Clifden Road, he passed through the heart of Connemara with all its barrenness and austerity. heep were everywhere grazing on grasses and berries. They created speckled dots on the bogland canvas, scattered among the lakes and ponds and illuminated by the morning light stretching over the weather worn mountains.

He turned left on R340 which took him to the coastal village of Carna, a place busy with tourists and hikers who stood around outside the shops and pubs. The views from the main street were spectacularly accented by the Twelve Bens Mountains and white washed houses dotting the rocky landscape. Sea air mixed with the scent of seaweed and sun-baked rocks permeated his senses. The parish church was located next to the edge of the ocean and the priest's house sat behind it. He parked in front of the church, pulled out his notepad, and scanned through his prepared questions for Fr. Tom.

Getting out of the car he walked around the church to the priest's house. He knocked on the door and waited for a few minutes before the door was opened by the priest dressed in his weekend clothes, no collar, a fleece jacket and slacks. Tomas guessed his age to be in the mid fifties with a kind face accented by blue eyes and reddish hair beginning to turn gray.

"Good morning," said the priest. "You must be Tomas."

"I am indeed."

"Go maith," said Father Tom, "Please come in. Would you like some coffee or tea?"

"Coffee would be grand, thanks."

The house was old but well kept and decorated with dated wallpaper and white painted trim. They walked into the large cozy kitchen where an oak table and chairs stood at one end of the room. Fr. Tom took two mugs from a cabinet over the coffeemaker and began to pour the black, tarry brew.

"There's some biscuits on the table in that tin if you'd like some."

"Thanks, Father."

They sat down at the table as Fr. Tom made some room amongst the books for Tomas and his coffee.

"So you're here this morning to ask me about the bishop?"

"Yes, Father, I hope you're able to give me some background on the man and his dealings with other priests in the parish. I understand that there were some issues that happened on his watch. You've been the parish priest here in Carna for ten years, and I'm sure you know about some of these cases."

"The abuse of children is despicable," said Fr.Tom, "by the clergy or anyone else. When I was a curate the bishop was dealing with many cases of abuse by priests and brothers. At that time, Bishop Cronin met with all the clergy and addressed this abomination. There were no charges filed by the abused children's families. The parents were persuaded by the bishop to take monetary settlements to maintain their silence. I've some real issues with the church on this matter."

"Did you personally know any of the children who had been abused?"

"I didn't. When the government set up the commissions to look into the abuse of minors, all the names of the abusers and their victims were kept confidential. There was no way to find out the identities of these individuals. We all had our suspicions but were unable to make any connections. The bishop made it clear to us that secrecy would be enforced."

"Have you ever been approached by any of these victims?"

Fr Tom thought for a minute and said, "No, I haven't. Do you think any of these abuse cases had anything to do with the murder of Bishop Cronin?"

"We don't know if they did or not," Tomas replied. "Do you know any priests who were accused at that time?"

Fr. Tom looked pensively at the ceiling, "If the priests were found out, they were reprimanded and transferred. Those records should be in the bishop's files. I had no personal contact with any of the abusers."

Tomas reiterated, "You didn't answer my question."

"That's all I have to say about that."

"Very well," said Tomas, "I respect your position. You may be called to make a statement later."

"I understand and will be happy to assist you," said Fr. Tom wondering how he would deal with the issue of the seal of confession.

"Do you know the bishop's secretary?"

"Yes, I know Teresa, she's a great organizer and has kept us all up to date with developments in the diocese."

"Would she have access to those transfer records?"

"I don't know. You'd have to ask her."

Taking another sip of coffee, he continued to write on his legal pad. When he was finished he looked up and said, "Thank you, Father, for your help with this case and for your time this morning. I may be calling you again as the process continues."

"You're welcome, I'm happy to help."

Tomas pushed back his chair, stood up, and picked his materials up off the table. Fr. Tom ushered him out of the kitchen and down the hallway to the front door.

"Thanks for coming to Carna this morning and have a great weekend. God Bless you," said Fr Tom as he closed the door and walked back into the kitchen, his mind now a whirl of questions.

Should I have told Tomas about Michael Godfree? I know he was transferred to another parish and protected by the bishop. Should I call Michael Godfree and tell him that his life may be in danger? There may be a connection between the man in the confessional and the murders in Galway. I can't divulge any information that I obtained in the confessional. I must be quiet and wait for further questioning from Tomas or others. My duty is to my God, my Church and the secrecy of the confessional. I must maintain this triune. But what happens if I have to make a sworn statement at the police station? Fr. Tom began to feel small beads of sweat on his forehead.

*   *   *

Conor studied the layers of evidence on his laptop, trying to connect the salient points of the investigation. There was evidence, both material and forensic plus possible motive based on the child abuse cases, but no suspects. *There must be a connection and I have to find it.* He took out his phone and dialed Tomas.

"Tomas, did you meet with Fr. Tom?"

"I did, but he didn't provide any new leads or information. He wouldn't answer some questions and refused to give me any names."

"What questions didn't he answer?"

"He wouldn't identify any abusive priests, told me that the records were confidential. I believe he has more information but is afraid to divulge it or he believes he should remain silent on the entire issue in order to protect the Church," Tomas replied.

"I don't understand. Two people have been murdered, surely that's enough motivation to have someone come forward and help find their killers. This is really frustrating," Conor replied indignantly. "We may need to take him to the station and force him to make a statement."

"Where do we go from here?" asked Tomas.

"I remember reading about the church in Wexford in the 70s, when they began to change the layout of the twin Pugin churches to conform to the Ecumenical Council. They locked the doors of the church and tore out the complete altar replacing it with slabs of marble. It looked like a men's urinal after they had finished. The community was incensed and architectural advisors from Dublin finally had the demolition stopped, but it was too late for one of the churches. That is an example of pure arrogance by the bishop in Wexford and his team of despots. Enough on that subject, for now, they protect their own so we have to keep up the pressure."

Conor continued, "I'll talk to Betty Duffy and Declan Cronin. I'll push them for information and get access to their computers. There has to be a connection between Brendan Duffy and the person he met with the bishop after their dinner. I believe that Declan Cronin knows a lot more but won't tell us. It may be attorney-client privilege, I don't know. Tomas, you need to re-examine the BMW for more evidence. There could be additional clues in the warehouse as well. We must have missed something. Did you check for security cameras?"

"Yes, we did. There were none on that side of the building," Tomas replied.

"Were there any cameras on the water side of the building?"

"Yes, one camera overlooked the docks, but it wasn't working," Tomas continued, "the cable had been cut."

"Is that the location where the car was dumped in the Corrib River?"

"Yes."

"Let's canvas residents on the other side of the river to see if they have any personal security cameras."

"We already canvassed the area and found one business that had a camera, but its field of view didn't show the other side of the river," Tomas paused and then added, "There was an empty loft apartment over one of the warehouses that we couldn't check. I'll get an officer to find the owner."

"That might be the break we need if it had a camera. It may show the car being pushed or driven over the dock on the other side of the river," Conor continued, "Let me know as soon as you find out one way or the other."

"I also met with Teresa O'Connor," Tomas continued, "She wouldn't give me any names either. I still believe she knows the name of the boy who was abused by the re-located priest. She's protecting the church and possibly her own involvement with the whole situation."

"We need to re-address the secret files on the abusers and the abused," Conor replied, "We'll need a court order for that."

"Will do, good job and have a great weekend," said Tomas.

Conor hung up and looked at his watch. It was 3:30. He needed to get ready for Brian's party and pick up Anne before setting out for Carraroe.

Chapter 34

Conor left the store with two bottles of French wine and placed them on the back seat of his car which was parked next to Eyre Square. He walked back down Market Street to Lydon's and bought some French bread, camembert and Dubliner cheese. *That should do it*. Returning to the car, he called Anne and got voicemail so he drove to Salthill and parked outside her hotel, waiting in the car. Soon his phone rang.

"Sorry, I was in the shower. I'll be down in a minute."

"No bother, take your time," Conor replied.

Anne got dressed in a short tweed mini-skirt. She pulled on a heather colored, fitted top and inserted her satiny legs into a pair of tightly fitting boots with four inch heels. She grabbed her large shoulder bag that held her Mac and walked down the stairs through the lobby and out into the afternoon sun. When she reached Conor's car he was waiting with the opened door, kissing her gently.

"OK, it's party time, let's hit the road!" he said. "You look great!"

"Thanks, what have you been up to?"

"There are hundreds of bits of data out there on this case and we've got to follow up on every one. Tomas is organized and thorough and stays focused. He's great to work with. I leave for Dublin next week so I've got to get my ducks in a row. What about you?"

"I finished the script for Peig's story and have scheduled the final audio mix on Monday at the studio. I've a lot of tweaking to do before I take it to the station," Anne replied.

"Writing a good story is a lot like a case, copious detail work which has to be carefully tended," said Conor.

"Yep, the devil's in the details."

They drove the coast road to Carraroe. It was a much more interesting drive than taking the road north through Maam Cross and inland through Oughterard. The CD player pumped out new style Celtic music that had strong connections to African and mid-eastern rhythms.

"I love that music," said Anne.

"Yeah, it's called Afro-Celt; an interesting mixture of Irish and other music genres. I downloaded it from Itunes last night," said Conor. "What did we do before we had all this technology?

"I don't know but I don't think we could work without it. I'm able to assemble the rough cut audio for Peig's show on my Mac and prepare for the final mix in a couple of hours. It's amazing."

"It sure is. I wish I could just enter all the murder evidence into my laptop and get all the answers but that'd be too easy."

They drove around the bay and approached Carraroe from the north side. Brian's house was situated on a three acre lot that bordered the lough on the northside with great views of the ocean to the south and the mountains to the northwest.

"Wow," said Anne as they drove down the gravel driveway scattering stones in all directions. "This is pretty spectacular!"

"Looks like we got here first," said Conor.

They got out of the car and walked to the edge of the driveway appreciating the view. The water in the lough was calm and large herring gulls wheeled over their heads, screaming their mournful cries.

"We always seem to attract the birds," Anne remarked, "Remember we had them around us on Inishmore? They must be a sign of good luck."

"They're good omens in this case, except for the crows. They're harbingers of death and magic," said Conor.

They turned around to walk to the front door and saw Liam approaching the driveway in his Jeep. He drove in and parked next to Conor's car.

"Hi guys, looks like you just got here," he said closing the door and picking up his supply of wine.

"I'm Liam, by the way."

"Hi Liam, I'm Conor and this is Anne."

"Pleased to meet you both. I've heard a lot about you from Brian," Liam answered.

The front door opened and Brian appeared.

"Failte!"

He walked over to the group, his feet crunching on the gravel.

"Brian, this is Anne," said Conor.

"Hi Anne, welcome to the real west!"

"Ceart go leor, you have a beautiful place here."

"Liam, Evie and Sean are eager to meet you," said Brian, "Come on in."

Conor went back to his car to retrieve the wine and cheese. They all went inside, entering an open foyer that connected to a great room with picture windows on both sides. A curved wooden stairs wound up to a mezzanine that ran along one side. Centered on one side of the great room was a big stone fireplace. Artwork was everywhere adding color and a variety of shapes to the rough textured walls.

A large weaving hung on the wall next to the fireplace and watercolors of Irish seascapes were placed strategically around the room to catch the eye of the viewer. On the wall ascending upstairs, hung a collection of mixed media, including some designs done with driftwood. Evie walked out of the kitchen, carrying Sean who was very interested in all the new people standing around.

"Conor and Anne, this is my wife, Evie and our son, Sean," said Brian.

"Cead Mile Failte, Brian's been telling me a lot about you." Evie replied.

They shook hands and the guys made strange noises at Sean who grinned back at them. Liam walked over to Evie and gave her a hug.

"Hello, "Uncle" Liam," she said, handing Sean to him. Liam threw Sean up in the air a few times as Sean's giggles got louder.

"We're having steak and lobster for dinner. How about we serve the lobster here in the kitchen, and if anyone wants to add a steak for surf and turf, feel free to be creative."

"Good, who wants a steak and how do you like it cooked?" Brian asked.

"Steak for me," said Conor, "medium rare would be great."

"I'll have a steak also medium," Liam added.

"Yes, and medium for me," said Anne.

"We have beer, wine and cocktails. Beer and wine are in a cooler in the wet bar and I can create any kind of cocktail," said Brian.

"Chardonnay for me," said Anne.

"Coming up, there's quite a collection here so be my guest."

He turned to Evie, "Would you like something?

"No thanks," she replied looking at Sean.

Conor and Liam each grabbed a beer and walked outside onto the deck taking Sean with them.

"I'll be out there in a minute," said Brian.

Anne went into the kitchen, joining Evie.

"What can I do to help?"

"How about mixing up the salad?"

"I love all the artwork, especially the watercolors with the boat scenes," Anne said looking at the walls in the great room.

"Thanks, I haven't done anything new in a while as Sean keeps me busy most of the time."

"I didn't know you were an artist."

"Yes, that's how I met Brian. I had an art show in a gallery in Galway when we were both students at UCG and we've been together ever since."

"Here's your wine," Brian said handing it to Anne.

"Thanks." Putting it on the countertop, she began to mix the salad.

"How did you two meet?" Evie asked.

"We're both in Galway because of the bishop's murder. I'm working for The Irish Times and since Conor is the lead detective on the case the opportunity to get together just opened up for both of us."

"Sounds like a great way to get to know each other," Evie remarked. "Conor is a great guy and a good friend. It looks like he's back to his old self again after that other relationship."

"I'm not naïve to think I'm his first relationship and frankly, he's such a great catch I'm having trouble understanding why he's not attached," said Anne

Evie continued, "We lost touch for a few years. He was involved with a woman who we found didn't have much in common with us. Conor, in trying to connect with her, grew away from us. We felt the loss but now he's back and seems to be really happy."

"Yeah, it's been a lot of fun getting to know each other and I've had a good opportunity to be up front with the facts as they emerge on the case because of him. We're both UCD alums so we also have that in common," she added, wondering what Evie meant about that "last relationship."

*   *   *

Brian walked out on the deck joining Conor and Liam.

"What a place! You really did a bang up job with this deck," said Conor.

"I had a little help," Brian replied looking at Liam who was on the floor playing with Sean.

"Teamwork and a lot of late evenings," Liam replied taking a slug of his beer.

"Conor, what's new with the case?" Liam asked, sitting down with Sean in one of the swivel chairs.

"We've got a lot of information and are making good progress, but nobody has been arrested yet. We know that both victims were poisoned and the type of poison used, but we're still working on a motive."

"Have you heard anymore from Dr. Somers in Derry about the Saxitoxin?" Brian asked.

"Yes, they're still investigating its disappearance from the lab."

"You know I'm going up there on Monday to meet with her about my research for the cod fishery," Brian responded, as he walked over to the grill and opened the lid.

"Looks like we're ready for the steaks, the coals are glowing," he said walking back inside the house, taking Sean with him.

Liam turned to Conor and asked, "How long have you been a lead detective?"

"Just over six years."

"It must be a very interesting job, solving crimes and coming up with answers using science."

"It's always a challenge and every case is new, with its own set of problems. That's what makes it interesting."

Brian returned with the steaks but without Sean.

"Boy, those look really good," said Liam, "did you get them in Galway?"

"Yeah, I got them at Walshes and seasoned them over the last few days," Brian answered as he lifted the lid and placed the slabs of meat onto the hot grill. Clouds of blue smoke emanated from each steak as they took their places on the ceremonial pyre. The smokey smell of garlic and seasoning permeated the air as each side of the meat was seared and then allowed to sizzle on the hot metal, promising a juicy, mouth-watering taste.

Brian turned to Liam and asked, "How's the new job going?"

"It's going great. I've an interested group of students. They're focused and really want to learn. I met a CAD teacher the other day at school. We hit it off right away."

"Really?"

"Yeah, her name is Niamh and we're getting together tomorrow night for a music gig in Spiddal."

"You don't waste any time!" said Brian. Liam laughed.

Back inside the house, Anne took another sip of her wine as she walked around the great room looking at the wide variety of artwork and sculpture. Evie returned from Sean's room to join her, "Got him down," she acknowledged. "I hope he'll sleep with all of us out here having a good time."

"He's so cute," Anne responded, "does he let you work?"

"He's getting a lot better with his schedule and I can squeeze in time for my art when he's sleeping. I understand you're producing a radio show about storytellers on the Aran Islands."

"Yeah, I got some great interviews from two seanachies while Conor and I were there recently. I'm producing two shows to air on RNG in the next few weeks."

"The station is just down the road from here, you know."

"Yes, this is the heart of the Gaeltacht after all. I love it," said Anne. "When can I get a tour of your studio?"

"How about after supper," Evie replied. "Let's see how those lobsters are doing."

"Wow, they smell great," Anne remarked. "I'm sure they're local!"

"I got them off the boat just down the road at Rosaveal, can't get any fresher than that."

"That's for sure," Anne began to toss the salad.

"I've baked potatoes in the oven and mushrooms on the stove," Evie remarked as she opened the lid to check the lobsters, letting the steam waft through the kitchen.

Outside on the deck Brian turned the steaks. "Looks like these suckers are done. Let's go inside and eat before they get cold."

"We're ready to eat," said Evie. "Let's do this buffet style, so grab a plate and we'll eat in the dining room."

They picked up their plates and filled them with steak, potatoes, salad and, of course, the lobster served with melted butter and a claw cracker.

"This is quite a spread," said Conor as he finished filling his plate.

"Who needs another drink?" Brian asked. "We'll have wine at the table and if you want anything else just let me know."

They finally all sat down with the food and Brian proposed a toast.

"To friends, old and new, may we have many more great times like this together!"

Glasses were raised and "Slainte" chorused in response to the toast as the conversation began to burble again.

"This steak is perfect," Liam observed, "and the lobster is the freshest I've had in a long time."

"Glad you like it. It pays to live by the sea. More wine anybody?"

The bottles made their way around the table accompanied by Brian who served it with an astute knowledge of wine etiquette. Anne and Evie were deep in conversation about the artwork and planning a studio tour after dinner. Brian sat back down and began another conversation with Liam.

"How's the house coming, I know it's getting close to being done?"

"I'm going to move in in three weeks, and if there are some things left to do, so be it. I'll handle them myself. Finbar'll be glad to help me out."

"What do you know about Finbar?" Conor asked, always the detective looking for information.

"He's a great craftsman and a good friend. He's done a spectacular job with my house."

"What do you know about him, personally?"

"He's a very private soul. I've known him for a number of years and have to admit there's a lot more to learn about him."

"I'd like to meet him when I get back from Dublin."

"I'll be sure to get you guys together."

The meal continued with more wine and seconds of food for some.

"How about dessert?" Evie interrupted. "We have ice cream and apple pie."

"Ok, that's something I can handle," Conor answered.

"Anyone else?"

"I'll have a small helping of both," Anne responded looking at the pottery. "Are those bowls made by Mosse Pottery?"

"Yes, they sure are. I got them last year when we were visiting the family in Bennetsbridge."

Conor and Brian cleared away the dinner dishes and brought out the Mosse bowls for the dessert. Evie appeared with a large homemade apple pie placing it in the middle of the table.

"There's a pie that needs to be eaten," Liam observed looking at the flaky crust.

Brian cut into the pie, releasing all the sugary juices that oozed slowly into the crust and on to the waiting plates.

"There you go, that's the best pie I've ever seen," he announced.

"I agree. Let's go back outside onto the deck and eat this pie while the sun sets," said Conor.

The three guys added a dollop of ice cream to their plates and walked outside into the warm evening.

Brian stopped, "What a sunset!"

They watched as the golden sky painted itself onto the rolling waves.

"Where did you get the plans for your house?" Conor asked Brian.

"They were designed by an architect in Galway and we worked together to create the space. Are you planning to build something too?" Brian answered.

"No, I already have too much to deal with," Conor replied. "I've a condo in Dublin and am remodeling a Martello tower off the southeast coast."

"That sounds like a fun project," Brian answered. "There are a few of those towers on this side of the country too. Is it the tower on the headland overlooking Baginbun Bay? I think I've seen pictures of it on a website."

"That's it. My uncle left it to me but it needs some serious work."

Conor asked Liam, "Have you seen Finbar's house?"

"I have," Liam answered. "He had a Dublin architect, Brendan Duffy, design it for him. Apparently the bishop gave him the contact."

"You know, Duffy was the other victim we found in the river," Conor exclaimed.

"Oh, that's right."

*   *   *

Anne and Evie continued to tour Evie's studio. She had located it upstairs on the lough side of the house in order to make the best use of the northern light.

"You've done some beautiful work here," Anne declared. "I see you work in watercolors and oils."

"I do, but watercolors are my favorite. I like the feel of a blended palette in this environment because the terrain tends to be very stark and the blending of watercolors softens the results."

Studying the painting taped to Evie's easel, Anne remarked, "This picture of the dolmen with the lichen all over one side of it is amazing. The contrast between the hard rock and the light on the lichen works perfectly."

"I tried something new with texture on this painting," Evie replied. "I used twigs of heather to make a brush and then spattered the paint onto the paper. It created an interesting effect."

"I'm sure you get lost up here with all the elements and that special western light. It must really get your juices flowing."

"Sure does and I take Sean up here so he'll get used to watching me work and I can keep an eye on him."

The western sky still glowed long after the sun had set. The guys decided to come back into the house and continue their conversation in the living room. A cool breeze had blown up from the water so Brian lit a turf fire in the big stone fireplace. The scent of turf smoke added the final touch to a cozy meeting place. Evie and Anne came down the stairs and joined them in the living room.

"Did you solve all the world's problems?" Evie asked Brian.

"No! Just some of the local ones!"

"I got the studio tour from Evie and her work's very innovative," Anne remarked.

"So, are you ready to buy one of her pieces?" Conor asked.

"I'm ready to buy them all. I can't decide which one yet."

"Anybody need another drink?" Brian asked.

"No thanks," said Conor, looking across the table at Anne, "We've got to drive back to Galway and its 10:30; time to hit the road. We have to do this again."

"Next time we'll get together at my house for the house warming," said Liam.

"That's for sure," said Brian. "We had a great time this evening."

"I'm so glad Conor brought you along tonight," said Evie giving Anne a hug.

"Me too!"

Conor, Anne, and Liam walked outside into the departing day. Liam walked over to their car. "Good to meet you guys, let's stay in touch. Conor! Good luck with the case."

"Thanks, Liam, we all need it. Slan go foil!" Conor replied starting the car.

Conor and Anne drove back to Galway through the warm August evening. They were quiet for a while as the motion of the car lulled them into a relaxed state after all the excitement of the party.

"That was a great evening," said Anne, breaking the silence.

"I enjoyed hooking up with Brian again, we were always doing something together in college in spite of the fact we were in different schools."

"I really liked Evie. She told me a lot of stuff about you, all good though."

"She did? I've known Evie for as long as I've known Brian. Those two are a perfect match and now they've got little Sean to complete them."

Arriving on the outskirts of Galway, they continued on to Anne's hotel in Salthill. Conor pulled up in front of the well manicured grounds of a charming old building.

He got out of the car and walked around to open Anne's door. Reaching out for her hand, he pulled her up into an embrace kissing her softly. Anne responded with a longer kiss as Conor's hands worked their way under her shirt. Feeling her warm body and soft skin, his kisses deepened into her. Gently, he released himself from her and said, "I need to get some sleep. We'll continue this journey later."

"Thanks for a great time," Anne replied regretfully pulling away.

"Uh... let's go hiking tomorrow," said Conor, changing the tenor of the moment.

"Great idea, what time?"

"I'll pick you up at eight, and we'll grab breakfast before we go."

"See you tomorrow," said Anne walking away.

Chapter 35

Fr. Michael Godfree checked the sacristy at his church in Bridgeville to make sure all the vestments were laid out and the altar-ware was ready for Sunday mass the following day.

The evening sunset cast an eerie light on the crumbling plaster of the parish house as he walked up the path and opened the front door. Two gray crows settled in for the night in the old yew tree above his head, cawing quietly to each other as the black figure of the priest below them glided between the stone walled church and the mildew covered walls of the old rectory. He made his way into the dingy kitchen illuminated only by the food spattered bulb in the microwave. Turning on the overhead light, he pulled open the refrigerator door and took out the remains of last night's dinner. The microwave hummed loudly as the leftovers rotated inside.

Before sitting down to eat, he made sure the front door was securely locked then checked the back door that led to the garden and locked it. *Someone was here I can feel it.*

Returning to the kitchen he sat down and began to eat yesterday's leftovers. The stale smell of a reheated meat pie permeated the musty kitchen as the naked light bulb illuminated the dirty dishes in the sink, the boiled over stains on the cooker, and the overflowing trash pile building in the corner of the room.

Finishing the leftovers, he rattled the plate into the sink leaving his mess for the housekeeper. It was time to move into the other room, sink into his stained leather chair to watch the Saturday night movie and try to forget the two Latin words he had seen earlier on the white card in the sacristy.

Later in the evening after some mind numbing televison, he donned an old pair of striped pajamas and went to bed reaching out for the forbidden book in the nightstand.

Pornography did something to his soul, not to mention his body which seemed to like the pictures better than the words. While opening the book another card fell out.

Dies Irae. Oh my God! They've been in here?

A chill ran through his tired body as he reached for the drawer in the sidetable. Pulling it open he searched around for the beat up flashlight he kept for emergencies.

CLADDAGH POOL

He slid off the bed and crept out of the room down the hallway. The dying flashlight led the way over tattered carpet into the spare bedroom where it lit up an ancient tubular bed covered with dust and more piles of paperback books.

Nobody here! He checked the other rooms opening all the closets but found nothing. Returning back down the hallway to the welcoming light of his bedroom, he climbed back into bed.

He sank back into the moth eaten pillows behind his head. Escaping into the next few chapters he satisfied his sick perversion before clicking off the light and blending into the safety of the musty darkness.

Hail Mary, full of grace . . .

Chapter 36

Sunday morning found Liam preparing a punchlist for his nearly completed house. Painters had finished their work and a final coat of polyurethane had been applied to the floors. Now it was just a matter of signing off on the final details before he would move into his dream house. He walked into the kitchen and found Finbar tweaking the trim work on the kitchen cabinets.

"Finbar! Looks like this job's about done."

"Just a few more adjustments with the doors and I'll be done with the cabinets."

"I'm going to bring one of my classes over here next week to look at the final project."

"Great idea, how's the new teaching job going?"

"It's going a lot better now that my students understand the basics."

Finbar continued, "As soon as I learned the difference between gouges and straight wood chisels, I was hooked. I couldn't wait to see the finished result and have someone appreciate my work. I learned from crafts-people working with their hands as well as using computer programs like CAD.

"Speaking of CAD, how long have you known Niamh?" Liam asked.

"Oh, I don't know, about six years."

"She and I are going to a gig in Spiddal tonight."

"You are? Great! She loves Irish music and plays a tin whistle. You'll have a good time. She's a lot of fun."

"Good. I understand she likes to hike and camp."

"Yeah, she'll walk your legs off and is really good with a fly rod, so if you guys hook up, she'll challenge you in lots of ways."

"That's just what I want, a good challenge."

"Well, I've got to get back to finishing this trim even if it is Sunday," said Finbar. "Have fun with Niamh this evening and tell her Hi from me."

"Thanks" said Liam. "I'll be here tomorrow to go over the punchlist and talk to Pat about a completion date. Don't work too late."

Liam found himself wondering what Niamh would think of his new house.

*   *   *

The alarm woke Conor at 7:30. Bounding out of bed, he showered, and quickly dressed. He laced up his boots, grabbed his backpack, and headed down to the car. It was a short drive to Anne's hotel and he waited in the parking lot. A few minutes later she appeared in her gear and climbed into the car.

"Morning!" said Conor leaning over to give her a kiss.

"Good morning to you. Did you sleep well?"

"Sound," said Conor, "The alarm woke me."

He pulled out a map of the National Park and they surveyed the area.

"Let's hike the long trail that goes up the mountain. We'll be able to see all of Connemara from there. It's a perfect day for that; the weather looks fair," said Conor.

"Good idea," said Anne as Conor started the car. "Let's go get breakfast."

They drove into the city. Nealon's was busy but they were able to get a table and began to look at the breakfast menu that they now knew almost by heart.

"I'm going to have the mushroom omelet with bacon," said Anne.

"Breakfast special, with rashers, sausage, black pudding and more brown bread," said Conor. "All that food should keep us going till dinner, don't you think?"

The food arrived and they made short work of it, finishing up with some special house ground coffee. They walked out the door and down the street to the car and drove off in the direction of Letterfrack to the park entrance.

"What a great day for a hike!" Anne remarked.

"I thought this would be a good idea, to get out and walk the mountain together," Conor added. "Have you ever been to this park before?"

"No, I haven't, but I've been to the park in Wicklow," she replied. "It was pretty spectacular and so close to Dublin."

"This is my first time also so we'll have this adventure together."

The drive through the heart of Connemara brought them speeding northwestward past ponds, lakes, and acres of blanket bogs with white sprigs of bog cotton blowing in the warm summer air. Ancient solitary trees stood with their backs to the stinging salt wind, their matted limbs giving shelter to the occasional crow or sparrow hawk looking for a meal on the barren ground below. Blue sky accented with grey clouds reflected images in the rippling lakes as the car sped on towards Letterfrack.

The travelers were quiet as they inhaled the stark beauty in the browns, greens and yellows of the scented gorse whirling by, punctuated by gaps in the lichen covered stone walls.

Soon they arrived in Letterfrack village, walked into the park. Their hiking boots gripping the stones as the trail led up the rising terrain.

"Conor, look at this!" Anne exclaimed. "There are the most amazing flowers here next to this turf cut."

"Yeah, they are totally different," Conor remarked. "This place sure has its own flora and fauna."

The trail continued up Diamond Hill and their pace slowed down a bit as it became harder to place their feet along the stony path.

"Glad the weather's good," said Conor. "This wouldn't be fun in the rain." Coming to a break in the wall he exclaimed, "What great view of the Twelve Bens! I've never seen them from this perspective before."

The hikers continued up the trail to the highest point and stopped for a drink. The view of the water spread out below as the mountain slid down to the ocean punctuated by small, rocky islands.

"Look at the color of the water!" said Anne. "I didn't realize we were up so high."

Sheep were everywhere chomping at tufts of grass, black heads and short horns topped by shaggy wool coats. Connemara ponies grazed close to the trail and were scattered below in the lower levels of the park.

"I'm glad we took all this stuff with us," said Anne as she fished some energy bars out of her backpack and handed one to Conor, his subtle cologne wafting in her direction.

"Thanks," he said looking into her eyes.

"This was a great idea, so far away from the daily grind of words and tight schedules," said Anne as they sat down on a flat rock.

"Just what we needed, some time together to unwind and get re-energized for the week ahead. This is so different from the situation I was in before," said Conor.

"What do you mean? Tell me about it," said Anne moving closer to Conor on the warm rock.

"I met this person through a friend of mine. She was in a sales position with a design company in Dublin and well connected. I was attracted to her and we began to see each other on a regular basis. She liked to be seen with all the right people at the races in Leopardstown, the hunt balls and fancy parties like the Trinity Ball.

"That doesn't sound too bad."

"It was OK until I realized that I was just her escort...an accessory. Someone she could brag about and present to her socialite friends as a different sort of person, a detective."

"How long did you go out with her?"

"About a year all together."

"What happened? And why did you stop seeing her?"

"One day we talked about going sailing and she seemed interested, so I set it up. She had never sailed before so I suggested dinghy sailing. She showed up in a fancy top, tight jeans and really high heels. I asked her, *"What are you doing?"*

She replied, *"Going sailing!"*

Then I said, *"Not dressed like that you're not."* She got pissed and I decided that this was the end of a relationship that was going nowhere."

"What did you do?"

"I drove her home and deposited her and her stuff on the front step."

"That was it?"

"Yep, that was the last straw. Brian and Evie didn't like her anyway, so that helped me make the decision to finish it."

"Sounds like you made the right choice."

"Looking back on it now, I know I did, but it hurt at the time."

Anne leaned over and wrapped her arms around him and said, "I'm glad."

He responded with a slow kiss on her soft lips. She moved her body into him, pushing her breasts into his muscular chest as she explored the warmth of his mouth with her tongue. She could feel his passion rising as he responded with a deeper kiss. Slowly they released and sat together relishing in the moment they had just created before beginning the descent down the circular trail. Hand in hand when the trail was wide enough, they descended through a line of stark trees and began to turn back towards the mouth of the park. The trail was rocky at this point so they stopped again and sat on a warm, moss covered rock to grab another drink out of the backpack.

"That was a pretty tough climb. I think there's an easier one through the blanket bog. We should do that next," Conor observed.

They finished their drinks and began to walk the other trail that led through wet blanket bog and dark pools. The footing was spongy and the going got tougher as the ground became softer.

"This is a little different," said Conor. "We went from stones and rocks to squishy and sometimes underwater. Look how the ground shakes when you walk on it!"

"This place has been here forever," said Anne. "It's amazing how old the turf cuts are and how deep they go into the ground."

They continued on through a wet spot and as the trail began to rise and become more solid and dry, it lead up to a field where the Connemara ponies stood at a gate which was held in place by lichen covered posts that had split many moons ago. Startled, the ponies cantered away down the hill. The hikers waited hanging over the gate but the ponies never came back.

"OK, let's head back," said Conor reaching for Anne's hand, we still have to drive back to Galway."

The return trek through the blanket bog was easier for them as they stepped carefully on the known trail. Arriving at the Visitor's Center, they cleaned their boots and got back into the car.

"That was spectacular!" said Anne looking at Conor. "What a beautiful day, I had no idea there was such variety on a bogland trail. It's nearly five o'clock, are you ready to head back to Galway? I'm not!"

"Let's go back through Clifden," said Conor, "I want to buy some flies for my fishing collection. There's a great tackle shop on the main street and they're open on Sunday catering to the tourists. The owner ties his own flies which work really well with the local trout."

"I'm up for it." said Anne.

Clifden was busy with lots of day trippers but Conor knew exactly where to go. They parked the car and he walked into the shop leaving Anne outside to peruse a craft store down the street.

The tackle shop was loaded with rods, landing nets, waders, bags and a whole counter of flies under glass. Conor asked the owner to show him some flies which were then ceremoniously spread out on the counter. The maestro explained the different fly tying techniques for the area and which flies to use when a hatch was occuring. After much discussion and haggling with the owner, Conor carefully stowed his selection in a plastic case and walked back outside.

Anne was sitting at a round table on the sidewalk with a group of people she had just met. "Conor," she exclaimed. "Come here and meet these guys! They're all in a band and will be playing later next door in the pub. Let's stay for the first part of it." Conor joined the group at the table.

"Hey Conor, I heard you were in the bogs today. I bet you're ready for a pint and some craic. This is Paul on the fiddle, Fiona on flute and Leo on the pipes and I'm Michael. I sing the vocals and play the bodhran. We'll be setting up in a few minutes, so come on in and I'll get you a good seat up front."

They moved inside and took a seat near the small stage. The place began to fill up as the players took their places, adjusted their instruments, and checked their mikes.

CLADDAGH POOL

Fiona began the session with a flute solo, joined by Leo on the pipes as Paul answered with his fiddle. Michael picked up the beat, using a well worn bodhran. The mixture was pure magic as Leo's chanter and register chords filled the entire room.

Anne listened enthralled feeling the ancient beat pulsing through her body. The number ended to thunderous applause.

They enjoyed the music and the company before heading back to Galway.

"There's a lot going on here," said Anne. "Clifden seems to be the place for action."

"Especially what we're into," Conor replied. "It's the music center of the West, I think."

As they got closer to Galway, Conor glanced over at Anne watching the world whizzing by outside, her blond hair tumbling over her face backlit by the evening light.

"Want to stay with me tonight?"

"I thought you'd never ask."

Conor grinned and added a little more pressure to the gas pedal.

Chapter 37

Arriving home after inspecting his house, Liam took a quick shower then left to pick up Niamh. He couldn't wait to hang out with her and listen to some great music. Before leaving his room, he slipped his harmonica into his pocket. *This could turn into a session and I might need it.*

The evening light cast shadows along the stone walls as he drove around the rocky coast. Niamh's house was where he thought it would be. He had driven by it numerous times and now knew who lived there. She was outside on her deck, reading the paper when he drove up.

"Catching up with the news," she said looking up as he walked up the pathway.

"Ready for the craic in Spiddal?"

"I'm ready, need one more thing and I'll be right out."

She disappeared inside grabbing her tin whistle off the shelf in the living room before locking the house and walking outside.

"It's a great evening to go to the Sunset Bar," she exclaimed getting into the car.

"Sure is and I'm sure the music and craic will be awesome."

"Who's this friend of yours?" Niamh asked as they got moving.

"Owen, I know him from school. He's a natural musician and plays keyboards and the uileann pipes."

"That's a lot of talent."

"Yeah, it's so cool to hear him play the pipes. He seems to have a personal contact with that instrument, like it was part of him," Liam replied.

"Can't wait!"

"So, I understand you play the whistle!" said Liam.

"Yeah, I do. I picked it up one day when I was a kid and have never put it down since."

*   *   *

Arriving at the pub, Liam parked the car across the road from the pub facing it towards the rocky coastline. Patrons had already gathered inside and were spilling outside the brightly painted establishment. The pub was painted blue with beige lettering "Bia, Ceol, Ol." *Food, Music, Drink.*

"Good timing", said Niamh."We'll have time to eat and get a couple of pints before the music starts."

"Hey Liam," someone shouted behind them.

Liam looked around and saw his buddy, Owen.

"Owen, this is my friend Niamh."

"Hi Owen, I understand you're part of the music action this evening," said Niamh shaking his hand.

"Yeah, I'll be doing a little work with the pipes and then we'll open it up to anyone who wants to join in."

"Good, I brought my tin whistle," Niamh replied with a little sparkle in her eye

"We'll have to have that for sure. I hope Liam brought his harmonica as well," said Owen.

"I did and can't wait to jam with you guys," Liam replied.

"Pressure's on! Now we really have to perform," Niamh answered as Owen laughed.

"What do you want to eat, Niamh?" Liam asked.

"I'll have fish'n chips and a pint of Swithwicks," said Niamh.

"Me too," said Liam.

"What a great night for a gig," Niamh remarked. "I can't wait to hear Owen on the pipes."

CLADDAGH POOL

They finished their food and brought their pints inside working their way next to the stage. Niamh watched Owen use the bellows to pump air into the pipes. Then it started, a low drone becoming steadier in demand, followed by the base chords created by the regulator. The magic notes on the chanter measured out by Owen in a musical blend of Celtic harmony. The mandolin joined in and the bodhran completed the sequence as the flute took the lead with the melody. The crowd was awestruck, listening to every beat and regulated chord, as Owen's fingers worked the pipes.

"Wow!" said Niamh. "I haven't heard a pipe player like that in years."

"That he is," said Liam.

The band played through the first session and then took a break.

"You're amazing on the pipes," said Niamh. "I've never heard such a variety of chords."

"Thanks, I really enjoy playing."

"I'd love to learn the uileann pipes. I know I could handle the chanter because I can play a whistle but the rest of the instrument requires so many skills," said Niamh.

"I'd be happy to teach you."

Turning to Liam she said, "Maybe if I got good enough Finbar could make me a set."

Owen interrupted, "Are you talking about Finbar Joyce? What a small world! These are his pipes," Owen excused himself to get ready for the second half.

227

While waiting for the band to continue Liam and Niamh went outside for some air. They discussed Finbar, wondering if he would ever be able to forget his past and decided to invite him to the next session with Owen's band.

"I think that's one of the ways we're going to help him, by bringing him back to music and the people that play it," said Niamh. "I think he plays fiddle as far as I can remember, so we could jam."

"Well, looks like the guys are getting ready to get back at it, so let's go back inside." said Liam.

Niamh sat on a stool next to Owen, putting the whistle to her lips.

"Any time you're ready!" said Owen.

After the first few bars of the song, the guitar picked up her rhythm, a fiddle added and then the bodhran. Owen picked up the melody and masterfully wrapped the entire piece with the drones, and chantered notes of the pipes. Liam pulled out his harmonica and added reeded accents when needed.

After a few more sessions the music ended. Liam and Niamh spent time with Owen and the band before driving back to Carraroe.

"What a great craic!," said Niamh. "That was some session!"

"We should start our own thing here in Carraroe," said Liam, "You never know, just put out the word in the right place and the players will come. Maybe we can ask Finbar and his fiddle to join us and be part of our group?"

"I think it would be a great idea to get him away from work and his hidden demons. I'm sure there's a huge amount of pain buried inside that lovable character. Finbar confided in me a few years ago that he had been abused by a priest and I promised to keep it to myself, but I trust you to help," said Niamh.

"I understand and will do all I can to hopefully get Finbar to open up. I'm sure that's his biggest trial every day even though I have worked with him over the past year. I read somewhere that an abused person has little or no confidence in other people especially when it comes to any form of relationship. I don't think he'll ever be able to have a normal relationship with a woman and that's so sad. It wasn't a woman who abused him and now his life is ruined," Liam replied.

"Yeah he's been self medicating with drugs and alcohol. I've seen him in bad shape at times, but I try and call him every few days and tell him he is loved. I think he has started to trust me. I just love the guy," said Niamh.

Moonlight illuminated the road back to Niamh's house as Liam turned into her driveway.

"I had a lot of fun tonight."

"Yeah it was a good craic. How about hiking the next time?" said Liam.

Chapter 38

Turning off the main road Conor drove south through Galway arriving at the hotel in Salthill. They grabbed their backpacks out of the trunk and made their way into the hotel lobby stepping into the elevator. Wordlessly they watched the blue numbers slide by as the elevator crawled its way higher into the maze of rooms. When they finally reached the third floor, tension mounting, they left the elevator and walked out and down the hallway. He slid the keycard into the lock and opened the door.

"I need a shower after all that hiking," said Anne walking toward the bathroom.

"Me too," Conor replied.

CLADDAGH POOL

She turned on the shower and waited until the room got warm and steamy. When the temperature was just right, she stepped out of her clothes now pooled around her ankles and walked into the shower where Conor joined her wrapping himself around her. The hot water permeated their two warming bodies and disappeared between their toes. Anne grabbed the soap and began to lather Conor's body, across his strong muscular chest, sliding her hand over his belly and around his fully erect penis. She cupped her hand around its head and squeezed softly, Conor moaned in response running his fingers into her crotch feeling her wet folds shudder with his touch.

They stayed in the warmth of the shower, clinging together until their desire for each other moved them into the bedroom where they sensually dried each other and climbed under the covers of the king sized bed.

Conor began to run his hands over her soft, velvet skin, his fingers finding all the curves and secret places of her body. His lips travelled around her neck and onto the special place next to her shoulder. She groaned and snuggled in closer to him as his fingers moved between her legs bringing her to building wetness. They kissed passionately, bodies entangling wanting the thrill of touch and stimulation to last forever. Conor would not give in, however as he continued the symphony of pleasure wanting to bring her to a crescendo higher than she had ever gone before. His lips were everywhere; her neck, her shoulders, her breasts, while his fingers continued with their magic.

She was ready and moaned loudly as he turned her over and entered her from behind, using slow, deep, silky strokes. They came together, losing all control. Afterwards they lay united and spent, whispering endearments until sleep overcame them.

*   *   *

Monday morning Conor rolled over and began to stroke Anne's neck. She responded by moving her hand down his belly and discovered that he was ready for her. He turned on his side and slid inside her as she came.

"Great way to wake me up," said Anne feeling Conor's strong body and smelling his morning scent.

"Better than a cup of coffee in bed?" asked Conor.

"Why can't we lay here like this, all day?" Anne replied.

"I wish we could, but I've got to get on the road to Dublin."

"I'm ready to take on the world," said Anne as she got out of bed and into the shower. Conor joined her for a few more minutes of wet entanglements. Later they got dressed and he drove her back to her hotel.

"See you when I get back," he said, kissing her longingly, and running his hands over her muscular posterior.

"Um .... You're such a good lover," said Anne, disconnecting herself from his body.

Chapter 39

T he route to Dublin was wide open. Conor had no delays other than the usual truck traffic around the outskirts of the city. He drove to Foxrock, a suburb on the south side of the city and continued on to Shanganagh cemetery, arriving about an hour before the burial.

The church next to the cemetery was packed for the funeral mass to be celebrated for Brendan Duffy. Conor walked through the carved stone doorway and stood in the rear vestibule. The priest had finished the service and was in the process of annointing the casket with thurible smoke and incense before it would be removed and placed in the hearse for the short trip to the burial site.

Reverently the pall bearers walked over to the casket in unison and began to carry the remains down the aisle and outside into the afternoon sun.

The family followed their loved one out the door and waited while the casket was placed in the hearse. Then they got into the lead car as all the mourners lined up to begin the procession to the final resting place.

Conor drove to the cemetery and waited for the entourage to arrive. Dark trees lined the walkways; gravel paths next to the ancient headstones lined up like soldiers about to make a charge into the next life.

The hearse drove up the driveway to the gravesite and the pall bearers took up their positions at the rear of the hearse waiting for the widow and her family to join them.

Betty Duffy stood motionless with her daughter and the rest of her family. She was a pretty woman with dark hair sculpted around her face and wore a well fitting, dark suit.

The priest recited the 23rd Psalm and completed the service by blessing the casket with holy water as it was lowered into the ground. Betty Duffy picked up a handful of dirt and tearfully scattered it on the casket. The loose dirt rattled on the wooden box as it disappeared into the ground. She stood back and said a short prayer before walking away and rejoining her family as Conor rounded the gravesite.

"Mrs. Duffy, I'm Conor Horgan. I was so sorry to have to call you on the phone about the death of your husband. I'm here today to offer my support and condolences to you and your family. We're doing our best to find his killers and prosecute them for this crime."

"Thank you, Detective. Can we meet tomorrow morning at my house? I'll call you this evening and set up a time."

Conor replied, "I'm always available to you. If you need anything else, please call me."

"I will, and thank you."

Conor walked away and noticed Declan Cronin standing by himself under an ancient yew.

"Hello again," he said shaking Conor's hand.

"Hi, Mr.Cronin, I'm glad to see you here."

"I needed to pay my respects to Brendan. He was a close friend of my brother," he replied.

"Do you have time to go over some of the the communications between your brother and Brendan?"

"I do," Declan replied. "Why don't you follow me to my house when the ceremony is over and I'll show you everything I have about Eamon."

"I'll meet you out at the front entrance of the cemetery and we'll go from there," Conor replied.

After the crowd dispersed, they convoyed to Dalkey via the Vico Road where Declan lived with his wife, Eileen in a Georgian style home. Conor followed Declan to the gated entrance and parked on the gravel driveway.

"What a great location!"

"It sure is," Declan replied. "We've lived here for fifteen years and love the view of the sea and the easy access to the city. I was able to buy it before the economy hit the skids and it is still maintaining its value because of the location."

Declan opened the door and Conor followed him through the spacious foyer into the living room. A tall picture window overlooked the sea with Dalkey Island in the foreground.

"I need a drink," said Declan pouring himself a stiff whiskey, "Join me?"

"Just water, thank you," Conor replied.

Declan returned with the two drinks and proceeded into his office which overlooked a flag stoned patio, framed by an ancient manicured fuchsia hedge trained to outline the blue sea in the background. The room was decorated with painted bookcases full of law books and novels that went all the way to the ceiling. They walked over to the desk and began the search process.

"Let me show you my email to Eamon before his death," Declan said opening up his laptop. "I'll be happy to give you copies of any of this information, so please let me know which information is of interest."

"Will do."

"I'm going to search for any communications between myself, my brother, Eamon and Brendan Duffy to see if there are any links to that person who may have contacted either one of them in Galway," he said scrolling through the history.

"Here's an email from Eamon indicating that Brendan Duffy would be going to Galway to meet him for dinner. It does mention another person who would be meeting them after the meal but no name was given." Declan continued to search.

"Do any of these emails have anything to do with the child abuse issue?"

"Let me search for that."

The hard drive whirred as the two interested parties waited for the results and watched the LED lights flash through the data hidden within.

"Here are two references to that issue; one is a question from Eamon concerning the ongoing government report on the abuse issue. Eamon asked if I thought he would have to testify. I replied that I didn't think he would because as far as I knew none of the cases that he was involved with were part of the investigation," Declan explained. "In the other reference, Eamon asked me if it was possible to gain access to records of the abused children because he wanted to check on a particular individual."

"Did he give you a name?"

"No."

"Those are all the email files that I have concerning my discussions with Eamon. I have an email from Brendan Duffy asking me to play golf but no other emails regarding Eamon and the Galway meeting. You may want to check with Betty Duffy to see if you can find anything in her husband's files," Declan suggested.

"I'm going to meet with her tomorrow," Conor replied. "She's gone through a lot and I didn't expect her to meet with me today."

"Good, I hope you'll be able to solve this as soon as possible so we can all get on with our lives. It's been a huge shock for all of us."

"Thanks for your help and for your hospitality," said Conor. "If you remember anything else, please give me a call."

"I will," Declan replied as they shook hands. Conor walked out the front door tasting the salty air off the Irish Sea. I need to get back out sailing again he thought as he got into his car and headed back to his condo at Longboat Quay in the Docklands of Dublin.

While driving he thought of his years at University College Dublin. Many things had changed since that time and now he was doing what he always wanted to do; solve crimes. The hardest part of the job had to be dealing with relatives of victims of crimes. A professor could not teach that in college.

He drove back into Dublin along the Bray Road to Rogerson's Quay beside the river Liffey and down the street to Grand Canal Basin where his condo overlooked the harbor in the Docklands area. As he turned into the parking garage his thoughts returned to Anne.

*   *   *

Brian left Carraroe for Derry early Monday morning. The road led him through Sligo, Bundoran, and across the open border into Northern Ireland where the highway passed close to the shores of Lough Foyle.

CLADDAGH POOL

The Foyle meandered northward out of the great northern mountains and flowed through the ancient city of Derry, a city mired in religious strife where freedom for the Catholics had been fought on the streets for seventy years and decades earlier a "No Surrender" battle ended victorious for the Protestants when the Jacobites tried unsuccessfully to take control.

Derry had recently emerged from the bombing and bloodshed on both sides of the conflict. Its history encompassed political and religious factions within its walls but since 1998 promised peace and political expression for the next generation. It lay like a sleeping dragon with its cratered battlements encircling the great historical city.

Brian continued the drive to the university built on the banks of the river. He had an appointment with Dr. Somers and the research team at UMR in order to finalize their joint research on the cod fishery. The project had been in the works for the past three years, but was now nearing approval. It had been rife with EU intrigue politics which had at times slowed progress to a crawl.

Entering the building he stopped at a security desk where he was searched and given a visitor pass into the lab. He continued down the corridor and walked into Dr. Somers office.

"Hi Susan," he said walking towards her desk.

"Brian, good to see you," she replied shaking his hand. "Glad you're here. It's a long drive from Galway."

"It is, but a beautiful day to make the trip."

"I got your samples and have included them as part of the research. They helped us speed up the process. We're now able to state to both governments that there is an abundant supply of marine organisms in the area, enough to begin a breeding program for the fishery."

"Brilliant! How's the hatchery program coming along?"

"Oh, they're ready to provide the first batch of adults as soon as the final agreement is signed."

"I understand the Taoseach is about to meet with all the parties as soon as we provide the scientific results of our research," said Brian.

"It's true. That's supposed to take place at the end of September."

"On another matter," Brian went on, "the missing Saxitoxin! Was the material really missing or simply mislaid? I remember we talked about it a few days ago when I was in Galway."

"Oh, it's missing all right. We don't know where it went. One of our staff is being questioned by the police as we speak. Apparently she has a friend in Galway or Dublin who may have been involved. I'm expecting to get an answer from the security branch at any time," Dr. Somers continued. "I've been in touch with Detective Horgan about it."

"How about some lunch?" she asked, changing the subject to a more pleasant one. "I know it's late but I'm starving, and I'm sure you must be also."

"I'm past ready."

"Good, let's get out of here. There's a deli down the street where we can eat and spend some time catching up."

They checked out of the building and drove about a mile to a small shopping area. Located on the first floor of an old mill was a deli overlooking the river Foyle. Architects had used an existing water wheel to create power for the building and designed the deli around the shaft which ran through the center of the restaurant.

"They have an interesting menu here."

"What an inovative use for an old mill," said Brian, watching the shaft rotating in the floor.

"Now here's an example of the EU actually working. The owner got a grant to turn this historical place into an eco-friendly business," said Susan.

Brian ordered soup and a sandwich and found a table where Susan joined him.

"What's the latest news about the bishop?"

"Evie and I had some friends over last Saturday night and Conor Horgan was there. He said there was no new news about suspects so the search goes on."

"Thanks for taking the time to drive up here by the way. Your help in developing the samples for the food-supply research has been critical to the establishment of the fishery project. Now all we need is for the politicians to do their job. It will create a lot of jobs and great opportunities for the fishing industry on both sides of the border."

They finished lunch and returned to the lab to discuss their report that would be presented to the politicians, making sure that the entire process was succinct and could be easily understood by political rather than scientific brains.

Chapter 40

Monday morning Anne got ready for the trip to the radio station at Cashla where she would present her show. She arrived shortly before noon and walked into the control room to meet Ronan, her producer.

"Ronan, the show's ready for air."

"Great! Let's listen to it in the edit suite. Want some coffee?"

"I'd love some."

They walked into the suite armed with her Mac and two coffees. Ronan booted up the system; plugged in her Mac and adjusted the volume with one of the slider controls on the audio board. Anne slid on a headset and listened intently. The show ended and Ronan removed his earpiece.

"That's one of the best productions I've heard in years. It really captures the story and tone of a place; and the best part of it, is that it's all produced in Irish. Nice work, Anne!"

"Would you change anything?"

"Not a thing," Ronan replied. "I'm ready to get it a spot on the station rundown for next month. I'll call operations as soon as we get finished here and make it happen. As soon as I get an airdate, I'll let you know. In the meantime I'll work on a promo for the story."

"Thanks for the opportunity to air it. I'll produce a print promo piece for it as well and add the airdate as soon as I get it from you." Anne stood up, shook Ronan's hand, and walked confidently out the door into the warm afternoon air. After a quick lunch she called Conor.

"How did it go?" he asked.

"It's going to air!" Anne replied, her voice going up an octave.

"Congratulations, we'll celebrate when I get back," Conor replied.

"Dinner, on me?" said Anne.

"Well that's an interesting visual! Is that a promise?" Conor exclaimed.

"Maybe dessert! That's a date."

"What are you going to do now?" he asked.

Anne replied, "I'm going to see if I can set up an interview with Finbar and get his back story. I want to see if he knows anymore about the bishop and Duffy."

"Hope it works out. I spoke to Finbar as well and plan to meet with him when I come back on Wednesday," said Conor. "Maybe between the two of us, we can break something loose."

"How was the funeral in Dublin?"

"Sad, but it's over. I met Declan Cronin and looked at his computer records, nothing new on that front, and I'll meet with Betty Duffy tomorrow and hope to get better results from her. It's hard not to get emotionally involved with this case, but I need to stay focused and find the killers. I'm driving back to the condo now and plan to stay the night here in Dublin."

"I'm going to call Finbar now. I got his number from Liam," Anne said. "Maybe he'll have time to meet me after work."

"Good luck. I heard he was a tough person to get inside. I know you can make it happen if anybody can. Call me if you make any progress on that front."

"We'll talk later, bye." Anne hung up and dialed Finbar.

"Finbar! This is Anne O'Gorman. I'm a reporter for the Irish Times and a friend of Liam Duggan and Brian Connelly."

"What do you want?"

"I'd like to meet you this evening and talk about the bishop. I'm writing a background story about his life and I know you worked for him in Galway. Maybe you can help me flesh out my story for the paper."

"Because you're a friend of Liam's, I'll meet you this evening, but I really don't know anything."

"Great, I'd really appreciate it, Finbar. Let's meet in Moran's at 6:30."

"OK, how will I know you?"

"I'm tall and have blond hair. I'll be wearing jeans and a black jacket."

"That'll make it easy I'm sure! See you then."

Anne continued her drive from Cashla to Clifden via Maam Cross. She turned left at Maam Cross and drove west passing Lake Shindilla where she stopped to take some pictures. She also recorded some audio of lapping water for her sound files.

The afternoon light softened the scene with warm tones and reflected the beginnings of a sunset in the rippling water. A large Scotch pine stood, sentry-like at one end of the lake, painting its scaly bark across the waves, its reflection broken by two rounded boulders that lay like ancient beasts submerged in the water.

Anne got back in her car and checked the drive on her camera. The pictures were all there and her digital recorder had stored the audio. She relaxed for a few minutes and then putting her car in gear continued on towards Clifden and into the setting sun. She wished she could be with Conor in Dublin but they would be together again soon.

* * *

The sun was disappearing when she arrived in Clifden and drove down the main street to Moran's. There was quite a crowd at the restaurant, but she found a parking spot and walked inside. It was 6:25. She took a seat at the window and gazed outside in deep thought. The waiter came over to her table and handed her a menu asking if she would like a drink.

She told him she was waiting for another person and would order when he arrived. She picked up the menu and began to read the entrees. Suddenly, she sensed the presence of someone standing near her. Looking up she said, "You must be Finbar."

"Yes," he replied, shaking her hand.

"Thanks for meeting me on such short notice."

"Yeah, it worked out," Finbar answered. "Liam's told me about you and about the party. Sounds like everyone had a good time."

"We had a blast, lots of talk, great food and good wine."

The waiter returned and they ordered drinks; Anne, a glass of wine, and Finbar, a Jameson on the rocks.

"Liam says you're doing a great job on his house."

"Yeah, I've had a lot of fun working on it. It's always a challenge to work on new construction and make the cabinets look like they've always been part of the house."

"Where did you get your love of woodworking?"

"From my Da, he was always working with wood; he used only hand tools to build his furniture."

"Did you learn shop in school?" Anne asked trying to direct the conversation to Finbar's earlier life.

"We had a small shop class at the Christian Brothers' School in Salthill, and that's where my interest in woodworking got started."

"What was it like going to a Christian Brothers' school? I've heard some pretty bad things about that place."

"What do you mean?"

"I read the recent Ryan Report about child abuse and that school in Salthill was named as one of the locations where abuse was rampant. Did you hear of any abuse there while you were a student?"

"Why do you need to know about that? I thought we were here to talk about the bishop?" Finbar asked a little concerned.

"You're right," she responded, realizing that Finbar didn't want to talk about it. I'm writing the story about the bishop's life and death and because of your connection with him, I need your help. The police seem to believe there may be a connection between his death and child abuse in the parish. You went to a school where abuse had been documented and may have seen instances of it."

Their drinks arrived and the conversation continued.

Anne tried another direction with Finbar, "I understand you did some work for the bishop in Galway at his house."

"I did, he had a huge amount of books and needed some custom bookcases, also a built-in desk area in the library."

"How well did you get to know him while you were working in the house?"

"He was a good customer and told me what he wanted, that was it."

"Did you know of any students at the school who were abused?" Anne asked redirecting the conversation back to the school.

"Yes, and I'm still in touch with them."

"Did you or your fellow students report the abuse?" she asked, zeroing in.

"No, we couldn't, nobody would listen anyway."

"By the way, Finbar, your name will never be mentioned in my story. I just need some background for it and will only use the general facts, not your individual story," Anne explained. "Your identity will never be known."

"Good," Finbar replied. "This is the first time I've ever spoken to anybody about that time in my life. It feels scary but liberating at the same time. I really don't want to get into a lot of details about that period. I've tried to forget it, but it's not possible until justice has been meted out. That's all I want to say about it."

Anne watched Finbar's expression change from calm to deadly serious.

"Very well, I won't ask you anymore questions. Thanks for being so helpful. I know it's hard to talk about this so let's eat."

"OK," Finbar replied, relieved that the interview was over.

They spent the rest of the time enjoying the food and talking about Anne's upcoming show about Peig, the seanachie.

"I remember Peig when I was growing up on Inishmore," said Finbar. "I always knew she was a seanachie and could shapeshift."

"You mean she had the gift?" Anne asked.

"Yeah, sometimes in your life you hear about those people, but I believe Peig has always had it and could move about as another being."

"I remember hearing something about Peig when I was a kid. One day I was coming home from school and walked past a small field of oats. I saw something really strange going on in the field. A murder of crows had gathered in a circle in the beaten down oats and were making a huge racket. Two big grey crows were standing in the middle of the circle, screaming and pecking at each other while the other crows outside the circle continued to crow loudly. Then they'd stop for a few seconds before starting up again. I didn't know what was going on so I went home. Later in the day I brought some brown bread over to Peig and told her about the circle of crows. She laughed and said, "Finbar, you just saw a crow court. *Cuirt na Preachain*,"

"She told me that crows kept order in their ranks by holding court and applying punishment to any crow that had broken their code, sometimes killing the offender.

That's when she told me that she had the gift, discovered it when she was a little girl and was able to change into a bird. I remember listening intently to her story looking into her blue eyes and asking her to fly.

"Can't do it just like that." I remember her saying."

"Then I went home and told this story to my mother and she said, "Finbar, that's not a story it's true. Peig also has a pet crow that lives outside her back door."

"During the school holidays I went back to Peig's house to ask her about an Irish composition that I was writing. As I walked up the pathway around her house, I saw two grey crows sitting on a perch. I walked to the door, but the crows didn't budge. One of them bounced over to me and sat on the half door. Then I saw it had blue eyes. I knocked on the door but Peig never came out. I looked at the crow and asked, "Peig, is that you?"

"Wow, I knew she was different, but really didn't believe it," said Anne.

"Well, now you know," said Finbar.

When they were finished, Anne thanked Finbar for his time and courage for reliving a dark time in his life. She left Clifden in darkness, but realized that she had shed a little more light on Finbar's life. She now had feedback from an abuse survivor, if there was such a person. *I got a lot closer to him than I thought I would.*

She left the restaurant and drove back to Galway. Thinking back, she realized Finbar was totally alone in his world as an abused soul.

CLADDAGH POOL

I have to talk to him again and maybe I'll be lucky enough to get some more out of him. Seems to me it's better to let that out than keep it bottled up inside, she thought watching her headlights dance along the stone walls as she drove back to the City of the Tribes.

Chapter 41

Fr. Michael Godfree turned off the lights, closed the sacristy door then walked up the stone pathway to the house. There was a light on in the hallway. *I don't remember leaving a light on.*

He walked cautiously now down the path, stopping at the door to get a key out of his pocket. As he slipped the key into the lock and turned it, he noticed that the door was already unlocked. He went on inside locking the door behind him. The light in the kitchen was also on, yet he distinctly remembered turning all the lights off before he'd left that morning. Fear immobilized him.

Has someone been here, again? I need to look around the house.

The bedroom door was open. He turned on the light and looked around. Nothing seemed out of order although the room was such a mess with piles of dirty clothes and magazines scattered beside the bed, it would be hard to tell.

He continued into the bathroom and reached for the light switch but his hand never made it to the lever. Someone roughly grabbed his arm and twisted it painfully around behind his back. He tried to elbow his attacker with the other arm but that arm had also been immobilized. He kicked and arched his back to throw off his assailant but it didn't do any good. A gloved hand was clasped over his mouth and he was wrestled onto the bathroom chair and strapped to it with duct tape.

"Good evening, Father," said a malevolent voice behind him. "We meet again. We're here to represent the innocent young boys you have defiled. You're scum! You prey on the young and innocent. Your church has allowed these crimes to go unpunished and has offered secrecy and silence as its only solution. So it's left up to us to rid the world of the likes of you."

The paltry light over the vanity mirror clicked on and Michael Godfree saw two imposing men standing in front of him. One was dressed in a black military sweater and black pants with side pockets. His head was shaved and his left ear pierced by a gold earring. The priest recognized the earring and had seen him once in his church but remembered him having hair on his head.

The other man also dressed in black was armed with a pistol. He was larger than the bald man and very muscular with a thin mustache. He also had a gold earring in his left ear. His weapon was aimed at the priest's head. Both men wore black gloves.

"You'll be quiet, now Father. If you scream, I'll tape your mouth shut," said the man holding the pistol.

The bald man spoke, "Did you think you had gotten away with your sick past time of abusing young boys?" he asked menacingly.

The priest began to tremble. A cold dribble of sweat ran down his back under his belt. He wondered how long it was going to take before they killed him. There was no escape, no way out. His life had caught up with him.

"Bishop Cronin gave you a free ride and a new life here in Bridgeville in order to continue with your perversions, pretending you were a pious priest. Now we'll have justice for them and retribution for you and the hierarchy which allowed these scurrilous crimes to take place."

The gloved hand was removed from the priest's mouth.

"How many altar boys did you rape, asshole?" asked the bald man.

"I...uh...uh...don't remember," stammered the priest.

"Oh you don't remember!! We found a list of names in this book beside your bed, you sick fuck! Does that jog your memory?" asked the bald man, his head now gleaming with sweat.

He handed the priest a dirty piece of paper with a list of names written on it, "Does this look familiar, asshole?"

"I kept this list so I could pray for them," whined the priest.

"Bullshit, you kept this list like a trophy, you bastard."

"I swear, I pray for them every day at mass."

"You better start praying for your own sick soul," said the bald man.

"I've something here that you need to read so you can prepare for your departure into hell; since you believe in such a place and believe me we'll help you get there. You've created a hell here on earth for the boys you have defiled."

The bald man handed the priest a sheet of paper.

"Read this," he said. "I'm sure you've used it before as a priest."

He held the paper in front of the shaking priest.

"I can't see it!"

"I'll get some candles," said the other man in black. The terrified priest could hear him rattling through the mess of things in the kitchen. Soon he returned with two candles.

A light flashed as a match exploded in the gloom. Its sulfurous flame lit the candles and the man held one of them in front of the priest. He gave the other candle to the bald man with the pistol, so the priest would have plenty of light to read what was written on the paper.

"Start reading, asshole," he ordered. The terrified priest began to read, his voice trembling with every word. He looked at the first stanza of the ancient verse and recognized it as *Dies Irae*.

The day of wrath, that day
will dissolve the world in ashes
as foretold by David and the sibyl!
How much tremor there will be,
when the judge will come,
investigating everything strictly!
Death and nature will marvel,
when the creature arises,
to respond to the Judge.

The priest's mouth began to dry up, "I can't do this anymore. Just get it over with!"

"Keep reading you sick bastard, like you ever had any mercy for them."

The sobbing priest continued to read,

The written book will be brought forth, in which all is contained, from which the world shall be judged.

"Stop! Stop! Please! I need something to drink!"

"No rest for the wicked, right Father? How 'bout some vinegar on a sponge!" said the man holding the candle. "Did you give the boys a drink when you abused them? If you did, I'm sure it was alcohol!"

The terrified priest continued to read the blurry lines realizing that he had lost control and could feel warm urine running down his leg. The liquid traced its way down the back of his right leg as it filled up his shoe and overflowed onto the floor. He continued to read.

I sigh, like the guilty one:
my face reddens in guilt:
Spare the supplicating one, God.
My prayers are not worthy:
however, thou, Good Lord, do good,
lest I am burned up by eternal fire

He fainted. They roused him with the butt of a gun to the side of his head.

"Keep reading, asshole!"

The priest, now reconciled, transcending the temporal, with blood running down his face and into his eyes, continued prayer-like, peering through the red mist.

Call thou me with the blessed.
I meekly and humbly pray,
my heart is as crushed as the ashes: perform the
healing of mine end.

Tearful will be that day,
on which from the ashes arises
the guilty man who is to be judged. Spare him
therefore, God.

"Shit! He actually thinks he's been martyred. Let's finish this!"

The terrified priest ended the reading as the flickering candles illuminated the three figures gathered together in the center of the room; their shapes waving up and down the walls like black shadows hovering over a funeral pyre.

"You'll be judged by a higher power when you leave this place," said the bald man. "The words that you just read will prepare you for your resting place in hell."

The candles were carefully placed on the window sill next to the bathtub as the next part of the ritual was about to begin with preparations for the execution and cleansing baptism by water.

The man with the pistol slapped a piece of duct tape over the priest's mouth, as the bald man in black began to fill the bathtub. The water crept upwards, past the first brown scumline then higher, covering the rusted metal where the enamel had fallen off on the inside the tub.

The priest uttered a muffled scream. The acrid smell of urine was now apparent and had begun to pool under the interrogation chair and reflect the flickering flame of the candle. He saw the bald man open a small wooden box, pull out a syringe and a small glass phial. The man stuck a needle through the rubber seal in the phial and slowly drew down the illuminated liquid into the syringe.

When it was finished loading, he walked behind the priest and waited. The tormented man tried to scream from under the duct tape.

"Go raibh a anamh ar an diabhal, Michael Godfree, may you burn in your hell!" said the bald man, as he jabbed the needle into the right side of the priest's neck pushing down the plunger until all the liquid had disappeared.

CLADDAGH POOL

The priest's body shook for a few minutes as the massive dose of Saxitoxin did its work, coursing into the carotoid artery and flooding the brain with heart stopping speed. His body shuddered and then went limp in the chair. The ordained one had met his fate.

The executioners watched as the water in the bathtub continued to fill past the higher scumlines of many weekly ablutions by the dead priest.

"That's enough. Let's finish it with the cleansing water. It's over," said the bald man.

They untaped the priest from the chair and carried his limp body across the room to the waiting font, where he was unceremoniously dumped into the sacrifical tub and slowly sank, disappearing into the murky water. They watched until the water covered his head. He lay there submerged; his eyes still open watching them as he sank lower into the font. The whiteness of his priestly collar glowed in the brownish liquid like a disappearing headlight on a rainy night.

The executioners left the candles burning, not caring that the hot wax dribbled onto the weathered windowsill.

As the men in black walked out of the room, they switched off the light and closed the door behind them. The bald man carefully put the syringe back into the box, taking it with him.

They walked down the driveway, got into a black car and drove away. The glowing green light of the digital clock on the dashboard read 12:15. Nobody was on the road as they sped away into the night. Their poisonous baptism completed.

Chapter 42

Tuesday morning Conor awoke to a bright sunny morning and looked around the room. It was true; he was home in Dublin. He got up and walked to the window overlooking the Grand Canal Harbor, its water glistened as a squall blew across the surface. Seagulls sat about on the lock gates and cried incessantly for food or attention from other gulls. Walking into the kitchen, he made coffee and foraged in the pantry, where he found an unopened box of cereal. He pulled it out, taking down a bowl, glad he had thought to pick up a small carton of milk the previous evening.

Today was his interview with Betty Duffy. Conor always hated interviewing survivors after a crime, and hoped she would be up to it. While sipping on his coffee he checked the email on his Mac. There were two messages, one from Anne and the second from Tomas.

He called Betty Duffy to confirm the appointment at 10:30, then took a shower and got dressed putting on a fresh jacket and khakis. Grabbing his notes, he opened the door deciding to walk down the stairs for some early morning exercise on his way to the car.

The drive to Betty Duffy's house took a little over thirty minutes. It was situated on a quiet street, surrounded by a loosely built stone wall along the front of the lot. It reminded him of the stone walls in Connemara and the other part of his life back in Galway. He drove into the driveway and parked on the raked gravel. A flagstone walkway led to the front door. He pushed the bell button and Betty opened it.

"Good morning, Detective Horgan. Please come in."

"Morning, Ms. Duffy, thanks for seeing me today. I hope you're holding up."

"Would you like some coffee?"

"No thanks, I just finished breakfast."

They walked into an office that had an antique desk on one end and a fireplace at the other. A drawing table was set up next to the desk with a half drawn plan taped to its surface.

She walked over to the desk sat down and tapped the mouse to wake up the computer. Conor watched her closely as she waited for the page to come up. He had not realized how pretty she was. Her sad eyes were set darkly now, in her unlined face. The page appeared.

"Here are the last emails that Brendan had with Bishop Cronin. Feel free to explore," she said pushing back her chair.

Conor moved closer to the screen. Scrolling down the list, he could see details of the proposed meeting with the bishop. One email indicated that an additional meeting had been set up with another person after dinner. This was apparently the person who had called Brendan with information concerning the safety of the bishop judging from the email.

"Do you know who this might have been?" Conor asked pointing at the screen.

"I've no idea and Brendan never mentioned that he and Eamon were meeting anyone else,"

Conor looked at the email string. There was a confirmation of the dinner date and an approximate time of Brendan's arrival in Galway. He thought for a minute and then hit the email search bar and typed "Finbar." Since Finbar had a business relationship with Duffy, Conor wondered if this unknown person could have been Finbar and there might have been a record of that communication.

A series of emails popped up. Conor scanned through them but they all seemed to relate to Finbar's new house. These emails were about a year old. There was nothing new between them. *If it was Finbar, he didn't discuss it by email.*

Conor sat back in his chair and stretched, "Thanks for letting me see these emails. I don't see anything here that identifies the person who called Brendan, but it was worth a try," he continued. "Do you know if he got any letters from the bishop?"

"If he did, I didn't know anything about them."

Conor stood up, "Thank you, Ms Duffy, I wish you all the best and am so sorry for your loss."

"Thank you, Detective Horgan. If I come across anything else I'll call you. I hope you find those bastards."

"I'll find them, believe me! I'll find them!'" said Conor confidently.

Betty walked him to the door and shook his hand.

"Bye for now," said Conor crunching across the gravel driveway to his car.

*　　*　　*

May Doyle, Father Godfree's housekeeper arrived in the late morning to clean the house. She had her own key and let herself in through the back door. When she entered the house she called for the priest to see if he was home as she had noticed on her drive up that his car was still parked outside. He was usually out of the house when she was there. She walked through the kitchen, down the hallway and looked in the living room, then walked into the bathroom where she found the priest submerged in the bathtub.

"Jesus, Mary and Joseph!" she wailed crossing herself, "What happened here?"

She went into the living room and called the police. Ten minutes later, two police cars arrived. Four policemen entered the house, went into the bathroom, and saw the ghastly scene before them. Two of the policemen went back outside to cordon off the house and the church next to it. They ordered everybody to leave the area and go home. The sergeant in charge called the NBCI notifing them that a priest's body had been found and that the area had been secured. He then called the coroner and went back into the house to wait for the detective branch to arrive.

"Don't touch anything. Don't move anything!" said the sergeant. One of the police officers sat with his arm around May Doyle in the living room, taking her statement.

"It's going to take some time for the Bureau to get here and go over the crime scene. Until then we are unable to do anything. Let's wait for the detectives and the Technical Bureau to arrive.

May sat motionless in the chair, her face frozen in shock.

Roger Bennett, one of the policemen began to type a report on his laptop. He started a case file and began to fill in the details.

*   *   *

Conor had just left Betty Duffy's home and was on his way back to the condo in Dublin when his phone rang. NBCI lit up the screen.

He answered, "Conor Horgan!"

"Detective Horgan, this is Lieutenant Davis in Dublin. There's been another death. A priest has been found drowned in a bathtub in the rectory in Bridgeville outside New Ross. We believe it's connected to your case. Where are you right now?"

"I'm in Dublin."

"Here's the address for Bridgeville Parish Church. It's located about eight miles outside New Ross on route N25, about an hour or so from where you are. I've notified the Technical Bureau and they're on the way."

Conor responded, "I'm on my way, Lieutenant. Have they locked down the scene?"

"Taken care of, thanks Conor, call me when you get there."

Conor hung up and called Tomas.

"Tomas, we have another body and I believe it may be Michael Godfree. I'm on my way to the location in Bridgeville in County Wexford and will update you as soon as possible."

Then Conor called Anne in Galway.

"Hi there, how did it go?"

"I'll tell you later. Listen, a priest has been found, drowned in a bathtub in County Wexford. I'm guessing it's Godfree. I'm on my way now and should be there in less than two hours. Get moving if you want the scoop. I'll text you the details as soon as I hang up."

"No shit! Another murder!" Anne interjected. "I'm leaving right now and will be in touch on the road. Thanks for the heads up. I think it's about a three hour drive from here."

"See you then and be careful!" Conor hung up.

He continued the drive back to the condo, collected some clothes and retrieved the current data on the case. Ten minutes later he was back on the road heading south towards New Ross and the murder scene. He called the Technical Bureau to find out their status and location, and discovered they were also an hour away from the scene.

He spoke to the team leader Detective Jane Doherty, "Jane, Take precautions at the scene," Conor emphasized, "There may be poison involved so HazMat suits should be worn."

"Understood, thanks for the warning, Conor. We have the equipment with us. I'll make sure everybody understands the situation."

Conor continued the drive and began to put the pieces together in his head.

If this is the priest who was transferred to County Wexford by Bishop Cronin, he has to be linked to the other murders. If the modus operandi is the same, then all three victims were killed by the same people. There's a common connection.

His journey continued southwards, paralleling the River Barrow as he approached New Ross, then turned east to Bridgeville and on to the church site.

New Ross, another ancient town with a history of Anglo-Irish conflict especially in the Rebellion in 1798 when a large number of the inhabitants were massacred by English forces. It was a major inland port on the river Barrow and had seen thousands of its people emmigrate to America over the centuries.

Before Conor reached the site, he noticed a number of cars and other vehicles including the press, parked outside the village. Driving up to the church he parked near the priest's house and flashing his ID, he stooped under the yellow cordon tape. He called the lieutenant in Dublin to let him know that he was on scene.

A tall woman dressed in a HazMat suit walked out the back door and saw Conor approaching, "Hi Conor, glad you're here. We got here about thirty minutes ago and are just about to begin the investigation. Here's a suit for you."

"Thanks Jane, I'll be there in a minute."

Conor donned the suit, gloves and booties before walking into the house and down the hallway into the bathroom. He stepped over to the bathtub and saw the partially clothed priest's body, still submerged in the water. The body looked bizarre with the contorted limbs gathered around the torso. The skin was shriveled and all the color had receeded from its texture. The coroner stood on one side of the tub as the Technical Bureau continued to look for evidence.

Conor began to absorb the scene before him. A chair sat in the middle of the floor with a piece of duct tape still stuck to it. A series of water drops and a pool of liquid dampened the floor around the chair; maybe water or possibly sweat. He had the team take swabs for the evidence book. The remains of burned candles were puddled on the window sill. There was no visible blood anywhere that he could see.

A piece of paper lay on the floor beside the chair and a book lay on a wooden cabinet next to the sink. Conor looked at the book covered in dirty brown paper. As he opened it, a small piece of paper fell out. He picked it up and noticed it had a list of names written on it. He had it photographed and secured as evidence.

The crime photographer took a complete panorama of the scene, creating a digital record of the area. Conor directed her to specific items for evidence as he identified them. He marked the location of another piece of paper on the floor by the chair. He picked it up and saw written on it some kind of verse. The first line of the verse read *The Day of Wrath*. He placed it in a plastic bag writing a description on the bar coded label before giving it to a technician. *My God! Dies Irae is not just a website anymore!*

The team checked the chair and tape for prints. He checked all the items at the sink, noting a glass which was processed for prints. The contents of a trash can, located next to the sink were catalogued. A piece of gum lay on top of a pile of tissues in the can. *Ah! There it is! Let's hope they're that stupid.* The contents were removed and tagged.

Then walking over to the bathtub, Conor had the photographer make a complete set of views of the body. He took samples of the water and gave the priest's body a close inspection. The left side of the face had some bruising, indicating he may have been tortured. Conor looked for the signature puncture wound on the neck and found it, located on the right side of the priest's neck. *Here we go again.*

He told the team that now there was the real possibility of a hazardous material being involved. Looking at the priest's hands, he noticed some bruising on the wrists.

A gurney containing an unzipped body bag was wheeled next to the tub. Conor instructed the team to lift the priest out of the tub and onto the gurney, recording the event with video.

The body was sealed in a bag and rolled out to the coroner's vehicle which would remove it to New Ross for the autopsy. After tagging the body, the coroner sealed the bag with official tape and the vehicle departed. The forensics team continued to check for fingerprints on the sink, the bathtub, the window sill and the door.

Conor went back to the priest's bedroom. The room was an unholy mess with clothes everywhere. It smelled of dirty linen. The bed was unmade and a stack of magazines were piled on a table near the window with other magazines scattered on the floor next to the bed. Conor examined the magazines and discovered that most of them were child porn. *This man was a sick fuck!* The photographer recorded the evidence as Conor identified it and forensics checked for prints and DNA.

Looking around the room again to get an idea of what was going on, Conor knew without a doubt that he was in the home of a pervert. The dichotomy between a priestly life of service to a parish and history of pedophilia was symbolized by the broken effigy of Christ falling off a dust covered crucifix. That said it all to Conor as he walked back into the bathroom.

Jane Doherty was finishing up her evidence collection when Conor entered the room.

"We're taking all of this evidence to the crime lab in New Ross. The coroner scheduled the autopsy for 9:00 AM. I'll be there for that as well. Looks like this guy got what he deserved!" said Jane.

Conor replied, "There's a definite connection to the other murders based on what I've seen here in the house. A poisoning and a body once again immersed in water?" he observed. "I'll see you, Jane, at the lab tomorrow, bright and early. This is getting exciting."

Conor exited the house just as Anne was walking up the driveway.

"You made it!" said Conor.

"It took longer than I thought, there was a wreck outside New Ross and I had to wait. What have you found?"

"A dead priest, Michael Godfree; looks like he was poisoned too and then dumped in the bathtub."

"More poison and water?" said Anne.

"Looks that way, another ritualistic murder? Now we have to put it all together. There are too many similarities for there not to be a connection," Conor said confidently.

"When is your press conference?" Anne inquired.

"Tomorrow evening," said Conor, "or as soon as we get the results from the autopsy, sometime tomorrow. I'm going back inside now to go over the entire house again and try to reconstruct the crime. I can't let anyone into the house at this point but you're welcome to take pictures outside."

"Right," said Anne walking back to her car. She began to type her notes to piece together the bones of a story.

Conor returned to the scene. The front door, showed no evidence of forced entry. The windows on the ground floor looked like they hadn't been opened in a long time. The back door was also intact.

"Jane, has anyone been in or out of the back door since you arrived?"

"No," she yelled from the bathroom.

Conor continued to put the pieces together.

The door must have been open or the murderers had a key. He reviewed the complete set of pictures taken by the Technical Unit and before anything else was removed, studied the scene one last time in order to fix in his head the final moments of this latest victim.

The priest seemed to have been alone in the house when he was attacked in the bathroom. It would have taken more than one person to subdue the priest judging by the size of him. He was duct taped to the chair, tortured and interrogated; very similar M.O. to the Galway murders in the warehouse. Looks like they gave him something to read, or read something to him, poisoned him, and dumped his body in the bathtub. There's a common ritual attached to these murders.

He continued to look around the house for other obvious clues or evidence. Besides the autopsy, he would have to wait for the forensic guys from the Bureau to provide blood, fingerprint and body fluid evidence. As far as he could determine, the bad guys left no physical evidence of their presence inside the house. *Except for maybe the gum.*

Checking the photographs again he noticed a partial footprint that had been found near the back door. It looked to him like the mark of a hiking boot. He asked one of the technicians to make a cast and searched the house for similar boots but found none. The picture indicated the sole part of the footprint impressed in the dirt next to the stone pathway but the heel was not visible. *Might be connected.*

Outside, Anne illustrated her story by taking pictures of the house and the church. She typed the story into her Mac and prepared to format the pictures into the text while googling a history of the church and parish to use in the introduction.

Conor finished his observations in the house and walked outside ducking under the crime tape and into the glare of lights from a TV crew that had taken up position outside the cordon. A reporter called over to him, "How did the priest die? Was he murdered?"

"Hope to have an answer at tomorrow's press conference," Conor replied. "We're still processing the crime scene and the autopsy is scheduled."

"Do you think the death of Fr. Godfree had anything to do with the murder of the bishop of Galway?" the reporter asked.

"I don't have any definitive connection to suggest that possibility at this point," Conor replied.

"Do you have any suspects?" the reporter asked.

"I hope to be able to answer that question at the press conference tomorrow. I'd like to ask the public if anyone saw anything out of place at the church or at the priest's house to call the police."

He concluded the impromptu interview and walked back down the stone pathway into the sacristy, behind the altar. He looked at the vestments laid out by the priest and called the Technical Department to come to the church to check for fingerprints on the door and the light switches. He also asked them to take fingerprints on the doors from the confessional box.

The body of the priest was taken to the morgue in New Ross where it was placed in a refrigerated drawer in preparation for the autopsy the next day. All the other evidence was taken to the forensics lab and logged into the system.

*   *   *

Later that evening, Conor drove to the lab to preview the evidence before the forensic department began their examination.

Arriving at the building he found the lab technicians still working. The evidence had been organized into specific areas in preparation for the team the following morning. He examined the book that had been found on scene and the card inside it. Both items were still in the plastic evidence bags, but he could see a list of names on the dirty piece of paper. He tried to read the list but was unable to see all the names because he could not open the book wide enough.

I wonder why the priest kept a list of names in a pornographic book?

The other piece of paper was folded up and he could see that the words were some kind of verse.

I'll look at all this tomorrow after the forensic team has dusted for additional prints and biological evidence. I'm not going to solve this thing tonight.

He remembered the first words of the verse that he had seen in the bathroom.

The Day of Wrath. Is that ever appropriate?

He walked back outside into the on coming darkness of the summer night.

Chapter 43

Next morning Conor met Anne for breakfast in order to compare notes about the death of Fr. Godfree with its possible connection to the Galway murders and to get the results of her interview with Finbar. She explained that it was the first time she had ever interviewed a victim of child abuse and hoped to meet him again when she returned to Galway.

"Let's see what happens today with the autopsy and all the other evidence," said Conor bringing Anne's focus back to the new murder.

"I'll be updating the story after the press conference this evening," said Anne, "if there's any breakthrough before then I'll put it on the website."

They finished breakfast and walked down the quay beside the river. The town was beginning to come alive as an army of vendors restocked the pubs and shops with produce. A pair of scullers rowed past going up river against the current, oars glinting in the morning light.

"Now there's a workout, against the current too!"

"Kind of like us with this case," Conor observed, as the rowers disappeared out of site under the bridge pylons.

"I've gotta get back to Bridgeville and interview the locals about the murder and see if I can meet with May Doyle," said Anne.

Conor looked at his watch, "Its 8:30. Time to get over to the morgue and then to the Bureau." He leaned over to Anne, leaving a long, wet kiss on her lips, then turned and walked to his car giving her a wink over his shoulder.

Arriving at the morgue he immediately went to the examination room. The coroner was already there as the clock ticked towards nine. Conor put on the protective suit and joined the group standing around the priest's body, laid out on a stainless steel table.

"Morning, all," said Conor introducing himself.

"Good morning Detective. I'm Toby Pierce, the coroner, and Dympna Powers will be helping me with the autopsy this morning, so let's begin."

Dympna unzipped the bag revealing the flaccid, white body of the priest. His clothes had already been removed and transferred to the lab. Hair was matted across his face, his eyes were shut. A strange rancid odor emitted from the body as the extraction fans removed the biological gases from the room.

Dr. Pierce examined the external body for trauma, wounds or any physical damage. The wrists showed bruising indicating that a restraint had been used. There was sticky trace evidence indicating that duct tape had been placed over the victim's mouth. The ankles also had tell-tale bruising caused by a restraint. The coroner examined the neck for signs of strangulation or other fatal causes of death and found a small puncture on the right side of the neck, noting it in his audio report. He commented that the puncture wound was a possible entry point for a substance injected into the body. Except for a bruise on the left temple, there were no other marks or wounds.

"Now, I'm going carry out the internal investigation," said Doctor Pierce. Making a "Y" incision in the body, he began to remove the organs one by one, checking each for signs of failure or disease. They were weighed and logged. The liver was placed in a plastic container and sent to the lab for analysis because poisoning was already suspected and the toxin would present itself primarily in that organ. The remaining organs would be examined later after the substance in the liver had been identified.

"This murder looks very similar to the other deaths in Galway," Conor observed. "We'll wait for the evidence, but I have to tell you that we may be dealing with Saxitoxin. How long will it take to get the results back?"

"We should answers later today."

"I'll wait for the call from the lab. Thanks for your help today," said Conor.

He discarded his protective suit, tossing it into a biohazard container and walked out of the morgue into the lab next door. The technicians were busily working on the evidence; the book, the list of names and the paper containing the verses. They found prints on the chair but none on the tape indicating the killers had worn gloves. Forensics also processed the prints found in the remaining rooms of the house including the door frames, bathtub and fixtures.

Conor sat in a vacant office reviewing the evidence. He began a timeline for the murder scene to establish the sequence of events leading up to the discovery of the body in the bathtub.

Crime solutions are all about connections, Motive, means, and opportunity.

He continued typing information into the file.

Motive: Possible retribution for child abuse.

Means: Poison and drowning as cover-up or ritualistic power and control over the individual.

Opportunity: Lone priest in house at night. No witnesses.

Suspects: None to date.

He looked at the piece of paper found in the book. Reading down the list of names, he saw a familiar name; Finbar Joyce.

There's the connection! I have to talk to him as soon as possible and get a warrant to search his house.

Moving on to the paper with the verses, he guessed, based on the content of the verses, that it may have been used by the priest as a confession or plea for forgiveness before the needle was plunged into his neck. Googling the first line, *Day of Wrath*, he discovered verses in Latin with an English translation. The Latin translation for *The Day of Wrath* was *Dies Irae*.

He recalled that no verses had been found with the other murders.

So why was this one so important?

Searching the internet, he found a site called www.diesirae.ie

That's it! This site must be the connection. It has resources for abused children. It offers legal support. It has downloads for all the Irish government reports on child abuse including the Ryan Report.

Sally Cullen, one of the technicians walked into the room, "Detective Horgan, would you like some lunch? I'm collecting a to-go order if you're interested."

"Yeah, thanks! I'll have a Ruben sandwich on rye," he replied pulling out some money.

Conor drilled deeper into the site looking for contacts and links. He clicked on the "Contact Us" bar and submitted a request for info about services using an anonymous email address. Before hitting send, he built a ficticious personal file in order to create a credible scenario for the webmaster.

Sally returned with the food. "Thanks for getting lunch," said Conor as he opened the paper biting into the well earned sandwich.

His phone buzzed and he recognized the number of Dr. Pierce, the coroner.

"Detective Horgan, we have the victim's cause of death and as you suspected he was poisoned. Saxitoxin was injected into his carotoid artery causing cardiac arrest. Death would have been almost instantaneous."

"Thank you, doctor."

"We'll send you the written report as soon as we've completed all the details."

*　　*　　*

Conor's press conference began promptly at 7:00 that evening on the steps of the county building. A cacophonony of reporters swarmed all over the place vying for position to get closer to the source of information and find out the latest on the case. Now overflowing onto the street they formed a tight group around the podium as Conor took charge of the event by introducing himself.

"Good evening. I've called this press conference to give you an update on the death of Father Michael Godfree. His body was found by his houskeeper in the bathroom of the rectory. When we found him, he was submerged in the tub. The autopsy indicated he had been killed and then placed in the tub.

A reporter blasted out, "Does this murder have a connection to the murders of the bishop and his friend in Galway a few weeks ago?"

"These three killings have the same M.O. We don't have any suspects at this point but we're following some promising leads that could help us solve these crimes. Now I'll take some questions. Two reporters began to talk over each other asking questions and Conor interrupted them saying, "This is not a cattle fair. I'll answer your questions, but if you continue to behave like a wild mob I'll terminate this event."

RTE News here, "Rumor has it that these murders may be connected to the child abuse issue. Can you speak to that?"

"I don't respond to rumors."

George Jones with BBC, "What do you know about this priest; was he a pedophile?"

"He was relocated to Bridgeville from a parish in county Galway."

The reporter continued, "Was this transfer hushed up by the Church?"

"I can't speak to Church policy," Conor replied.

Joe Mellon with the Independent Newspaper, "Do you believe these murders were committed as retribution for child abuse?"

"We have no proof of that. I've given you all I can give you at this point. I'm returning to Galway tomorrow to continue with the investigation," Conor concluded and walked away from the podium.

A priest took up position at the microphone saying, "I'm Fr. Byrne, the curate here in Bridgeville. I'm here to express my sorrow at the death of Fr.Godfree and to give my condolences to his family. I have details on the funeral arrangements. It will be this Saturday at 10:00 AM at the church here in Bridgeville. There will be a requiem mass followed by burial in the church cemetery."

The lights were turned off and the reporters began to disperse. As Conor walked back to the building, the press jumped on the unwitting priest like carrion, peppering him with questions.

Anne joined Conor at the entrance to the building, "That was short and sweet!"

"Yes it was," Conor replied,"I'm going back to the lab to continue with the report and plan to drive to Galway tomorrow morning. What are your plans?"

"I'm staying here in Bridgeville and hopefully dig up some more background about the priest from the locals."

"Let's get together for supper when we're done here," said Conor.

"Where are you staying?" Anne asked.

"I've a room at the Ross Inn just outside the town."

"I'm booked into a hotel close to Bridge Street," Anne replied.

"I'll call you as soon as I'm done at the lab," said Conor giving her a smile.

He returned to the lab and continued to update the file of evidence on the latest victim.

- Card with handwritten names, in the book.

- Paper with verses.

- Latent fingerprints on all the items including doors and windows of the priest's house and also in the sacristy of the church.

- Other forensic evidence, body fluids, chewing gum in trash can.

- Footprint near pathway.

- Duct tape with possible fingerprints.

- Analysis of poison- Saxitoxin. Compare its DNA signature with Galway poisoning.

I have to figure out the connection between the Galway murders and Michael Godfree. That's the key. It's really starting to come together. These crimes are premeditated which make them hard to solve. The bad guys planned a clandestine operation. They planned not only the murders but also a clean getaway not leaving any clues. But every criminal eventually makes a mistake; every crime has a signature and because there's a ritual in these murders, there's a footprint. If we solve one, we've solved them all. We already know how the next murder will happen – poison and water, and there will be another!

He went back into the evidence room and re-examined the chair, finding duct tape marks around the back and sides. Looking at it more closely, Conor noticed a short strand of hair in the residue of the duct tape glue and placed it in a plastic container for DNA analysis.

There was also evidence of black fibers on the glue, indicating that the killers wore gloves.

Match the fibers to the gloves! Match the gloves to the killer?

Conor updated his crime tracker software, backed up the data, then closed down before calling Anne on his way out.

"I'm done here; where are you?"

"Just finished the Godfree story for the morning edition," she replied.

"Let's meet at the Rosemount Café for supper. I'll be there in about fifteen minutes."

"See you then," Anne replied. "Is it the one located on the quay next to the river?"

"That's the one; I just googled it!"

Conor approached New Ross from the south side driving along the river Barrow. The restaurant was on the river overlooking the bridge. He parked outside the building noticing that Anne's car was already there.

She was waiting for him at a table near a window. A waitress approached and took their drink order.

"I'm glad today is over," said Conor with relief. "There's a lot of evidence with this crime, but still no suspects. Forensics will make the connections with both crimes, I'm sure, and then we'll have them."

"I hope to talk to some more of the locals tomorrow and get some background on the priest for the story," said Anne. "Now I'm ready to eat and relax."

"Me too," Conor replied as he scanned the menu.

Their drinks arrived and they ordered.

"I think Finbar could be the key to solving this case," said Conor. "He's obviously been abused according to your interview with him, and now we have his name on the list of boys that was found in the priest's house. I'll question him as soon as I get back."

"He has a deep rooted issue of abuse in his past life I know it. Maybe I can talk to him again as well. We seemed to connect," added Anne.

"That's a good thing. I'm sure he doesn't talk about any of this to just anyone," said Conor.

"Yeah, I've read that people who have been abused have physical as well as psychological after effects. Besides colitis, there are a host of mental issues like; insomnia, guilt, anger, depression, PTSD. In Finbar's case, I think it's a huge step forward for him to even talk about it, especially to a stranger."

"Maybe he feels more comfortable talking to you because you're a woman,"

"Maybe, at any rate, he certainly opened up and I like to think that he sensed my sincerity. I hope he can get help and I'm going to contact a friend of mine in Dublin to see if she has any suggestions. OK, enough on that subject. Don't forget we have to celebrate my radio show broadcast when we get back to Galway!"

"Oh, I haven't forgotten our dinner date. I'm sure dessert will be spectacular!"

The restaurant recycled customers as Anne and Conor talked on into the evening. When they finally walked outside they were surprised to find that night had fallen on the slowly flowing river outside the stone building.

Street lights cast pools of light on the cobbled streets.

"Let's walk across the bridge and burn off some of this food," said Conor, "I'm so glad to have you in my life to bounce ideas and theories off and help me come up for air."

"Which is worse for you, Conor; the murders or the abuse issue?" Anne saw the answer written on his face.

"I don't understand how Catholics can continue giving money to an organization that ignores abuse by priests. Don't they see that their financial support allows the hierarchy to maintain the status quo with secrecy? If the money dried up, maybe they'd pay attention. Now we're here, investigating the results of that cover up."

Anne interjected, "I was brought up Catholic. We would go to mass when I was a kid but my parents weren't drunk on the mindless words of an organization too interested in its survival alone. I stopped going to church when I was in high school, but I still have my personal beliefs. I don't need the church to tell me what to believe or how to live my personal life. I can see, though, how some Catholics are unable to disconnect from the church."

"Why can't they understand the difference between faith and belief," Conor asked.

"Which is?"

"Faith is something not based on proof. It's something to hang on to; to hope for."

"What's wrong with that?" said Anne, "sometimes you need something to hang on to!"

"It's called blind faith for a reason. I don't blindly follow anything. It's not in my job description. Faith is an illogical trust in something. Where did that trust get Finbar?"

Anne responded, "The Catholic church is part and parcel of many Catholic's faith. They grew up in the church. They have a recipe in the church cookbook. They've attended each other's baptisms and funerals. It's part of their social fabric."

"It's just that I watch what's going on with the Catholic Church and wonder if they will ever change anything. Their priests and bishops have been put on a very high pedestal by the people and it's going to take a lot to bring them down to earth," Conor replied.

"Enough on that subject," said Anne moving closer to Conor.

Warm hands met as they crossed over the bridge and turned left continuing down the quay to a replica of the sailing ship, *Dunbrody*, moored at the dock.

"Too bad they had to weld this beauty to the dock," Conor remarked. "They built it to sail and now it's just a museum. You know there's a replica of another ship the *Jeanie Johnson* in Dublin just down the quay from my condo. That one still sails however. That's another thing we could do when we get back to Dublin, go sailing!"

Returning across the bridge to their cars, Conor followed Anne to her hotel waiting until she was safely parked.

Anne came over to his window, kissed him and said, "We've both got a lot of work to get done tonight. I'll talk to you in the morning."

"Right," Conor answered. "I won't get anything done with you around to tempt me!"

Chapter 44

Thursday morning dawned over the river town of New Ross. A warm wind swept up the river Barrow and rattled the window of Conor's hotel room. He looked at the clock and saw that it was 7:00 am, got up, showered and went down to breakfast carrying his laptop and some paperwork.

Breakfast was served buffet style and he made good use of the generous spread, loading his plate with scrambled eggs, rashers and fruit, and topping off the meal with coffee. He sat at his table for a few minutes entering more data on his laptop.

Conor's drive back to Bridgeville took about twenty minutes. He parked outside the rectory at the end of the driveway. The police cordon around the building indicated that it was still an active crime scene.

Once inside the house he took a final look at the entire scene before leaving for Galway trying to cement the image in his mind. Two technicians were completing a final clean up of the bathroom and kitchen area before entry restrictions would be removed. His phone rang. It was Anne.

"Morning! Missed you last night. When are you leaving for Galway?"

"Good morning to you. I'm leaving in about an hour," he replied. "I'd like to get back there as soon as possible to hook up with Finbar."

"I'll call you later this afternoon. Have a safe trip back," said Anne.

"Thanks. See you soon."

Conor signed off on the paperwork releasing the crime scene and walked back down the driveway still thinking about the murder of Fr. Godfree and the image of the dead priest lying in the dark waters of the tub.

His drive back to Galway would give him time to prepare his interview with Finbar. He didn't want to force him to testify but all the evidence seemed to point to Finbar as the centerpiece in this case.

He drove westward to Galway city stopping at the courts for a warrant to search Finbar's house.

*   *   *

Meanwhile, Anne was on her way back to Bridgeville to meet with May Doyle, the dead bishop's cleaning lady.

I'm sure she knows a lot more about Godfree and his life. I just need to get it out of her.

Arriving at the rectory she pulled up next to the priest's car still parked beside the house and walked to the open front door.

"May, are you here, it's Anne O'Gorman?" she asked directing her voice in the direction of the kitchen.

"Yes, come in Anne, I'm back here."

May was sitting at the kitchen table looking at the pile of dishes in the sink considering the onerous task before her.

"Where do I start with this mess?" said May.

"Don't you need some help with this?" said Anne.

"No, I'm the only one who can put all this back together. The police cleaned up the bathroom so I don't have to go in there."

"Are you ready to talk about this?"

"I have to talk to someone," said May, "And you're the only one who's offered to listen. I talked to my husband last night but he's too close to all of this and just wanted me to stay home and feel sorry for myself. But I can't do that. I want to tell someone what I know. Someone needs to hear it."

"Let's get out of here and go somewhere else," said Anne.

She drove May to Kennedy Park, stopping at the start of one of the trail heads overlooking the rolling parkland where they sat on an oak bench in the morning sun.

"Thanks for getting me out of there. I come here often to walk the dogs and love this place."

Anne put her backpack on the table and took out two bottles of water.

"Where do I start?" said May. "Fr. Godfree came to Bridgeville years ago when I was looking for a part time job as a housekeeper. He'd been transfered from Galway and was starting up as a parish priest. I got to know him pretty well but began to hear some things from other people in the church."

"What kind of things?"

"They'd heard he'd been moved here because of something he'd done in Galway, but it was just a rumour as far as I could tell. Then I read in the paper that the Bishop of Galway had been investigated for hiding information about abuse in a Galway parish and I made the connection even though no names were mentioned. I assumed it was all over."

"What kind of person was Fr. Godfree?"

"Very untidy. He never cleaned up after himself. I found a lot of stuff in his bedroom, dirty books and magazines and told him he needed to get rid of that stuff because sometimes people would come to the house and I didn't want them to see any of it."

"Was it pornographic stuff?"

"Yes. He told me to mind my own business and that's when I asked him if he had a problem.

I'm getting help, he said."

"Did you tell anyone?" asked Anne incredulously.

"No, I kept quiet. That's what everyone does He's not the first and only priest to bugger little boys!"

"Did you hear anything about him and altar boys here in Bridgeville?"

"Just rumors. He had a team of altar boys who helped serve mass and did the sacristy work every week but that was normal. I didn't notice anything different about that."

"What kind of "help" was he getting," Anne asked digging deeper.

"He went to retreats with other priests every few months, and I think that may have been part of it. The Auxiliary Bishop of Galway has started a program to fix priests and I know Fr. Godfree was part of that. I think he was going to attend one next week in Galway. Guess that's not going to happen now."

When I get back to Galway, I need to contact Teresa and find out what's going on with the program. Maybe meet the auxillary bishop.

"Did you go to the rectory every day?"

"No, I went on Monday, Wednesday, and Friday. I never went at the weekends and the place was always a pit on Monday mornings," May replied. "Sometimes he'd leave for a few days and then I wouldn't go at all."

"Did you know any of his friends?"

"He had a few priest friends who visited once in a while, but I wasn't there all the time so I don't know if people came by when I wasn't there. Now, I need to get back to the rectory, clean it up and get ready for the funeral."

"You seem to be taking this really well," said Anne.

"I'll never forget what I saw in the bathtub as long as I live, but I have to try and get on with my life. A girl's got to make a living!"

"I hope your next job has a better ending. Let's get back to the rectory. I need to get back to Galway this afternoon," said Anne.

"I'm kind of glad it's over. The Lord works in mysterious ways."

"You were in a tough spot May, but you're in a position to cooperate now. It'll be the best for everyone."

Leaving May at the rectory, Anne began her drive to Galway.

What's wrong with these people?

Chapter 45

Next morning Conor drove to Liam's house where Finbar was finishing up the cabinetry, having called him earlier to make sure that he would be there. He didn't want to make a big deal of his first interview with Finbar. He wanted to take advantage of a non threatening environment by catching Finbar on his home turf.

When Conor arrived he found Liam in the kitchen admiring Finbar's handiwork, "Man, this guy does great work. There's not one missed step. Look at the reveals on these doors. They're perfectly lined up," said Liam.

Conor walked over to the cabinets, rubbing his hand on a door and said, "I really like the hand rubbed finish on this door. It says a lot about Finbar's love of wood. I wish I could get him to help me with the tower in Wexford."

"Well, let's go ask him," said Liam.

Finbar was working in the living room when the two men entered the room.

"Finbar," said Liam. "This is Conor Horgan. He's a fan and wants to know if he could persuade you to go across the country and help with the remodel of his tower on the Wexford coast."

Finbar responded, "A Martello Tower? I've always wanted to try my hand with the interior of a tower."

"I'm going to leave you two. I know Conor has a few questions for you," said Liam. "He's the detective working on the Galway and Bridgeville murders."

"I don't know anything about them," said Finbar defensively.

"Let's sit down over here and see if you can help me with some background," said Conor pointing to a worktable and two benches on either side of it. The men sat down.

"Did you know Father Michael Godfree?"

Finbar's face became taut, "I did."

"Where did you meet him?"

"When I was growing up in Connemara," Finbar replied. "Why are you asking me these questions about this priest?"

"We found your name on a list of boys in Fr. Godfree's house."

He handed Finbar a copy of the list. Finbar glanced at it, his face changing from stern to angry.

"Why do you think your name was on this list?"

"I've no idea."

"Did you know these other boys?"

Finbar looked back at the list.

"Yes, I knew one of them, Dermot Murphy."

"Were you and Dermot altar boys for Fr. Godfree when he was a parish priest here?"

"We were."

"I think you were abused by Father Godfree. Is that true?"

Finbar stood up, enraged by the question.

"That's none of your business!"

Conor continued, "Did you ever talk to anybody about the abuse?"

"I don't want to answer any more questions."

"Did your parents know?"

"I don't want to talk about it."

"Did you get any help?"

"I told you, I don't want to talk about it!"

"Finbar, you gotta help me here. There may be a connection between the murder of Father Godfree and the abuse of boys in his church. The list indicated that you were one of Fr. Godfree's altar boys. Did he hurt you? Did you kill him? God knows no one would blame you!"

Finbar collapsed on the bench, "I had nothing to do with his murder."

Conor's phone rang and he answered, "OK, thanks, Tomas." and hung up. "Finbar, we're going to have to talk about your past life and I have more questions. Did Bishop Cronin know about your problem?"

"I don't want to answer any more questions," Finbar stammered, getting more frustrated.

"Did Bishop Cronin transfer Fr. Godfree out of the parish in Connemara?"

"I don't know. Godfree left the parish and that was it. And I was glad for it."

"Did your parents know?"

"Leave my parents out of this!" Finbar replied angrily.

"Did they receive any money from the bishop, to keep quiet? I can ask your parents that question as well."

"Then you better talk to them about that."

"Did you promise not to tell?" Conor continued with his persistent questions.

"I didn't have a choice."

"Did anybody report this to the police?"

"That would've been a total waste of time. The police look the other way. They don't want to get involved with the church."

"I have a warrant to search your house."

"I've nothing to hide."

"Let's go find out," said Conor.

*   *   *

They drove around the coast through Roundstone arriving to find Tomas Ashe parked in front of the house. He emerged from his car when Conor and Finbar drove up. Conor followed Finbar to his front door.

"Glad you could be here on such short notice," said Conor to Tomas.

"No problem."

Conor introduced him to Finbar who stood waiting in the living room. Tomas began to search the upstairs while Conor searched Finbar's emails. He found a number of old contacts with Brendan Duffy who had been the architect on Finbar's house. He was not surprised to find a number of emails between them, mostly work related.

He looked through Favorites on Finbar's computer and found a site called *Dies Irae* along with two other sites relating to assistance for individuals who had been abused.

"What do you know about these sites?"

"I belong to these groups," said Finbar. "I was able get free counseling and legal advice from them."

"Do you meet online or in person with them?"

"Both."

"Tell me about *Dies Irae*. That site is one you seem to visit often," Conor observed. "I see here that they have only Christian names, do you know their surnames?"

"I only know them by their first names," Finbar replied. "They don't want to be identified."

"I understand," said Conor. "Where did you meet them?"

"We met at different pubs in Clifden and Roundstone."

"I'll need the names of these pubs. Do you know where these people live or have you been to their houses?"

"No, I don't and have never been to their homes."

Tomas came down the stairs into Finbar's office.

"I didn't find anything upstairs, but took hair samples in the bedroom and in the bathroom," Tomas advised, "I'm moving on to the workshop."

"Be careful in there," Finbar ordered. "I've a lot of cabinetry still set up in there for gluing, and I don't want any of it moved."

"Right."

Finbar walked Tomas through the kitchen to a door at the end of the hallway which when unlocked automatically lit up. The room was set up with work benches as well as drying racks for painting and staining. A vast variety of shop tools were laid out around the floor and connected to a dust removal system. The windowless space created a cave-like hideaway.

"Thanks Finbar, I can take it from here."

Finbar returned to Conor in the office.

The interrogation continued, "How long have you known about *Dies Irae*?"

"About four years."

"I want you to set up a meeting with them now and do it on their webpage."

Conor typed in the URL for *Dies Irae*. A message appeared "Unable to find website." He tried again, still the same answer.

"You searched this site earlier today, Finbar," said Conor. "I see the search records on your computer. Now it's down! Don't you think that's strange?"

"Could be a server issue," Finbar replied.

"Call your contact at *Dies Irae* and set up a meet."

Finbar searched his phone and hit the contact name DI, getting a voice message. "This number is no longer in service."

"Shit! Do you have contact numbers for anybody else in the group?" Conor asked.

"That's the only number I've ever used."

"Give me your phone!" said Conor, growing increasingly frustrated as he searched through the contacts.

"I'm getting your phone records. If you're lying to me it's not going to go well for you."

Conor tried the number again and got the same result. He called his IT back in Dublin and found that the phone number was attached to a disposable making it impossible to trace.

In the meantime Tomas returned from the workshop with a metal stamp in his gloved hand.

"What's this?" asked Conor looking at Finbar.

"It's a prototype for a metal stamp that I designed for a customer."

Conor looked at it and recognized the entertwined Celtic scroll design with a snake wrapped around the letters "D" and "I", mounted on a background of waves.

"I dusted for fingerprints on this piece," said Tomas.

"I'm sure you'll find some," said Finbar, "They're mine!"

"Did you make this piece for *Dies Irae*?

It has the letters D.I. on it, so it must be their stamp; not just a coincidence, don't you think?"

"I designed this stamp for them in return for counseling."

"I also found a note to Finbar from someone called Fergus, concerning the design for this piece," said Tomas.

Finbar was visibly upset at the mention of Fergus's name since he thought he had destroyed all reference to the group.

"Fergus! Is he one of the group?" asked Conor.

"Yes."

"OK Finbar, I need your fingerprints and DNA," Conor said exasperatedly.

"I had nothing to do with any murders," Finbar replied, despondently, "I'll give you anything you want. I'm innocent!"

"We're done here, Finbar. Now we're going to Roundstone and you're coming with us," Conor demanded.

"And if I choose not to go?"

"Then I'll take you to the station in Galway."

"Who are we meeting in Roundstone?" Finbar asked, unaware that Conor had been in contact with *Dies Irae* and that a meeting had been set up with Colm at Grogan's Pub in Roundstone.

"You'll see when we get there."

*   *   *

Grogan's was always busy on Friday night. The parking lot was full and Conor heard music pulsing out the doors of the pub.

He parked his car close to the entrance. Tomas and Finbar pulled in at the end of the parking lot next to the road.

"We'll wait here until we hear from Conor," said Tomas.

The music swelled as Conor opened the door. He approached the greeter to tell her that he was looking for a friend. She directed him to a man seated on the deck overlooking the harbor. He was dressed in a black polo shirt, black pants and a fisherman's hat covering his bald head.

Conor approached the table and introduced himself.

"Are you Colm?"

"I am," said the man, "You emailed me yesterday?"

They shook hands and sat down.

"How about a beer?" Colm asked, waving at the waitress who came over and took their order.

"So, you found us on the internet," said Colm looking intently at Conor.

"I did and I can't handle it anymore by myself. I want justice. I want that son of a bitch to pay for what he did to me."

"Keep your voice down!" said Colm.

"OK" said Conor. "How can you help me?"

"Conor, that's what we do. We're not only going to get you some psychological and legal help, but we're also going to get you some justice."

"How are you going to get justice?"

"Believe me. We'll rid the world of this dirt bag one way or another."

Colm continued, "I'm going to give you a few minutes to decide if this is really what you want. There'll be no going back!" Colm excused himself and went to the bathroom.

Conor quickly texted Tomas; *5 Minutes*; then picked up a table knife that Colm had been playing with and put it in his pocket.

Colm returned and took another slug of his beer, "Are we on the same page here, Conor?"

"I don't want this prick to bugger anyone again," Conor replied.

"OK," said Colm. "I'll be in touch with the details."

Colm was seated with his back to the door of the pub so he didn't see Finbar and Tomas walk onto the deck.

"I have someone here I'm sure you'd like to meet," said Conor looking at Colm.

Colm turned around and froze when he saw Finbar walking towards him.

"What are you doing here?" Colm asked.

"I brought you both here to help me solve the bishop's murder," Conor interrupted.

"Shit! You're the law!" Lights went on in Colm's brain as he scanned the deck looking for a possible exit.

"We are," said Conor. "Let's walk outside."

Standing next to his car, Conor looked at Finbar, "Is Colm a member of *Dies Irae*?"

"He's here isn't he?" Finbar answered.

"Let's take a ride, boys," Conor continued, "Maybe we can loosen up your tongues a bit at the station in Galway."

*   *   *

Friday night traffic had dispersed when the two vehicles arrived outside the police department in Galway and Conor realized it was going to be a long night.

The four men walked into the building, down the corridor into the Detectives office. Conor asked Colm to follow him to the forensic records department where they met with a technician.

"Colm, we want your fingerprints and DNA. I have a warrant to carry out this procedure and also to search your house," Conor was bluffing.

"Where's the warrant?"

Pulling the knife out of his pocket, Conor replied, "I already have your prints and something tells me I won't have any trouble getting a warrant after running them."

"Get on with it then!"

The technician processed hair and DNA samples; then took them the lab to begin the identification process. Conor took Colm into the interrogation room and sat down opposite him placing a pad of paper on the desk.

"Has your group had anything to do with the murder of the bishop of Galway and his friend, Brendan Duffy?"

"No."

"Have you ever met the bishop?"

"No."

"Did you ever talk to or meet Brendan Duffy?"

"No."

"Have you ever been at a warehouse on Quay Street in Galway?"

"No."

"Do you know Father Godfree?"

"No."

"I believe you do, according to our information. Do you still deny you didn't know this priest?"

"I do."

"Where were you last Monday night?"

"I was at home in Rosaveal."

"Can you prove that?"

"I'm sure my wife, Sheila, would verify that fact."

Conor left the room and went next door where Finbar was sitting at a desk with Tomas Ashe.

"Finbar, thanks for your cooperation so far with this investigation but I've some more questions for you."

Conor continued, "Did you communicate with Colm, either in person or online regarding Fr. Godfree?"

"Yes."

"Did Colm know that you had been abused by Fr. Godfree?"

"Yes, I told him early on in our relationship; that was one of the first questions he asked."

"Did Colm ask you about the transfer of Fr. Godfree to another parish?"

"He did, but I didn't tell him the location."

"Did Colm or his group offer any sort of counseling service or group therapy?"

"They did and I took advantage of it."

"Where did that take place?"

"We met in the office of a warehouse in Galway."

"How well did you get to know any of the other abused while you were in the group therapy sessions?"

"I got to know some of them."

"Do you remember their names?"

"Some."

Conor's phone rang and he walked outside the room to answer it. It was the forensic technician asking him to come to her office.

"What do you have?"

"We identified Colm's fingerprints on the chair in the warehouse in Galway. His hair matched a sample from the crime scene in Bridgeville. His fingerprints were also found on a light switch in the sacristy in Bridgeville."

"Did you find any evidence of Finbar, the other suspect, at any of the crime scenes?"

"No, there were no links to Finbar."

"Thanks, call me if you find anything else."

We've got him!

Conor returned to the room where Colm was being held. He walked around the table standing behind the dark figure with the shaved head.

"Colm McDaid, stand up. I'm arresting you for the murder of Fr. Godfree in Bridgeville, County Wexford. Anything you say may be used as evidence. You'll be remanded to the county jail until a hearing is scheduled for your case."

An officer placed all of Colm's personal effects in a plastic bag snapping handcuffs around his wrists, as he led him out of the office and placed him in a cell.

Finbar waited in the other room, wondering when all the questioning would end. He had spent the last few years of his life trying to come to terms with his demons, and now the lid had once more been removed from the hell-hole of his life and the heat was becoming unbearable.

The door opened and Conor returned, "Finbar, you're free to go at this point but don't leave the area. I may have more questions for you. I'll have one of our officer's take you home. Thanks for your cooperation."

Finbar felt a huge weight being removed from his shoulders as he listened to Conor's words of freedom.

Now what do I do? I've betrayed my friends.

"If you remember any more about *Dies Irae* I'd like to have it as soon as possible."

Finbar walked out the door with the officer into the on-coming night breathing a sigh of relief.

Chapter 46

It was a cloudy Saturday morning when Conor and Tomas drove to Rosaveal to search Colm's house. Tomas went around the back and Conor knocked on the front door waiting for a few minutes until someone answered.

The door opened to reveal a woman with long dark rooted blond hair, tight shorts and a beat up tee shirt.

"Who are you?"

"I'm Detective Conor Horgan and I've a warrant to search your house. You must be Sheila."

"I am."

Conor produced the warrant and couldn't help noticing the form fitting tee shirt as he showed her the warrant.

"Now I suppose you want to come in. Where's my husband?"

Sheila ushered Conor into the kitchen. An Aga cooker was located on one of the shabby green walls and an ancient sink with beat up drainer took up space under one of the windows. Broken tiles accented the floor and the place smelled of old food and cigarettes.

"Where's Colm?"

"He's been arrested."

"Arrested? For what?"

Conor watched as Sheila became enraged. The long ash on her smoking cigarette dropped onto the kitchen tiles as she glared at her visitor.

"What gives you the right to come in here and fuck with me," her pierced tongue spit out the words.

"This piece of paper," Conor replied. "What do you know about Colm's connections with *Dies Irae?*"

"I don't know what you're talking about."

"What are their names?" Conor asked becoming more impatient. "You know damn well what I'm talking about."

"Fuck you!"

"It's just a matter of time before you tell me! Where's Colm's computer?"

"You're the one with the warrant. You find it."

They walked into an office next to the great room where a laptop sat on a desk. An old fireplace, still filled with an exhausted turf fire filled the wall opposite the desk. Conor pulled up a chair and began searching the files, looking for any connection with the other three members of *Dies Irae.* Producing a flash drive, he stuck it in one of the USB sockets. The first file appeared "Marine ecology." It contained information about fish life on the west coast of

Ireland including shellfish and episodes of red tide. He drilled deeper and found information about algeal blooms and a list of poisons created by the shellfish that ingested it.

That's what Colm does. He's in the fishing business.

Then he found a contact "Beth4". One of these emails included a reference to the poison Saxitoxin and its derivation from shellfish. Another email from Beth4 indicated a meeting between Colm and Martin, regarding a shipment.

Who's Beth4?

Then he searched *Dies Irae*. A number of files appeared. The first showed a logo design with a PDF of the finished product. The sender's name was Finbar. It indicated that the design was complete and Finbar would expect payment in the form of on going counseling.

Now, we're getting somewhere.

Conor called Sheila, "Do you know the addresses or locations for the other three members of *Dies Irae*? Remember this is a murder case and you will be considered an accessory to the crimes, if you don't cooperate."

"Pog mo thoin!"

The doorbell rang. Sheila got up and answered it, "There's some guy here, says he's with you."

"Hi Conor," said Tomas. "How's it going?"

"Still looking at computer records," said Conor. "Can you search the bedroom, the garage and the attic?"

"Sure."

"Do you work with Colm, in his business?" Conor continued.

"Yeah, I keep the books and handle all the ship's manifests and crew schedules."

"How did Colm become part of *Dies Irae*?"

"Why don't you ask him!"

"OK, smart ass, that's it, I'm taking you in," said Conor.

"You're arresting me? No fucking way! I haven't done anything!"

"I'm taking you to the station for questioning and then I'll decide if any charges will be filed."

"What about my daughter, Siobhan. What am I supposed to do about her?"

"Where is she?" Conor asked a little perturbed.

"She's over at a friend's house. I can't leave her here!"

"I'll take care of that," said Conor as he called the local police station and explained the situation.

"A female police officer will stay with her here until we finish our investigation in Galway. Call your daughter and ask her to come home," said Conor.

"You have no right to mess with my daughter. I'm not going with you."

"Sheila, you have no choice. Either you go quietly or I'll take you in handcuffs. Your choice. Now make the call."

Sheila pulled out a beat up cellphone.

Tomas continued to look in the bookshelves and cabinetry around the stone fire-place, but found nothing. Looking in the utility room he found two pairs of hiking boots.

He remembered a footprint listed in the evidence from the Bridgeville crime scene, "I found two pairs of hiking boots."

"Good, we'll take them back to Galway," said Conor.

"Has Colm been hiking lately?" Conor asked Sheila.

"Not with me!"

"That's interesting!" said Conor. "Do the boots look like they've been used lately?"

"Possibly, there's a little dirt on 'em," Tomas replied.

The front door opened and a teenager stomped in.

"Siobhan, these men are the police. They've arrested your Da. They're taking me to Galway."
Siobhan ran over to her mother.

"Where's Da? Is he OK? Why was he arrested? Who's going to stay with me?"

"Da's in Galway and a policewoman will stay with you. I'll call you as soon as I know what's happening."

"I want to go with you. I don't want to stay here."

"It'll be OK. I can take care of myself," said Sheila.

Sheila and Siobhan sat together on the couch looking at Conor. A few minutes later a policewoman drove up and walked into the house.

"OK, we're done here," said Conor. "Let's take all this evidence and get back to Galway."

Chapter 47

The funeral of Fr. Godfree was carried out with little fanfare in the village of Bridgeville.

The bishop of Clody led the ceremony with a requiem mass, assisted by a local priest. The old stone church filled with parishioners as the smell of burning incense wafted into the guoined ceiling above the altar.

The service ended and the bishop briefly spoke to the collected mourners about the life and death of their priest, praising the man for his service.

A lone figure stood quietly at the back of the church as the cloud of scented blessings rose over the wooden bier. Fr. Tom had made it to Bridgeville to see his fellow priest pass into the next chapter of his life.

I could have saved him. I knew he was a pedophile and maybe he could have been rehabilitated. Now I begin my new mission.

The faithful gathered around their pastor as his body was lowered into the ancient soil of saints and scholars. Another evil life had been hidden away, leaving the wounded to mourn for each other and move on as best they could.

The bishop returned to the sacristy and removed the sacred vestments of his station. He dusted off his soutan, placed the purple skullcap on his head to signify his patriarchal importance, then opened his portfolio and stuffed the sermon inside the leather bound pages. Walking down the aisle, he exited the rear door which shut with a bang as a pair of startled crowsflew like scattered messengers into the sky.

*   *   *

Sitting at her desk at the hotel room in Salthill, Anne continued to write her Bridgeville report. She included interviews with two of the parishioners adding local color to the story and more research into the background of the man who had provided spiritual service to Bridgeville for of years. She learned a number of the parishioners refused to believe that their priest was a pedophile.

Calling Conor, she discovered he was returning to Galway with Colm's wife, Sheila and would soon be arriving at the police station. Her excitement building, she gathered up her notes and laptop and drove to the police station to prepare for the next phase of the investigation.

Conor arrived within minutes of her, carrying a laptop and a bundle of files while Tomas escorted Sheila into an interrogation room.

"I'd like to make this as easy as possible," said Conor. "I need to know about the other members of the group. Either you give me the information or I'll get it from Colm.

"Where were you last Monday night and how is Colm connected to *Dies Irae*?" his questions met with a stony silence. He left Sheila to ruminate on the answers, knowing that she would be a hostile witness at best. Maybe he could play her against Colm?

"Sheila's in the other room," said Conor to Colm.

"Why did you bring her here? She's got nothing to do with any of this."

"That's up to the district attorney," said Conor taking a sip out of his drink before turning to Colm.

"I'm waiting," he said, his patience beginning to run out.

"Have you got a statement from Sheila?" Colm asked.

"None of your damn business. Let's start simple. What is Fergus's last name?" Conor asked, eyes piercing into the man seated across from him.

"No comment!"

"Who's Beth4?" Conor continued to probe. A shrug.

"Where were you last Monday night?"

"At home," Colm finally answered.

"Have you ever been to Bridgeville?"

"Where's that?"

Conor walked to the door, slamming it behind him as he strode down the hallway to the room where Sheila was being held.

"Have you finished your statement?"

"Yes, here it is."

Conor picked up the piece of paper. It was blank. "Colm wasn't home last Monday night," he said. "Are you still insisting he was?"

"Yes, I am," Sheila replied.

"I've got Colm here at the station and he's giving me a different memory of that night."

"Bullshit! I know what you're doing. Trying to work us against each other, but it won't work."

"Ok, Sheila, I've had it with you. I'm arresting you as an accessory in the murder of Fr. Godfree."

"What's going to happen with Siobhan?"

"She'll be placed with the children's agency and you know what could happen to her if she's put in an orphanage," said Conor.

"You can't do that," Sheila replied.

"Oh yes I can."

" Alright, give me back the paper. Do not put my daughter in child care."

*   *   *

Down the hallway Anne continued to flush out the murder of Fr. Godfree including some quotes from the locals who had various opinions of the man who seemed to have lived a double life. The interview with May Doyle gave her some insight into the priest who lived in a filthy house with a filthy habit.

The picture she was painting was not pretty and she felt the depraved evil of the man creep into her bones as she tried to find something positive to say about the pervert. According to May Doyle, he had been getting help from a group and spending time away from Bridgeville. Anne also learned from May that the Auxillary Bishop of Galway had started a rehab program in the diocese and apparently Godfree was part of that program.

I need to call Teresa and find out what's going on with that.

She dialed the number, "Hello Teresa, Anne O'Gorman."

"Hello, Anne. How are you?"

"I'm great. Do you have any comment on Fr. Godfree's murder?"

"I hope they find the murderers who are preying on the priests."

Anne continued, "When I was in Bridgeville I found out about a rehab workshop for the clergy that has been started by the Auxillary Bishop in Galway. What do you know about it?"

"That's right. I'm working on that program for the diocese. The bishop wanted to show the country that at least one diocese was working with the clergy to fix the problem."

"How does it work?" Anne asked.

"Well, we've started group meetings with priests and psychologists here in Galway."

"Does the bishop want to promote this program or is it all being done on the quiet?"

"Yes and no. He would like the credit for creating the program but would like to keep its members private at this point."

*　　*　　*

Saturday afternoon moved slowly towards evening as Fr. Tom sat in the stifling confessional offering forgiveness to his flock. Michael Godfree's death weighed heavily on his mind as he remembered the morning funeral he had attended earlier in the day.

I could have prevented this crime. I knew that someone was about to do something to this man. Now the deed is done and the priest is dead. I've committed the unforgiveable sin of silence.

He half listened as his parishioners confessed their sins through the wooden frame of forgiveness provided by his holy orders. This could not go on much longer. He needed to act and take a stand; these crimes against innocent children had to stop. The heinous murders of priests had to stop. He had to tell the authorities what he knew about the man who had visited him earlier in the month.

If I do this I'll no longer be a priest or be able to receive any of the sacraments from the church. I'll be cut off, alone.

He sat in the dark, airless confessional realizing that his decision to become a priest was based on faith and his belief in God, together with his adherence to an organization that now was taking care of itself at all costs.

I've got to get in touch with the police and give them my information and also contact the auxiliary bishop about my decision.

Confession was over. He pulled the drape back to reveal two scalloped doors. Pushing his way through he reflected, "**That** was my last confession."

The church was empty and quiet now. Another day of service completed as he walked to the front door and locked it. Returning to the sacristy, he stopped and knelt at the altar rail and bowed his head in prayer.

Dear God, I have kept my oath of secrecy as a priest in the confessional, but now I have to break it and free myself from its strangling silence. My belief in justice is more important than my muted offering of obedience. I must resign as a priest and continue with my life as a lay person. Have mercy on me.

He visited the sacristy one last time, removing the purple stole from around his neck. Then he un-buttoned his collar and bib tossing them into a black garbage can. The evening was strangely warm as he walked out into the fresh air, slamming the door behind him. Two grey crows roosting in the yew tree screeched loudly in protest as he walked down the walkway back to the rectory. He was free.

Chapter 48

I'm glad we had some time off yesterday," said Conor pouring more coffee into Anne's cup as they finished breakfast on Monday morning.

"Me too, but we ended up working anyway," said Anne

"That's our life at this point but I can see light at the end of the tunnel with the arrest of Colm. And now Sheila has talked," Conor replied. "What's on your schedule today?"

"I'm going to meet Teresa O'Connor at the rectory this morning to find out about this rehab workshop for the clergy. It looks like the Auxiliary Bishop is driving this event. I'd like to understand just how the church thinks they can rehabilitate their home grown pedophiles when all the best psychologists in the field of modern psychology can't. I think its just window dressing," Anne replied.

"I'm back at it with Tomas at the Bureau so call me if you dig up anything at the workshop."

Leaving the restaurant, Conor gave Anne a hug and walked to his car, "See you later."

*　　*　　*

Numerous cars were parked behind the cathedral when Anne drove into the small parking lot and made her way to the conference center entrance.

Boy this is a bigger deal than I thought.

Finding a parking spot, she backed into the space and took a notepad and bag out of the car. As she stepped up onto the walkway she noticed a number of priests making their way to the entrance.

Why do they always have to wear black? They seem to lives their entire lives mourning something.

Anne walked through the solid mahogany doorway stepping onto the plush red carpet. She looked for the direction sign. Teresa stood sentry-like on the left side of the lobby.

"Anne, you're not supposed to be here!"

She was visibly upset and after ordering Anne to leave, turned on her heel and made her way down the aisle to the table in front set up to accommodate notetaking.

There's quite a crowd here. I had no idea there were so many perverts in this part of the world.

Anne slipped into the shadows at the back of the conference room, disregarding Teresa's directions. Lights dimmed over the crowd as the bishop moved to the podium positioned in front of a black backdrop.

"Good morning all and thanks for coming. Today is a new day in the parish of Galway, we're here to heal and be healed by the goodness of God's grace. We're weak and unable to overcome our earthly desires without the help of our creator. Let us pray. Loving father. . . ."

Anne watched in horror as a man in a black ski mask, dressed in black like a priest, jumped out from behind the drapes, grabbed the bishop and immobilized him. Two other men posing as priests and wearing black masks, appeared at each side of the bishop brandishing automatic weapons. They made their way across the front of the crowd and down the aisles.

Sliding back farther into the darkness at the rear of the room, Anne texted Conor, "*Under attack Three men send help building behind bishop house.* Send. Edit. Clear All.

"Do not get up. Don't try to escape. You will be shot!" shouted one of the men.

"You! What are you doing back there?" demanded the man in the left aisle pointing his weapon at Anne.

"I'm a reporter."

Teresa turned around glaring at her.

"Good, that's exactly what we need. Get up here!"

Carefully Anne walked across the back of the room, the weapon still pointed at her.

"Move, Move!"

The person holding the bishop pulled out a roll of duct tape and taped the bishop to a chair as one of the other men secured the entrance door at the rear of the room.

"Get up here!" said the bishop's attacker to Anne.

One of the men grabbed her. Holding her hands behind her back, he looked in her bag, finding her phone.

"Did you call someone?"

"No, I didn't."

"If you're lying I'll put a bullet in your head!"

He checked her phone and found no recent communication.

"Must be your lucky day," said the man holding her phone.

Then the leader pulled a silver canister out of his backpack.

"We're not done with you people. This is the end. I have the cure in this container. You came here to get help and we'll make sure that happens. Your bishop made it easy for us by getting all you in one place."

Placing the canister on the podium, the leader hit a switch and red LED numbers lit up showing a countdown clock.

"Don't anyone try to be a hero," then turning to Anne, "So you're Anne O'Gorman the one who's been writing about this filth in the church. That's a good thing, the public needs to know the truth but you've picked the wrong story today."

Where's Conor, did he get my text?

Then turning to the bishop, "Bishop, you're the reason we're all here today. Where's the justice in this room for all the victims. Somebody needs to pay and pay you will." He turned toward Anne.

"I've read your articles in the paper just another murder story to you, but now you'll see it happen for real."

With a vision of Finbar's court of crows flashing through her mind Anne remarked, "You're not going to kill us are you? Who made you judge, jury and executioner?"

The man in black hit her with the butt of the gun. Anne staggered backwards, blood streaming down the side of her face.

"Shut the fuck up. Enough!" he shouted walking back to the podium and picking up a small device.

Oh my God, that's the trigger, the canister must be some kind of gas or a bomb!

As the masked man turned to face the crowd the side of his head exploded. As the trigger went airborne Anne dove across his falling body snatching the device before it hit the ground. Two men in combat suits burst through the rear door grabbing the man at the back of the room and knocking away his weapon while the third man wheeling right in reaction to the intrusion, was tackled from the side and brought down still clutching his weapon.

Pandemonium broke out as people began to dive to the floor and behind each other. Groggily, Anne realized she was lying across a body and could feel something warm soaking through her shirt.

Reality hit and she remembered what had just happened; the trigger was still in her clenched fist.

"I'll take that," a familiar voice said behind her as she rolled over watching Conor pry the device out of her hand.

"Oh Conor!" said Anne. "I thought we were all going to die!"

Conor knelt down and lifted her off the bloody body.

"You OK?" he asked.

"Now I am," she exhaled, tears welling up in her eyes. "I thought it was too late.   He was going to kill us all."

"We got'em. They're not going to hurt anyone anymore. Now let's get you out of here," said Conor wrapping his arms around her.

"You were hit!" panicked Conor, "Where's all that blood coming from?"

"Yeah, that bastard hit me across the face!"

Conor ran his fingers softly across her bruised face, feeling for broken bones, "Let's get you to the hospital."

Anne staggered to her feet with Conor's help and began to walk towards the rear door.

Teresa O'Connor came running, "Oh my God Anne, we'd all be dead if it weren't for you. Are you OK?" she said, noticing the blood all over Anne's shirt.

"I am, just surface, thanks. These guys did all the work," she replied looking into Conor's eyes.

"Anne, you're so brave, God bless you!" said Teresa squeezing Anne's hand.

*   *   *

Later that evening Fr. Tom sat in front of his television watching the latest news on the arrest of the three murder suspects with a picture of the fourth man who had been killed in the assault.

That's him. The man I spoke with in the confessional!

He picked up the phone to call police headquarters in Galway and asked to speak to Tomas.

"Detective Ashe."

"Good evening Tomas, this is Fr. Tom."

"Good evening Father, what can I do for you?"

"I understand you have the murderers. I've information about one of them," said the priest.

"What do you know?"

"A few weeks ago, a man came to me in confession and asked about Fr. Godfree. I told him that the priest had been transferred to a parish in County Wexford. Then I asked him about the death of the bishop and the answer he gave me, indicated that he was involved with that event, this man was Martin Meagher. Since I had acquired this information under the seal of confession, I was pledged to secrecy but now, realize I need to give you this information."

"Wow! What can I say?"

"I cannot live with this. I could have saved Fr. Godfree's life but I couldn't break the confessional seal. Now he's dead, and I feel responsible."

"You know what this means Fr. Tom. I can't protect you."

"Yes I know and I'm at peace with that."

* * *

Next day the District Attorney, Fintain Lynch, arrived at Conor's office in Galway PD to go over the charges and evidence.

"Looks like we've a very strong case here and I'm sure the judge will confirm our findings for the trial," said Fintan.

"We'll be adding more forensic evidence in the days to come," said Conor.

After lunch the three suspects appeared, shackled and handcuffed in front of the judge who charged them with the murders of the three victims. Television crews from Ireland and Britain had taken up the space in front of the courthouse and reporters were busy trying to get more details of the arrests and more background information about the suspects. Conor walked up to a battery of microphones and began to speak.

"This afternoon, three men: Fergus Fox, James Collins, and Colm McDaid were charged with the murders of Bishop Cronin, Brendan Duffy and Fr. Michael Godfree. They have been remanded to the county jail and await trial. Martin Meagher was killed in the assault at the diocesan headquarters. We believe all four were members of a group called *Dies Irae*. I'd like to thank a very brave person, Anne O'Gorman who put her life on the line today to save all the people in that room. She's recovering well from her ordeal."

Conor walked away from the crowd and got into his car.

Now, let justice take its course. I need to check on Anne.

Chapter 49

Liam and Niamh, returning from a long hike in Connemara National Park, decided to drop in on Finbar to see how he was doing since the arrests. They hoped to catch him at home and suggest a time for their first music jam. Liam walked up to the house and knocked on the door. There was no reply.

That's strange! Finbar should be home. He told me he was going to finish up all the trim work.

Niamh walked around the back of the house and up the steps onto the deck. She cupped her hands over her eyes in order to see through the glare of the glass and saw Finbar.

He was hanging by a rope attached to the railing on the mezzanine.

"Oh my God," she screamed. "Liam come here, quickly. It's Finbar! He's hanged himself!"

Liam came running and tried the door on the deck. It was locked so he scrambled back to the front door. It was also locked. He picked up a small wrought iron sculpture at the front door and smashed in one of the side windows. Running upstairs he took out his knife and cut the rope around the railing. Finbar, released, fell to the floor where Niamh had positioned herself to break his fall. Liam looked for a pulse, but his body was cold. Finbar was dead.

"Oh my God!" cried Niamh, "We got here too late!" cradling Finbar in her lap.

Liam called the local police and then dialed Conor who responded immediately.

Finbar was dressed in jeans and a tee shirt. His black hair cropped short above his unshaven face. They laid him carefully on a rug and waited for the police to arrive. Liam held Niamh as she sat sobbing next to Finbar's dead body.

"I never thought it would come to this. He seemed so happy the last time we saw him," said Niamh.

"There's a note on the countertop," said Liam opening the folded sheet of paper.

"What did he say?"

DENIS HEARN

To my family and friends.

After many years of hiding my shame and guilt, I have decided to take my own life to end this torture. I'm sorry it came to this but I can't go on. There might be justice, but I'll never find peace here. Maybe I'll find some now. May God have mercy on my soul.

Finbar

Chapter 50

Liam opened the front door and welcomed his friends into his new home. The house was spectacular, allowing the golden western light to spread into its very bones.

Conor and Anne, her bruises now faded to a pale yellow, Brian and Evie with Sean on her hip, spread through the house like bees entering a new hive. They joined Finbar's parents and Niamh on the deck.

"Liam, this was such a good idea getting everybody here to remember and honor Finbar," said Brian.

"It all strangely seemed to come together at the same time. The house was finished and we lost Finbar, for me it's a kind of spiritual experience. I have this great home and every part of it was touched by him," said Liam.

"I understand Peadar and Moira have established a foundation in his name," said Brian. "What a great idea!"

"Yeah, it's designed as an advocacy group to help victims, to educate the public about the issue and to make sure the perpetrators are brought to justice whoever they are," Liam continued.

"A lot of innocent people suffered and it is a fitting tribute to Finbar to have the foundation named for him. We couldn't have come this far without him. He let us into his tormented world and helped to expose not only the evil in the church but also the evil of the misguided group that wanted to carry out vigilante justice."

Peadar and Moira Joyce stood silently on the deck, watching the rolling ocean before them. Turning around, Peadar spoke to the group, "Thank you all for being here in our lives today. We truly appreciate everything you've done. Finbar was a victim of the group that wanted to help him just as much as the priest and the church that took away his innocence and belief in his God. Fr. Tom is going to head up the foundation in Finbar's name. It was his way of donating his time and experience to carry on Finbar's legacy of rehabilitation."

CLADDAGH POOL

*   *   *

When the party was over Conor and Anne left through the back door. Stepping out onto the gravel driveway, Conor heard a noise above his head. He looked up into the tall, storm worn, pine trees behind the house to see two large crows bowing and cawing to each other in low scratchy voices. As he shut the back door, the two gray messengers flew up into the salty air disappearing into the setting sun.

One circled back and landed in a tree close to where the car was parked. Anne edged close enough to notice its intelligent eyes.

"Conor," she exclaimed. "That crow has blue eyes! I think its Peig!"

She watched as the gray shape opened its wings into the rising wind and flew west-ward over the waves in the direction of Inishmore. A slow smile appeared on Anne's face as she watched the old seanachie fly back to join her mate.

"Let's drive back to Dublin and get away from all of this," said Conor wrapping a strong arm around Anne's now healing body.

DENIS HEARN

Acknowledgements

Thanks to Cinda Skelton, my first editor
for her technical and literary support.

Art Mauer, a fellow author who gave me the
encouragement to complete the book.

Alan Vaughn for his support and artistic advice.

Anne and Andy for their words and encouragement.

Pete, for keeping me on track.

Please turn the page

for a preview of

Denis Hearn's

newest novel

Bagger Island

Available in 2013.

Bagger Island

Chapter 1

"Midships! Take in the net!"

Bill Blake pulled the throttles back and slowed *Girl Anne*, the Norwegian built trawler. The crew hustled to their stations as the giant winch slowly began to coil the grinding cables spooling them over her rusty stern. As the dripping net rose higher into air, the catch appeared from below the green surface like treasure sparkling in the evening sun.

Girl Anne lolled slowly in the ebbing tide of the Celtic Sea off the southeast coast as the waning sun slid westward over the spine of Ireland. The crew had completed two runs up and down the Channel and now, as the end of day drew to a close, it was time for the last haul of the day before they returned to the shelter of Kilmore Quay and the cool taste of a few pints at Moran's.

"Stand by for the end of the net," shouted Eamon, the lead seaman, his red beard glistening with sweat as he directed the crew to manhandle the purse onto the deck. The net moving inboard high over the stern, shimmered with the rustling silver herring inside.

"Wait! Stop the winch!" shouted Eamon. "There's something stuck in the net!"

"What the hell is that?" shouted Declan, the chief deckhand as he moved closer to the pile of quivering scales.

"Looks like a person! My God, it's a man!" said Padraig, the first mate, seeing the body of a mangled man inside, "or what's left of him!"

The crew tore into the meshes, cutting, hacking, scattering herring and orange net everywhere. The body slid slowly out from beneath the massed pile of shivering fins and glazed eyes; it was decimated. Pulverized beyond recognition with the arms weirdly wrapped around the remaining semblance of the person who had once been attached, his face was still recognizable as a portal into the body. A dark smeared mass of hair lay across the chapped and beaten face. One eye was terribly bruised and the other lay wide open, staring at its saviors. Eamon rolled the body over and noticed on the upper back a Celtic Knot tattoo emblazoned along the dead canvas of the body beneath it.

Skipper Blake continued down the aft companionway past the berthing area. Grabbing a digital camera he hustled outside onto the rolling deck. A busy crew was trying to stow the haul of fish and at the same time separate the body from the catch.

"Drag the body over here," Blake shouted to the crew. "Let's examine it and I'll take some pictures so we'll have a record of the boarding!"

Eamon moved the body away from the pile of fish that had been streaming around it. "Let's see what we have here," he said.

They positioned the body onto its back so they could see the face. The head slowly rotated around more than usual it seemed and ended up with the good eye staring vacantly at the two men.

"My God, what happened to this guy? His body looks like it has been beaten!" said Blake as he moved the man's arms from behind his back. The flash of the camera interrupted the frozen faces of the crew as Blake snapped the scene into memory.

"That should be enough," he said. "I'm sure we'll need all of these for the police investigation."

He pulled out his cell phone and dialed the emergency police number; no service. He walked back up the stairs and onto the bridge. *I'll try VHF that should work.* Lifting the mike, Blake called in his location, the name of his craft and a brief description of the event.

"*Girl Anne*, did I hear you say you had pulled a body from the water?" answered the radio operator.

"Roger," said Blake.

"What's your closest port of call?"

"Two hours from Kilmore Quay."

"Make for KQ and the police and coroner will meet you there," the operator replied.

"Roger and out," Blake answered, placing the mike back in its cradle.

"Stow all the catch," said Blake over the intercom, "and prepare to make port at Kilmore Quay in two hours. Put ice around the body and put it in one of our tarps until we get to port."

Girl Anne's throttles pushed forward, black smoke belching out of her two stacks as her bronze propellers bit into the rising sea and drove her bow towards the approaching land on the waiting horizon.

The crew worked feverishly piling the catch into the already full hold, washed down the decks and stowed all the gear. Eamon and Declan carefully slid the body onto the green tarp and wrapped it in ice, preparing it for the final journey back to the mainland. Moving back from the scene, the crew stopped work for a minute and cast down their heads in a moment of silence.

Blake sat transfixed in his seat on the bridge as *Girl Anne* wallowed her way back to port. Eamon, his first mate, opened the door onto the bridge and sat in the other big sea chair.

"We're all shipshape on deck," he said sipping from a large cup of coffee.

"I've never seen anything like that in my life," said Blake, "and I've seen a lot of bizarre stuff."

"It looks like the man was beaten and dumped or fell in. It also looked like he had been cut by something," Eamon replied.

Blake remained silent along with the rest of his crew, joining in their self-imposed respectful vigil for the person lying in ice under the tarp, as *Girl Anne* steamed slowly past Bagger Island.

As the island disappeared astern, Blake looked aft, his eyes fixed on the bubbling stern-flow flowing southwards under the hull. A strange thought wandered into his head. *I wonder what's happening on Bagger these days. I've seen a lot of diving activity off the south coast. It seems to be a busier place. Maybe the Chief is in residence?*

13557309R00188

Made in the USA
Charleston, SC
17 July 2012